Peter Zaccagnino

Relevant

Peter Zaccagnino was born in New Brunswick, New Jersey. Passionate about aviation from a young age, Zaccagnino has flown over 23,000 hours in more than 270 aircraft types and flight tested over 680 aircraft. His sixteen years of racing have included four gold championships, including the fastest qualifying lap, and induction into the Aviation Hall of Fame. Zaccagnino is also the owner of High Performance Aircraft Group, which performs flight test services for several manufacturers, including the U.S. and foreign militaries. Zaccagnino's latest endeavors include writing, production, and aviation filming. He has produced and been involved with multiple Discovery Channel pieces, the Smithsonian Channel, various documentaries, and several shorts and race productions. *Relevant* is Zaccagnino's debut novel.

Relevant

Peter Zaccagnino

RELEVANT

A novel inspired by true events

ISBN: 978-1-7347-5930-3

Thank you to everyone who has disagreed with me over the years. As citizens, we have a duty to social discourse. I have learned much through our many contentious, yet civil discussions. A special thank you to all the people who can't share their stories. You may not get a star on a marble wall or similar recognition, but you deserve great honor for your sacrifice. Special thanks to my supportive family members, especially my mom, who inspired us to do anything imaginable. Thank you Jen for the great debates and introspective view on things, particularly when I'm reluctant to see your point of view.

You know what I look for in a book? You know what I need to justify the hit on my credit card and the valuable time it takes to read it? I need a fine story with compelling characters I care about and who are tasked with doing interesting stuff.

And to me, a fine story is one in which a seemingly typical person is placed in unusual circumstances and accomplishes remarkable things. A story in which we chase our main character up a tree, throw rocks at him, and then see how he gets down out of that tree.

As you are about to see, Peter Zaccagnino has written one fine story. A look at his biography confirms he has the knowledge and experience to write such a fast-paced, tension-filled, bit of fiction, and that what he describes could actually happen. Hell, it probably already has. But who knew he was such a fine writer…storyteller…character builder…describer of the hard-to-describe?

Strap in, keep the oxygen mask handy, and get ready for a twisting, turning ride straight through today's headlines and out the back side, where few of us ever go. But thank goodness the guys Pete introduces us to do just that.

Don Keith

rel·e·vant

/ˈreləvənt/

adjective
1. closely connected or appropriate to what is being done or considered.

PROLOGUE

BEIRUT, LEBANON

OCTOBER 1983

There was no evidence that the nineteen-ton yellow Mercedes-Benz stake-bed truck had even been there at all. Like everything else that morning, it had been reduced to a screaming, grotesque version of its former self, ripped apart on a molecular level and melted into the piles of twisted metal, concrete, and corpses that now replaced the barracks. The wails of the dying crushed beneath four stories of concrete pierced the black air and created a harmony that sounded like some terrible perversion of the muezzin's call to prayer. In that final agony, your life doesn't flash before your eyes, your future does. Everything that should have been hangs there in the dark flesh behind your paralyzed eyelids, taunting you.

LANGLEY AIR FORCE BASE

HAMPTON, VIRGINIA, U.S.A.

Abbott Mazuski carefully ran his manicured hand over the tape player, his finger hovering over the play button, not yet pushing down.

Abruptly, he turned his attention to the newest batch of recruits. He adjusted the temples of his wire-rimmed glasses to fit more precisely over his ears and nose, then cleared his throat. "This is the tape that has authorized your actions."

Mazuski pushed play. A man's voice, clear and considered, unfurled with the tape. "A workaround like this will keep the tinpots at bay."

A low, gruff voice responded. "And ensure our liberty, peace, and prosperity. And for our friends in the community of democratic nations, Mr. President." The gruff voice belonged to Abbott Mazuski.

"It's a go."

Mazuski swiftly pushed down on the stop button and ejected the tape, immediately moving it into the pocket of his starched white shirt. "President Ford curtailed the CIA's ability to assassinate with impunity. Our current Commander-in-Chief takes a broader interpretation on Executive Order 11905, but international law and diplomacy makes certain mission objectives unsavory. That's where you come in. You are not part of the foreign intelligence community. You and your missions officially do not exist. If you are expecting medals and glory, you will be disappointed. If you expect to protect and serve this great nation against the most insidious threats with humility and focus, welcome."

The four recruits focused on their instructor and his message. Their attention grasped each consonant and braced at each breath between his words. They were the dictionary definition of focused.

Mazuski coughed. He reached into his pants pocket and procured a lozenge. As methodically as he executed every action, he unwrapped the lozenge and placed it on his tongue. Then, folding the wrapper into perfect eighths, he disposed of it in the nearby wastebasket.

"Any questions?"

1

Chris Hodge was kicking a hornet's nest. He accepted that the conventional stance amongst the faculty and students at MIT was doveish, to say the least. Though unfashionable, Hodge's analysis of the probability of foreign policy challenges stemming from the radicalization of Muslim populations had to be presented. To Hodge, it was simple: there were facts and there were emotions. The emotional appeal to peace and equality, while at its core a just one, was not tenable. It lacked universality. Hodge believed that to operate based upon anything other than the facts as they are, not as one would wish them to be, was a fool's errand. And Hodge refused to play the part of the fool. Surprisingly, his professors and classmates treated him less as a pariah and more as a curiosity. While they rarely conceded to Hodge's arguments, they did extend a measure of respect for his perspectives, which Hodge appreciated. Hodge knew that the gods of wisdom would not enchant his audience today, but even if it was a losing battle, he would not sanitize his message.

The auditorium smelled like chalk dust seasoned with the faint burning smell of a furnace a half century past its prime. Hodge stood in front of the podium and surveyed the classroom. The room's ascending rows of seats were half-filled by the faculty of MIT's political science department, graduating seniors in the department, and a handful of other interested parties. Bodies moved in their seats in bored anticipation. Academicians carried on quiet conversations. A professor's vinyl coat rubbed against the knees of her colleagues as she squeezed through to a center seat in the third row. Hodge began his defense, "In this contextual analysis of just war and counterterrorism framed within traditional war theory, this paper seeks to extrapolate the effects of Islamic radicalization, not as a pretext, but as a sociological underpinning of the United States' current Middle East engagements. I argue herein that there is differential violence inherent in these present conflicts that does not exist outside of these particular religious and cultural norms and any war theory employed at the governmental and policy levels must therefore combine both soft and hard power exercises in the context of any ground war to eradicate this growing threat."

Hodge continued his thesis defense for fifteen minutes, drawing a handful of examples from the United States' past entanglements in Iraq, Iran, Lebanon, and Libya, the continuing Israel-Palestine challenge, and the history of Islam's bloody initial expansion through military conquest of subjected peoples in Jerusalem, among the Berber people of North Africa, and in Spain. He ignored the occasional eye rolls and sneers, and the loud groan from Mirele Sofer, the most ardent leftist amongst Hodge's graduating class. Her behavior was unprofessional, but Hodge knew better than to sink to the level of his opponents, especially ones to whom he was attracted. He knew that reason would always win. Of course, human nature being what it is, reason usually won after the die had already been cast.

With his defense presented, he prepared for questions. Richard Sales, former Director of the State Department's Bureau of Legislative Affairs under two Democratic administrations, opened the floor up to questions from the audience. Hands shot up. Hodge smiled. He appreciated the bit of celebrity that his unorthodox positions afforded him on campus. To him, none of his classmates were enemies, just amusing rivals who hopefully would one day realize the grave consequences of inaction in the face of the statistically significant growth of terrorism. Whether they would admit so publicly once their academic reputations had been established, well, Hodge understood that reputations were funny things.

Hodge chose Mirele to be the first Kalashnikov in his personal execution by rhetorical firing squad. She had acid on her tongue and a special hatred for everything he stood for. Hodge appreciated a worthy battle and couldn't deny the strange magnetism between them. Hodge was no stranger to female attention, but, like most of his peers, all of his on-campus relationships had been casual. Most of his classmates' only long-term bonds were to their studies. Hodge was no exception. Still, to say that the thought of approaching Mirele after a particularly contentious argument for a continued debate over a bottle of wine hadn't crossed Chris Hodge's mind would be an outright lie. Hodge was the furthest thing from the crass vulgarity of a college "bro," but he did share their wisdom in one respect: the only thing better than sex with someone you love is sex with someone you despise.

Her words came out like .50 caliber rounds. "So you view Islam as an exogenous threat unrelated to other precepts underlying conflict or radicalization, such as underdevelopment and poverty. How do you see the current problem of Islamic radicalization as distinct from other holy wars like the Crusades or any other war fought on the bases of hardline ideologies?"

No, Mirele never disappointed in serving counterpoints to Hodge's points. In his own mind, Hodge's arguments were airtight, and while on an instinctual level he understood that one can see things from an entirely different perspective, he found it surprising that people often did. Sentiment versus reason. Sofer versus Hodge. It was almost a game to him. "It's an excellent question. First, regarding your mention of the Crusades, I question whether you have internalized a false narrative of these events as predicated on imperialism and Christian chauvinism. That narrative is inaccurate. Within one century after the rise of Islam, two-thirds of Christendom had been wrested from Christian control by violent means. Islamic attacks continued against Christian territories through the eleventh century. The Crusades are to be understood as the first series of counterattacks from a population under consistent threat of forced conversion, political upheaval, violence, and murder. Now, addressing whether Islamic terrorism in its present form is distinct—"

Mirele cut him off, "So you find the radicalization of a tiny minority of the contemporary Muslim population as distinct from the murder of every Muslim woman and child on the Temple Mount in 1099?"

"The Christian communities of the Middle East were destroyed one year after Muhammad's death. The entirety of the Jewish and

Christian population of the Arabian Peninsula were involuntarily expelled, converted, or killed. Perhaps you view that as an inconvenient narrative for public discourse, but it is a factual narrative nevertheless. Now, if I may respond to your initial inquiry: research into the subject does differentiate the violence of Islam in this current era and other ideological wars—for example, the Viet Cong—along several sociological normative lines. Modern warfare has changed. Islamic radicalization and the terrorist trend may simply run concurrent with that change, but it may be something else altogether. Only time will tell."

Hodge hoped that Mirele Sofer and her contemporaries were correct, that he had misjudged the facts, that America and the West would not have to face a near-unstoppable menace from Islamic radicals, but Hodge knew enough to not confuse hope with logic and evidence. The use of terrorism by Islamic populations had steadily increased after World War II, but remained marginal. After 1979, there had been a statistically significant acceleration in instances of terrorism. Furthermore, by then the nature of terrorism had shifted from seizing aircrafts and kidnapping for ransom to unleashing carnage intent on inflicting maximum casualties. After 1983, the ever-present challenge had solidified. The Lebanese Civil War had unleashed—to devastating effect—the favorite weapon in the modern terrorist's arsenal, the suicide bomb.

With his friend and fellow hawk Spencer Miller away at an academic conference in Madrid, Hodge assumed he was a minority of one in the auditorium, but he was mistaken. There was one man, perhaps a product of a bygone era, who shared Hodge's views. Hearing all that he had needed to hear, the man rose from a center seat in the back of the lecture hall and exited, leaving as silently as he had entered.

2

MOGADISHU, SOMALIA

DECEMBER 2001

Guuce Duale was not the most religious Muslim, but he made it a habit to attend the masjid for Friday prayers every week with his five-year-old son Sharmaarke and his older brother Erasto. His wife Jamilah stayed at home. Once, Guuce had asked his imam about why women were not permitted to enter the masjid. The imam quoted a hadith wherein the Prophet said, "I know that you women love to pray with me, but praying in your inner rooms is better for you than praying in your house, and praying in your house is better for you than praying in your courtyard, and praying in your courtyard is better for you than praying in your local mosque, and praying in your local mosque is better for you than praying in my mosque." Guuce Duale and his wife sought to be good Muslims, but neither was familiar with any of the hadiths. While Guuce could recite some parts of the Qu'ran from memory, he had left the madrasa at a young age to provide for the family that took him in after his mother died in childbirth and his father died overseas. The loving couple, trusting their imam to have a better conception of Islam than they, followed his dictates.

The imam walked up the golden steps of the minbar to deliver the first of his sermons. He recited a prayer in Arabic and began his lecture in Somali. "Atheism and liberalism. Two of the most prominent trends in the world today. These are Western trends, but they are not limited to the West. These trends have taken root in the Muslim world, among the deen, even here in Somalia, in Mogadishu. Both of these trends are completely incompatible with Islam, with the sharia. It is foolishness. Do you know that in the West there is an idea that mankind was not created from Allah, but that they, that all of us, were once monkeys? That over millions of years we became men from monkeys? This theory is called evolution. This is foolishness. Some have even gone so far as to say that if enough monkeys were given enough time and enough typewriters, they would be able to create every chapter and every verse from the Qu'ran. It is evil, is it not, my brothers? The Qu'ran addresses this foolishness in Surah Al-Baqarah, chapter 2, verse 135." The imam switched to Arabic, before translating the verse into Somali for the few worshippers who did not understand the message in its original language, "'O you who believe! Seek help in patience and the prayer. Truly, Allah is with the patient ones.' We need patience, brothers. The foolishness of the West is its liberal ideas that claim their world became free after what they call "the Enlightenment," which was their rejection of Allah. But their world is not free, it is a world built on foolishness and lies. The prophet, peace be upon him, said in the hadith that 'A wise man is the one who calls himself to account and refrains from doing evil deeds and does noble deeds to benefit him after death; and the foolish person is the one who subdues himself to his temptations and desires and seeks from Allah the fulfillment of his vain desires.' Brothers, I ask you today to reject the vain desires and foolishness of the

West, the foolishness that seeks to claim that Allah is an invention of man and man is but a monkey."

Guuce Duale tried to listen to the khutbah, but his mind drifted. He respected the imam's flawless command of Arabic and his impeccable memory for delivering the verses of the Qu'ran. Sharmaarke had started his education at the madrasa, financed by the Americans in exchange for travel and information about some of the warlords and extremists in the area. While he agreed with the imam that the Americans and the West seemed to have an excess in their desire to separate themselves from Allah, his own experiences made him skeptical of painting with too broad a brush. There were plenty of problems in Mogadishu, and while some were the effect of the legacy of outside control from the Italians, the British, the French, and the Americans-not to mention the Somali land stolen by the Kenyans and the Ethiopians-most of the problems for him or anyone else came down to the choice to do good deeds rather than foolish ones. Yes, to believe that we were created from monkeys was stupid, but the actions of those who were so misguided was hardly his concern. Allah knows best and he makes those who He wills follow a straight path. Guuce hoped to follow a straight path, one free of error and just in his dealings.

The second khutbah of the day was on the topic of how to increase one's faith in Allah. Guuce Duale found this to be of far more practical interest. The imam's message was simple: Strive to increase your good actions and decrease your evil actions and you will be rewarded with more emaan, with the gift of faith.

After the second khutbah, Guuce, Erasto, and Sharmaarke performed their midday prayers in perfect unison with the hundreds of other men in the masjid. With their outside devotion to Allah complete for the day, Erasto returned home with Sharmaarke, while Guuce headed towards the park with Cabdi and Abdullahi. These cousins raised Guuce and Erasto as if they were their own kin, despite them having no bond beyond their belonging to the same tribe, faith, and nation. As a close friend of Cabdi and Abdullahi, Guuce and Erasto's father had instructed them to take care of his children should a terrible fate befall him. Honorable men that they were, Cabdi and Abdullahi upheld his father's wishes. They were like uncles to Guuce and his older brother.

It was one hundred and two degrees outside, a hot day even by the standards of a city only a couple hundred kilometers north of the Equator. When the men reached the litter-infested park adjacent to the dusty and bullet-ridden Dhagaxtuur Monument, Guuce and Cabdi sat down opposite each other. They began to create the board for Shax, their favorite game. Cabdi grabbed a nearby stick, while Guuce used the tip of his sneaker to draw his half of the board. "Always an innovator," Cabdi quipped.

"And innovation is of Shaytan, you know," Guuce quipped. "Perhaps it is not Allah, but Shaytan who has granted me four victories to your zero this last week."

"Perhaps that is so," Abdullahi interjected as he threw his collection of decades old Coca Cola and Fanta bottle caps onto the ground. The men used these artifacts as their game pieces.

Guuce and Cabdi began digging small holes into the ground to complete the set-up of the board. When it was finished, the board, with its squares inside squares, resembled an abstract artist's conception of a sniper scope. The men squatted near each other and started the game.

"We could play layli goobalay." Guuce Duale had a smirk on his face. It was his fifth victory in a row. "Or sing children's songs, the songs your wife used to sing to me when I was young. I do not want you to be discouraged, my friend."

"I shall play you next." Abdullahi crouched down next to Cabdi. His opponent may have changed, but Guuce was unstoppable in this ancient tactical game. With ease, he earned his sixth victory in a row.

3

BOSTON, MASSACHUSETTS, U.S.A.

JANUARY 2002

Landmark was an anomaly amidst the meat market of Downtown Boston's bar scene, a place with more than a touch of class. Its proprietor, John Howell, was a Yankee to the core, with ancestry that he could trace back to the first pilgrims at Plymouth Rock, although Howell was hardly a snob. His ebullient personality and friendly disposition were evident to all, but he upheld certain standards. Landmark never got too loud, the bar's patrons never got too disorderly, and despite how it hurt his bottom line, Howell always ensured that unlike most of the other bars in his area, ID was always checked, not just after news of a recent raid from Boston's finest made the rounds. John took pride in his establishment and was a regular behind the bar. In his way, he embodied both the best of America's egalitarian instinct and his forbearers' British politeness.

Tonight, Landmark was filled with familiar faces. Most of the bar's clientele skewed older and more established than the ambitious but still youthfully reckless BC, BU, Tufts, Harvard, and MIT students who often used alcohol to mask their inept social skills. John preferred it that way.

It had been six months since John had to deal with any of the typical challenges that faced the proprietor of a nighttime establishment, and even then, the incident was relatively minor. A graduate student from BU had started a shouting match with his girlfriend. He gave her a push. Derek Bradford, the U.S. Army combat veteran who was one of the men John had hired to encourage Landmark's sophisticated environment both intellectually and physically, had little patience for men like that. Without a second thought, Bradford grabbed him by the scruff of his neck and threw him outside. John didn't expect that an incident of that sort was in the cards tonight, but he did have an uneasy feeling that he couldn't shake. Maybe it was the stranger at the end of the bar. The stranger had arrived two hours ago, ordered a glass of pinot grigio, and was still nursing it two hours later. John observed that he'd barely had a few sips. Perhaps he was an alcoholic, walking the tightrope between sobriety and returning to the chaos of a life out of control. The stranger did seem rather stiff for an alkie, former or current. Maybe he had just left his spouse. Maybe he had lost hundreds of millions of dollars. Maybe he was just a loon. Whatever it was, something about his demeanor made John uneasy. His mother wasn't a religious woman by any means. She and his father attended their Episcopalian church not to grow closer to any Lord or savior, but as a way of maintaining an active social calendar. Still, one thing that John's mother always told him as a boy was that he had a sixth sense. *Bull. That's all it was*, John tried to reassure himself, but still the feeling lingered throughout the night, rising every time he glanced at the too-composed-to-be-real man who sat at the end of the bar.

John's discomfort had him wondering if it was too late to call Bradford in for an impromptu shift. As he was just about to shake off his misgivings about inconveniencing Bradford, Chris Hodge entered Landmark, his arm around an attractive young woman with unruly dark curls and playful cat-eye glasses sunk low on the bridge of her nose. John now felt at ease. Hodge had been a welcome presence since his first visit five months ago when he came in on his twenty-first birthday with his then-girlfriend Shannon, a spitfire if ever there was one, and his friend Spencer. Despite Spencer's decade as a Marine and crew chief on a CH-46 Echo during Operation El Dorado Canyon, he played the perfect clown to Hodge's straight man.

In their conversations, Hodge relayed that he'd been a champion shot on MIT's rifle team. John was comforted by the knowledge that Hodge would volunteer himself to handle any unwelcome disturbances.

Hodge and Spencer had enrolled in John's course. While Spencer Miller generally eschewed his family's privilege with their penchant for monogrammed shirts and feigned empathy, he seemed to inherit his father's predeliction for fine wine. Spencer was frankly shocked that the blue bloods didn't disown him when he enlisted in the Marine Corps as a fresh-faced eighteen-year-old. As a teenager, he and his friends at the prestigious Groton School would drive into Boston on the weekends and raid Newbury Comics and snag the latest Ramones and Misfits albums. After Groton, Spencer found the perfect punk rock middle finger to his parents' effete lifestyle; he enlisted.

"A 91 Margaux for the grad and his friend?" John procured a bottle of his finest for Hodge, holding it out like a proper sommelier to show his friend the label. Hodge nodded and John deftly opened the Margaux and poured a soupçon of wine into a stemmed, wide-bowled Bordeaux glass. He offered it to Hodge, who lifted the glass to his nose and closed his eyes, swirling the glass counterclockwise to allow oxygen to react with the tannins and releasing hidden aromas. John smiled. How rare it was to find a young person who preferred to savor a bouquet of a fine Margaux over slamming bottles of Brubakers until he was incoherent. Perhaps there was hope for humanity after all.

After Hodge delicately swirled the glass and took a sip, John poured him and his companion a full glass of the Margaux. "It only took you three and a half years, Chris. In a hurry to get out of this town?"

Hodge flashed his trademark half-smile, his lips turned upwards and his jaw relaxed. "More bang for my buck."

Hodge enjoyed the repartee with John, and while he was as moderate in his drinking as he was in all his habits, he did try to make a regular stop at Landmark when the mood struck. The ambience suited him and the owner and his staff possessed a rare element of class. For Hodge, it was the type of bar that suited a man of his caliber, one who was destined for the ivory tower of academia, but Landmark was also a throwback. The bar had standards and Hodge appreciated that.

"Duty calls." John remarked, heading towards another patron.

"Your personal sommelier seems to have a penchant for you, Chris Hodge. I've heard close quarters in a wine cellar can make for a surprisingly romantic evening. Is it true?" Mirele asked once John was out of earshot.

"Oh, Mirele, a gentleman never tells," Hodge said, a glib smile on his face.

"He's cute." Mirele jabbed her finger on Hodge's chest a few times as she drove home her point. "And probably not a reactionary neocon who just wants to bomb every Muslim into the stone age."

"John's a good back-up," Hodge smiled.

"You know this isn't a date. You're not going to be my boyfriend."

"Roger, captain." Hodge mock saluted Mirele, a trait he had picked up from Spencer. "Thank you, but I'm already aware that although opposites attract, they don't last."

"It's just a shame." Mirele tsk-tsk-tsk'd. "You're charming and attractive, but your politics are to the right of Genghis Khan. Why? You're not some ignorant hillbilly who masturbates to Fox News." She paused. "Wait. I assume you don't masturbate to Fox News. Do you masturbate to Fox News, Chris Hodge?" Mirele gave Hodge an impish grin. She was a woman who knew how to eat men alive, but Hodge was ready for a challenge tonight.

"I do. Daily." Hodge was surprised that a woman from Israel would be so naïve about politics, especially about the points he had raised in his thesis. "You're from Israel."

"I am."

"Your country knows how to handle Islamic extremists. Ariel Sharon is—"

"Don't talk to me about Sharon. The settlements and aggression will get us all killed eventually. You can't piss off over a billion people and expect Mossad and the Army to take care of the fallout. The house of cards will fall. Can't you see that?"

"Will you answer a simple question for me," Hodge asked, a half-smile on his face.

"Alright. Sure. But I have to say I'm disappointed that's the only type of question you have, Chris Hodge."

Hodge ignored her bait. "What would happen if terrorism wasn't addressed?"

"Terrorism is being addressed, albeit in an indiscriminate fashion that harms innocent Muslims."

"You didn't answer my question." Hodge's entire premise for his argument about Islam was based on an inconvenient truth. The fact that defenders of the politically naïve, doveish-bordering on-pacifistic chokehold on the topic, like Mirele, would evade as their first instinct was expected.

"There would be an increase at first from the lack of a military response, and then a dramatic decrease once the Muslim world understands that Israel, the United States, and Europe have developed tolerance for Islam."

"You've been in Boston too long. Tell me, would that be before or after Israel is wiped off the map?"

"There are solutions. If Muslims don't feel like they're under siege then there wouldn't be these terrorist attacks. By the way, in case you aren't aware, Muslims are far from the only people to commit acts of terrorism."

Hodge laughed. "I thought you were an intellectual equal. Your argument is reductive."

"You're not Israeli. You're not even Jewish. What gives you the nerve to even comment on this situation?"

"So you have to be Jewish to comment on this situation? We're all citizens of the world. And if you were intellectually honest, you would admit that the Democratic Party doesn't have Israel's back. I can't fathom how they garner Jewish voters."

"Uhh, maybe because we're an oppressed people and we don't want other disenfranchised people to continue to be systemically oppressed."

"You are aware that I attended MIT with a single mother who makes less than one year's tuition, right?"

"Yeah, but you're a white male. You don't have barriers in place to your success." Hodge scoffed. "No, you don't," Mirele continued. "The entire system is designed to allow people like you to succeed. It's not equal."

"Nothing is equal. Skill isn't divvied up equally at birth. Work ethic isn't divvied up equally at birth. Outcomes can't be equalized. It's foolhardy to even attempt it and history shows how dangerous that can be."

"Look, we have a responsibility to work towards equality, Chris Hodge, whether you believe so or not." Mirele kissed Hodge on the cheek. "Do me a favor."

"What's the favor?"

Mirele whispered in Hodge's ear. "Don't tell anyone I'm really a Marxist until after my term as Prime Minister is finished. Could you do that for me, Chris Hodge?"

"Sure, if Israel still exists after you're done leading her," Hodge retorted. "Look, Mirele, not only shouldn't we try to equalize outcomes, but we can't. Social engineering doesn't work. You're too sharp to not realize that people aren't equal. Everyone isn't born with the same talents. It's the Marxist in you that won't admit it and tries to go against nature."

"Right. The Marxist in me. I go against nature. Right, Chris Hodge," she bristled.

"If I mention how Islam has a foundation of murderous conquests, rape, and pillage since the 7th century then I'm scorned for living in the past. If a Muslim mentions baseless claims about the Jews or the Crusades then it's perfectly acceptable – courageous even. A Muslim can say whatever he wants and we have to bow to his perspective, but an infidel speaking the truth is politically unacceptable."

Mirele drank the rest of her Margaux in one gulp. "You know we're going to hook up, right?"

"Are we now?"

"No, not now, Chris Hodge. Tonight, you better hope Bill O'Reilly's makeup artists do a good job." With that said, Mirele left. Enamored of her combination of beauty and sass, Hodge hadn't noticed the man at the end of the bar, but the man at the end of the bar had been waiting for just this moment. With the lady gone and the bartender having to attend to other business, the eye could now chase its rabbit. The stranger slowly rose from his stool, leaving his barely touched pinot grigio behind as he approached Hodge.

"I knew your father." The stranger slid Hodge a dirt-stained and cracked black and white photograph of two smiling young men in combat fatigues standing in a jungle. Hodge stared at the photograph. The same blond hair. The same ice blue eyes. The same mesomorphic physique. Hodge wondered what this man was doing with a photograph of his dead father, presumably from his service as a Marine during the Vietnam War.

The stranger coughed. "When my lungs were intact." Before Hodge could even think of a suitable reaction, the stranger left the bar.

"Hey. Hey, Chris. Hodge." John remarked, panic in his voice. Hodge turned to John. "Was that guy giving you any trouble? I had a strange feeling about him all night."

"No. Everything's fine. Don't worry. Thank you for the Margeaux."

"Hey, you sure you're alright, Chris?"

Hodge left the bar without answer or explanation of any sort. His father had always been an enigma. Christopher Hodge, Sr. had died in the Beirut barracks bombing when his son had just turned four years old. Hodge the elder always seemed a vague presence to Hodge the younger, rarely home, always away on military operations. The only clear memory he had of his father was the airplane that he had brought back with him one day after a few months away in some far off location. He played with it every day until his older brother Dennis broke it in a jealous rage. Weeks later, his father was dead.

Now, some strange man had given him a photograph of his father in a military uniform and claimed to have known him. Why? A cold gale from the Atlantic blasted Hodge in the face as he turned the photograph over. Written on the back were instructions in neat cursive: "Let's take a walk. Congress and Farnsworth."

It was three days into the new year, but downtown Boston was still lit up for the Yuletide season. It was six o'clock on a Saturday night, the time of the great line shift. Happy families heading into the city from the suburbs were being replaced by the mixture of students and townies seeking to drown themselves in cheap liquor and cheaper sex. Abbott Mazuski waited on the corner of Congress and Farnsworth on this unseasonably cold night, shivering in his camel cashmere bouclé topcoat. Though his posture betrayed a man whose life was lived in shadow, Mazuski stood confidently. The prospect of learning more was too alluring to resist. To lose one's father at the age of four is to live with permanent mystery. Mazuski had considered all the variables that would bring these two men to the corner of Congress and Farnsworth that night. Of all the combinations of variables, this outcome was assured. Chris Hodge could not abide a variable of permanent mystery. He would, with high probability, always act to reveal hidden truths. He would choose action over passivity if given the chance. He would come.

Only ten minutes. Hodge arrived at the corner of Congress and Farnsworth. He was greeted by an identification card that Mazuski flashed in his face, too quickly for Hodge to ascertain which agency he was associated with, if any, or if the ID was even valid.

Mazuski coughed. It was a dry hacking cough and had been a common occurrence for him for the last couple of years. He had been diagnosed with small cell undifferentiated carcinoma of the lung one year ago and was continuing to undergo chemotherapy and radiation therapy, which transformed his naturally slim figure into a sickly, almost grotesque physique.

"I'd like to borrow your brain for some analytical work, Chris," Mazuski said in a low voice after his coughing fit had reached its conclusion. He began to stroll up Congress Street, motioning for Hodge to follow him.

"My brain for some analytical work?" Hodge had entertained the idea of entering the intelligence community. He had applied to positions at the NSA and the FBI and had received letters in the mail stating that his candidacy had been rejected. Hodge wondered if those letters were a ruse. Could this caricature of a spook be recruiting him for work in the IC? "What does that have to do with my father? Did you know him?" Hodge was spitting venom as he handed the worn photograph back to Mazuski.

Mazuski looked wistfully at the photo. He had enjoyed serving in Vietnam. There was a peace in the battlefield that civilian life, even throughout his service in the Central Intelligence Agency, could not offer him. There, the objective was simple, kill the Viet Cong and their allies. He had been an O-5 in the United States Marine Corps and relished the opportunity to lead his men from the front. Most of his men were exceptional warriors, though they lacked the strategic mindset or power to alter events outside of a rice paddy or some other malaria-ridden hellhole of a landscape. When President Nixon cowed to the demands of the peace and love generation, Mazuski had become a warrior without a battlefield. In one short month, he changed that situation, transitioning to strategic control over global conflict, but in an altogether different capacity. His new allies were masters of tradecraft, not war. Deception was ammunition. It was an adjustment, but Mazuski knew that even if his base inclination was more suited to the life of a Marine than an intelligence officer, his demeanor suited just fine.

"Who are you?" Hodge asked. His rage had begun to manifest. His father's ruddy Scotch-Irish complexion came to the forefront, partly in response to this baffling situation and partly due to the sub-freezing temperature.

"Those were better times," Mazuski remarked as he handed the photograph back to Hodge, his mind on the jungles of Vietnam and the men with whom he served.

"What do you know about my father? About his death? About Lebanon?"

Mazuski grinned. That same temperament. A true line-animal if ever there was one. "Deep down you must have known you'd follow in his footsteps. Intelligence is the highest calling."

"How did you find me?" After the words came out of his mouth, Hodge balked at the ignorance of his statement. Apparently Mazuski did too; he laughed in response, setting off another coughing fit. Hodge knew that whoever this shadowy stranger was, he was somehow connected to the intelligence community. Finding people is their bread and butter and Hodge wasn't exactly a tinfoil hat-type living off the grid. Hodge knew that even if he were, he could be found. That's just what these people do. "I'm not following. I'm not a military guy. I didn't apply for this," Hodge continued, hoping to trigger a clue as to the stranger's intentions.

"We've followed your progress."

"My progress as an academic?"

Mazuski laughed again. He hated to laugh because invariably it led to a coughing fit, but there was a distinct humor to the situation. He wondered if he was wrong about the boy. The boy fluent in Italian,

Spanish, French, and Russian with working proficiency in Arabic, the boy who quarterbacked The Aquinas School for Boys to the NJISAA Prep "A" championship, the boy who shot a 396 in the NCAA Air Rifle competition, the boy with 68 hours already logged flying – he couldn't possibly be this dense, could he? But family was a touchy subject. All logic gives way to emotion where family is concerned, Mazuski supposed. When Mazuski's flurry of laughs and coughs had reached their denouement, he began to search for the right words. He knew that reeling Hodge in would require a delicate touch. His voice softened, adopting a fatherly tone. "You do know that you can't save the world writing policy papers from an ivory tower, don't you, Chris?"

Hodge stared at the photograph. He could see the resemblance between this man and the other man in the photo, and he knew without a doubt that the other man in the picture was his father. His mind obsessed on the thought, desperate for even a hint as to his father's military life and the enigmatic way in which he died. "You worked with him? You were in Vietnam together?"

"Your father was a good man, a good soldier, a patriot."

"What the hell happened to him?" Hodge asked through gritted teeth.

"I won't put you in harm's way." Not this time. Not again, Mazuski thought to himself. Once again, his cough sputtered out, weak, dry, and ever present.

"Harm's way? Two weeks after graduation and I get some spy novel spook recruitment speech and a bunch of bullshit about my dad? My brain for some analytical work? Just tell me what the hell you want." The weather was too cold, the crowds too boisterous, and the neighborhood too charming for this conversation. The odd juxtaposition added to the fraying of Hodge's nerves at this intrusion into his life. It was supposed to be so simple. Pursue his Ph.D. in the fall, trek through the Yukon with Spencer and his girlfriend for a month or so, and in his spare time, brush up on his chess and do some freelance software development for a professor's startup. Hodge knew that those plans would have to be delayed, if not altogether abandoned, now that this new catalyst for some as-yet-unknown objective had emerged.

Mazuski knew that he had to ante up or risk a clusterfuck of this situation. He always preferred that objectives be met in the simplest way, whenever possible. "We're looking for a Ph.D. that can win a barfight. You're smart, you're capable, and this runs in your blood. I need an answer." Even that singular sentence had strained his lungs. Mazuski began to cough again, this time producing a thick mucus, which he wiped up with a handkerchief that he had stored in his coat's pocket.

"I want answers," Hodge demanded.

"I need an answer."

"You haven't told me a damn thing about him."

Mazuski smiled. The boy had fire in his belly. That was a good thing. "He didn't think twice. Honor. Commitment. A true Marine."

The men reached the corner of Congress and East Service Road. Without notice, Mazuski broke ways with Hodge, turning down Service. Hodge watched with bewilderment as Mazuski's silhouette disappeared into the darkness. He took another look at the photograph, placed it into his pocket, and then went on his way.

4

EAST COAST, U.S.A

FEBRUARY 2002

Persistent awkwardness was the phrase that Chris Hodge would use to describe every visit back home. At one time, his mother Donna and brother Dennis were part of his world. Now, they occupied a different plane of existence. Hodge had grown accustomed to the intelligentsia at MIT and the moneyed Boston Brahmin set. He had been groomed to associate with the upper echelon at prep school, yet Hodge had remained grounded by returning home to his receptionist mother and wayward older brother each night. After four years at MIT, including living in Boston through the last three summers, the distance between Hodge and his family had started to surface. He loved his family, but Hodge found it difficult to relate to their hardscrabble working-class New Jersey existence. It was not the life that had been set up for him, but family was family regardless of the inescapable vastness between them.

He planned to spend a week back in South Amboy. It would be enough time to try to spark his mother back into some semblance of a life. It would also be just about the limit of how much of his brother's crap he could handle. Hodge loved Dennis because he was his brother, but he had no respect for his choices. Dennis was not as bright as he was, but his brother was sharp enough to do more than have a life that consisted almost exclusively of visiting AOL chat rooms, playing Gamecube, and watching pornography whenever he wasn't at his entry-level job selling computer equipment. His brother was a failing example of modern manhood, or the lack thereof.

Chris Hodge had arrived at his mother's bungalow around one o'clock. When he was a child, the front door had been gleaming white; now, peeling paint hung from what was once shiny and new. Prior to 1983, the lawn had always been impeccably manicured; today, it was terminally brown from lack of care and too many winters with too much uncleared snow cover. A remnant of old vinyl ribbon from a balloon remained around the mailbox, a permanent reminder of his deceased eldest brother's ninth birthday. Hodge rubbed the ribbon between his hands. Now, he was ready to return.

Just as Hodge had expected, the house was empty. His mother was at work and Dennis must have continued to put forth the bare minimum effort necessary to remain employed in his entry-level sales job. Hodge lugged his suitcases up the stairs and dropped them off in his bedroom. The room remained the same in perpetuity. The rough, old blanket on his bed was folded tight and neat in hospital corners. Hodge ran a hand along the blanket to smooth out the lone crease. On his desk was a copy of *Revolutions in Physics* by Casper and Noer that he had read during his first Christmas break at MIT. Sticking out from the end of the book was a baseball card. It was his 1989 Topps Rookies card of Gregg Jefferies on the Mets. Hodge took the card out from *Revolutions in Physics*, then slid his binder of 1989 Topps cards off a side shelf tightly packed with binders of laminated baseball cards from the late

1980s and early 1990s. Hodge found the empty space after he sorted through the alphabetized catalog, then put the card back in its proper location.

It had been over two years since Hodge had visited Princeton. Since his time at The Aquinas School for Boys, Hodge had remained in touch with several of his favorite teachers and old football coach via email. Coach Hays had always been there to guide him as both coach and mentor, and Hodge was disappointed that it had been so long since he had made the effort to visit him on campus. Time spent with Coach Hays was worth the repeating variations on a theme that was the tour of strip malls and decaying suburban houses that marked the drive between South Amboy and Princeton.

The Aquinas School for Boys hadn't changed at all in the four years since Hodge had graduated. He imagined it hadn't changed much since 1914. Even the student body felt the same. Pubescent teenagers hovered on the precipice of adulthood, bundled up in North Face jackets over a uniform that no one had taught them how to clean and they didn't yet know how to launder themselves.

The students, like the stone facades and stained glass, screamed Ivy League. In the still gray light of the frozen February afternoon, the cold and academic architecture embodied an even greater majesty. Hodge took a deep breath, easing into relaxation as he entered Coach Hays' office.

The first thing Coach Hays told him was that the lineup this year was almost better than the one he captained his senior year. Of course, Coach Hays ran a hand across the fine blond hairs on Hodge's scalp. Hodge had started buzzing his hair every Sunday morning with a

#4 clipper ever since Coach Hays called him out for being a hippie after they had just won the New Jersey prep championship. At the time, Hodge's hair was tapered and gelled like Zack Morris from *Saved by the Bell* and was only about two inches long. Hodge never would allow his hair to grow that long again. Coach Hays had been like a father to him, and he wanted to meet his expectations in every way.

Coach Hays' office was sparsely decorated aside from the artifacts of the successful students he shepherded through Aquinas' athletics program. Ribbons, trophies, plaques, and championship cups adorned every available surface. As they chatted, Hodge's attention drifted past his mentor to the glass case behind him. A photo of a broad-shouldered, jovial-looking young man in Aquinas football regalia smiled above his school record for most touchdowns in a single game and his name etched in gold leaf, Jacob Matthew Hodge. Coach Hays crossed his arms and lowered his gaze, shifting his weight slightly.

"Jake was one hell of an athlete."

"Could have gone on to play college ball." Hodge echoed an easy, familiar refrain intended to avoid the platitudes that ubiquitously accompanied this topic: "He was taken too soon," "he's in a better place," and the worst "time heals all wounds." *Time couldn't punish the scumbag who killed him*, Hodge thought. The drunk driver who had run a red light and plowed into Jake Hodge's driver-side door had evaded justice with the help of a silver-tongued defense attorney and the alleged mishandling of evidence.

"Seems like no one's been over to see him in a while. I swung by last week and freshened up the flowers."

Hodge appreciated the gesture. His mother could barely control herself at the funeral. He knew she would be unable to bring herself through the gates of the cemetery.

Hodge returned home. His mother was in the kitchen preparing spaghetti with red sauce and meatballs with a side of eggplant parmigiana. It was classic Italian-American old world fare and though Hodge had a fine palate that had dined at more than a few Michelin-starred restaurants, his mother's food grounded him. The day started well enough, until Dennis emerged from his sticky cave upstairs. Dennis had a way of making even the most appetizing food unpalatable.

Seventeen years of employment as Doctor Pieter Wouters' receptionist had programmed Donna Hodge. She rose, unaided by alarm clocks, at precisely six in the morning. For years, she prepared her sons for school. She cooked them breakfast, fixed their bagged lunches, and took care of her own routine afterwards. By the age of eleven, Chris had enough courtesy and responsibility instilled in him to prepare himself for school in the mornings. Even though Dennis was four years older than Chris, he remained attached to his mother's preparations through his teenage years. Chris Hodge suspected that his brother couldn't even cook a package of ramen for himself. In a way, his mother was somewhat responsible for allowing his brother to remain trapped in his perpetual adolescence. She could kick him out, or at least choose to not prepare his daily feast, but where would he be without her? Donna Hodge was the daughter of immigrants from the island of Sicily, a place of lawlessness and murder, where family has remained the only stabilizing force for millennia. To her, some things were beyond personal responsibility, they were a question of blood. She had lost both her husband and oldest son to untimely deaths and her youngest son's future was too bright to remain in South Amboy. She didn't want a life here for him anyway. Dennis was all she could hope to hold onto.

Donna Hodge was an early riser by habit, but the constant hole of familial death sapped as much energy out of her tonight as it did seventeen years ago when her husband and oldest son died within months of each other. By nine o'clock, Donna would be in bed, drugged into a dreamless sleep by a Klonopin or two. Chris Hodge worried about his mother's reliance on benzodiazepines, but curing her constant anxiety and insomnia was beyond his reach. Every time he tried, she would shut down the conversation by telling Chris that she needed them ever since his father and brother died.

Chris Hodge knew that his mother kept a stack of photo albums in the living room closet. It was ten o'clock. By now, his mother should be fast asleep and Dennis wouldn't be seen again besides for the occasional bathroom break. Chris Hodge didn't want his family to intrude. He didn't want to subject his mother to the pain and didn't want the hassle of having to explain himself to his brother.

Hodge stared at a picture of his father cradling him in his strong arms. His father was wearing the red shirt with gold lettering given as a uniform for Marines to wear during PT. His father must have been halfway through his thirties at the time the picture was taken, but as Chris Hodge examined the photograph, he felt that he was staring into a mirror. His father had the exact same blond hair, cut in a high and tight, the same blue eyes. Dennis had the dark hair, brown eyes, and dusky olive complexion of their mother. Chris Hodge loved his mother, but as he gazed into the photograph, he knew that he was his father's son.

It had been weeks since the Klonopin worked at her alarmingly high maintenance dose. Sleep, Donna's one respite from the pain of loss that gnawed at her every day, had now failed her. Donna thought that perhaps a change of scenery might trick her mind into shutting down. She had splurged on a down-filled sofa as a Christmas gift to herself this year. There were advantages to sleeping on the sofa, she thought. The living room had a cable box rather than just network television. She could turn on Cinemax or Starz and find an interesting movie to fall asleep to instead of 20/20.

Donna was startled to see Chris in the living room, poring over a stack of her photo albums. His mother in the room, Chris shut the albums like a young boy caught with his hand in the cookie jar. Donna Hodge may not have had the privilege of her youngest son's education at MIT and one of the finest preparatory schools in New Jersey, but she was intelligent enough to know exactly what he had been doing. "Why are you torturing yourself like that?"

"I want to know who Dad was."

"You know your father. You know how he died."

"Do you think it could have been foul play?" Hodge wondered if the strange man that he had met at Landmark knew something about his father's death. Hodge knew that maintaining national security meant that sometimes the public could only be half-informed at best on matters with geopolitical importance.

A tear began to form in Donna's eye. "Chris, why are you asking me these questions?"

"How did I get that private school scholarship? You didn't even apply for me. Did Dad have friends in high places?"

A few tears trickled down her cheeks. Donna Hodge wiped them away with her fingers, trying to dam the river. "I don't know. Who cares? You got a great education, Chris."

She must be hiding something, Chris Hodge thought, as he pressed on, "Did Dad ever have strange men around? People who looked like G-men?"

Donna spoke with great rapidity, "No, Chris. What are you talking about? Why are you?—"

Before she could continue, her son cut her off. "After he died, did anybody come visit? Maybe from the government or the military?"

The tears started to cascade down Donna Hodge's face like a waterfall. "Of course. Two men came. They told me how sorry they were. And that's it. I never heard from anybody again after that. Never." His answer received, Chris Hodge put an arm around his mother's shoulder. He knew it was painful, but after his experience with the stranger, it was necessary to ask.

Dennis bounded down the stairwell and immediately positioned his pudgy frame in front of his younger brother. "What the hell's going on, Chris?"

"Nothing. Go back to your video games," Chris Hodge replied with a dismissive wave of his hand. Hodge enjoyed video games occasionally, with a special fondness for adventure series like *The Legend of Zelda* and *Metroid* that required a combination of snap reflexes and an agile mind; however, his brother's gaming habits struck him as pathetic. Dennis played in excess of six hours every night, racking up every achievement in these virtual worlds while ignoring even the most modest of achievements in reality.

Dennis turned his attention to the stack of photo albums. He moved in close enough to notice the photograph of Chris and his father, then slammed the album shut. "Asshole. You trying to make Mom upset?" Dennis gave Chris a shove, but it barely registered. Chris Hodge spent five days a week in the gym and ran a few miles almost every morning. Dennis Hodge spent five days a week in fast food establishments and almost never woke up before ten, the ability to make his own schedule being the main reason that drew Dennis to his current job.

"Dennis! Please don't fight with your brother," Donna's words were impotent. Dennis had hated his brother since they were children. Chris was strong, like his father, and put up with his brother's rage with what she thought was the patience of a saint.

"You see her? You see how she is? I live with her. I care for her. You run off to your fancy college and stop in whenever the hell it suits you. You don't give a shit about family. You don't give a shit about Mom. Never have."

Chris Hodge had planned to stay for a week. He realized that he would have adjust his plans. He couldn't make it through a full day. "I'd better go." He hugged his mother and then walked out the door.

Hodge had meant to get on the Turnpike; he'd made this drive so many times, his brain was on autopilot when he found himself turning into St. Joseph's Cemetery. He sighed and went to put the car in reverse. *I'm going to get back to Boston so late now.* He put the car in park and set out through the rows of stones towards an anemic-looking tree. Donna had insisted Jake be buried under the tree, becoming overwrought when she was told that the plot had been taken. In the end, he was buried under the tree with a headstone that Hodge always found distasteful. An artist's rendering of the photograph of Jake in his football uniform had been laser-etched into the granite flanked by large crosses. Underneath it read "Loving son and brother." The flowers Coach Hays had put in the vase a week or so before had already perished in the cold. Hodge took them from the vase. *What a waste.* He discarded them in a trash bin at the edge of the cemetery and got back into his car, reversed, and made his way to the Turnpike.

It seemed to Chris Hodge that every state trooper from New Jersey to Massachusetts had been stationed on speed trap duty on the New Jersey Turnpike that night. Hodge kept himself alert, careful to avoid assisting an officer in fulfilling his quota. When he merged onto I-84 East, traffic slowed to a crawl. About eight miles up, a woman in a neck brace was being carted into an ambulance. Orange flares around the scene of the emergency lit the ambulance and police vehicles like radioactive candles. The blinking lights of the emergency vehicles reflected her blood, blood that had speckled the sooty remnants of half-melted snow piles on the side of the road. The woman's 1999 Suzuki Grand Vitara was a mangled heap of metal and glass. Rubberneckers slowed down to watch, hoping to fulfill empty lives through gawking at a horror show at two in the morning. After assessing the scene, Hodge averted his eyes and waited for traffic to move, knowing there was nothing else that could be done.

It was a quarter past three when Hodge reached Exit 18. The lights of the Boston skyline illuminated the night sky like millions of fireflies, casting the city in limbo, neither dark nor light. The Charles River was still and glimmering. *There was no life in it*, Hodge thought.

A fish couldn't survive in it, beautiful as the river seemed at this moment. Nothing and no one could survive in such a toxic atmosphere.

Long as it was, the drive from South Amboy to Cambridge was routine for Chris Hodge. Once he drove off Exit 18 and merged onto Cambridge Street, he would continue onto River Street, then Prospect, and drive a few blocks until he reached his front door. Tonight was anything but routine. Upon entering the city limits, Hodge clocked that he was being tailed by a black BMW.

Chris Hodge had a sneaking suspicion that he had been watched for most of his life. Everything had lined up just a bit too perfectly. His mother earned a modest salary as a secretary, yet he was able to take advantage of the opportunities presented to him at every turn. Why was he so fortunate? Hodge knew that his mother wanted the best for him, the same as any loving parent does, but she was only a high school graduate with a smattering of junior college coursework from before she met his father. Her father was an immigrant from Trapani who had worked as an iron worker until he threw out his back when he was in his fifties. Hodge's grandmother was a homemaker originally from Italian Harlem. She had moved to South Amboy with her illiterate parents when the Italian spoken in the neighborhood had begun to change to Spanish. Hodge knew that he should not have been able to study at MIT, that he should not have been able to learn multiple languages. His life should have ended up closer to his brother's mediocre existence. But it didn't. Chris Hodge knew that his father must have been involved in something, but as to whatever that something may have been, it was a mystery. Hodge wondered if tonight was to be a night of reckoning. Do terrorists drive BMWs? Maybe members of his own government had come to take him out. Perhaps his work was sending up red flags to make them think that he knew more than he did.

Trying to lose his tail, Hodge took a sudden right turn, then sped up for a left turn that made his tires squeal, but the BMW remained two cars behind his 1996 Ford Mustang. Hodge took another left down a narrow alley. The BMW followed behind, the only other vehicle on the road. It wasn't even trying to be inconspicuous anymore. "Screw it," Hodge said to himself. The day had been long and the night even longer. Whatever was going to happen would happen whether he wanted it to or not. Hodge pulled over. The BMW parked right alongside his Mustang.

An extremely tall man in a dark suit, white shirt, and blue tie emerged from the BMW. "We'd like you to take a ride with us, Chris."

Hodge wasn't surprised to find the stranger from Landmark in the back of the BMW, but he was astonished by the stranger's first question. "Chess. What's your rating?"

Hodge scoffed. The big guy was driving and there was another spook riding shotgun. Neither looked back or said a word. "You tailed me to ask about my goddamn chess rating?"

"A friendly question. No need to be defensive," the stranger replied, setting off a coughing fit.

"I'm a 2200 player now. In high school I devoted more time to it and had a FIDE rating of 2500." Mazuski already knew Chris Hodge's score. Twelve years ago he had commissioned Doug Smith, a good player in his own right, to train Hodge in order to develop his asset's tactical and strategic intelligence. Doug had left the Agency shortly after his cover had been blown while trying to gather intelligence on threats to the government from a death cult that believed life had started on Mars and the true knowledge of humanity's origins was being suppressed by the government. Luckily, they averted another Waco with the space cadets, but it was a close call. By that point, Hodge was already three years into his tutoring and had a FIDE rating of 2100, which Mazuski figured was solid for a twelve-year-old.

"How many languages do you speak?"

"I'm fluent in Italian, Spanish, French, and Russian, with professional working capacity in Arabic." He had surpassed Wouters. The Dutchman that Mazuski convinced to hire Donna Hodge and press her talented son into developing foreign language skills only spoke four languages and one of them was his native tongue. Wouters continued to try to persuade the local school board to place a heavier emphasis on foreign language education. The civic leaders still ignored him, always icing him by stating that they would take his request into consideration, but Wouters' enthusiasm for languages had rubbed off on his employee. She was only too eager to send her son to language camp and Chris Hodge was as quick a study as Mazuski had hoped.

"What did you shoot in the tournament your senior year?"

"A 396." Bob Woodhull was a Scout leader. He was a family man and nervous type who owned a video rental store that sold black boxes that bypassed pay-per-view protections. Mazuski had some fun with that guy. He had put on his thickest Mafioso accent, a New Jersey Nets Starter jacket, and a Yankees hat to dress the part. He tracked Woodhull down outside of St. Mary's after he had dismissed his Scouts and was on his way to his car. Mazuski implied that Woodhull's cable descramblers were cutting into his trade and he would have to tell "the boys" to do something about it if Woodhull didn't do him a favor. He needed Woodhull to spend an hour a week developing the shooting skills of his second cousin's son. Mazuski told him he had plans to make Chris Hodge his man with the big guns, even though the boy was only three-quarters Italian. Woodhull was only too eager to comply.

"When did you enter your gifted program?" Mazuski knew the answer to that question as well. Nine months before his asset started kindergarten, Mazuski had struck up a relationship with Adrienne McAlarney, whose brother was the principal of Hodge's elementary school. He didn't even need to convince Jim McAlarney to place Chris in gifted education, as all he talked about during Thanksgiving was Hodge's exceptional intelligence. Mazuski only had to endure one Thanksgiving with that dull ignoramus before he called the relationship with Adrienne quits. If he had to listen to one more joke at a McAlarney family gathering about how he couldn't speak because his every word was classified, he would have devised a plan to make Jim McAlarney a desaparecido.

"In Pre-K." Hodge rolled his eyes. "Do your questions have a point?"

"What did you like best in camp? Tug of war? Wrestling? War games?" That one was easy, Mazuski remembered. Uncle Sam financed twice the camp's usual fees and in exchange the camp agreed to mail a special coupon and adjoining letter to the Hodge household. The letter stated that Chris Hodge had won a school contest for a free summer at their camp. Hodge was too excited to attend camp that summer to mention to his mother that he never entered any contest of the sort.

"What do these questions have to do with my father?"

The stranger ignored Hodge's question. "What's the worst moment of your life?"

Hodge glared at Mazuski. *The Babe Ruth card. It was him. He orchestrated the event. He was there. Dressed like a nerd. Loser cover story, a set-up. Same face. Maybe Richie Martino's stepmom too. Maybe Richie Martino's stepmom was a spook. Maybe Mazuski got her to tell her son to tell me that she was a nudist. I got away that time. Dropped to the grass and crawled. Climbed the fence. The long way home. Panting, heart pounding the whole way. I got away that time.*

Mazuski coughed and then answered his own question. "Stealing the Babe Ruth card at St. Mary's. Humiliating, wasn't it?" For all his exceptional abilities, Chris Hodge was still a normal American boy of the late eighties who loved collecting baseball cards. The local Catholic church opened its basement once a month to vendors who sold comic books and sports cards to an audience of young boys and eccentric men. Mazuski and Tom Graf dressed in full nerd regalia for that occasion. Mazuski goaded Hodge with a story of how he had bought the card for only a hundred dollars off a poor sap with a sick mother and no job who was desperate to fund her medical treatment. He could still recite the lines that he and Graf came up with to prod Hodge into stealing the card. "You know, if I were your age and some older guy showed me a card like this, I'd a stole it. It'd be easy to steal a card from some old fart like me. But you wouldn't do that. You look like just a harmless little punk. You don't have the brains or the ability to steal a card as valuable as this one." Graf played his part, approaching Mazuski with a sob story about how his girlfriend dumped him because he wouldn't get rid of his collectibles. Mazuski, good friend that he was, ignored his wares and soothed his friend's ego. Hodge scooted off with the card as planned and Mazuski raised all hell afterwards. There were many aspects of the job which Mazuski appreciated, but the acting components were up there on the list.

"You've been tracking me," Hodge asserted.

"Those rejection letters from the CIA and NSA must have hurt. Academia is a terrible fallback for someone as talented as you, Chris."

"You've been steering the course of my life since I was young. Why?" Hodge asked, his suspicions confirmed.

"Because you're relevant. I," Mazuski paused for a moment to choose his words, "We have guided you by our hidden hand. We have been preparing you for this role your entire life."

"And if I say no," Hodge replied, a defiant grin on his face.

"You won't say no, Chris, because to say no is to make me disappear and to make me disappear is to forever bury your father's story." Hodge couldn't fathom the nature of the role. Were they recruiting him into one of the conventional agencies? Was this his induction into the FBI, NSA, DoD, or CIA? Given the strange nature of the events, Hodge wondered if he was being recruited for a shadowy subgroup - false aliases, fake passports, that whole deal. The whole chess rating deal was what he started with tonight. Maybe he was being recruited for an all-intensive chess camp to take out Garry Kasparov. It wouldn't be any stranger than everything else that had transpired. "Well, Chris, what's your decision?" The stranger asked as blood and mucus flowed out of his mouth.

5

CAMP PEARY

VIRGINIA, U.S.A.

MAY 2002

Camp Peary outside of Williamsburg, Virginia was an AFETA, or area for Armed Forces Experimental Training Activity. In the official records it was listed as being under the Department of Defense. The existence of Camp Peary and its training facility for covert officers of the CIA and other intelligence agencies, colloquially known as "The Farm," was never publicly acknowledged. Camp Peary was Chris Hodge's first destination for the role he was being groomed for, covert contractor. He would be charged with leading teams into terrorist hotspots and eliminating high-value targets when the U.S. military's hands were tied by bureaucracy, political expediency, international agreements, or traditional rules of engagement. While the thought of joining the military had crossed his mind on more than one occasion, he had instead decided to protect his country through academic discourse. Abbott Mazuski, who had identified and developed Chris Hodge since the age of four for this role, steered Hodge's decision and guided his rabbit into a different hat.

Hodge sat in a classroom with around twenty other potential covert operatives. The room felt like a byproduct of the Cold War and contrasted sharply with the hallowed halls of the classrooms that had preceded this one. Mahogany, large wrought iron and stained glass windows, chalk dust, and professors in unkempt corduroy suits gave way to a stark concrete box with halogen lights, the smell of industrial disinfectant, and twenty-odd laser-focused crew cuts. The slide projector whirred as the instructor, a mid-fifties straight-laced analyst type in khaki slacks and understated cobalt tie, focused the lens on a slide that read: "Interrogation Methods and Procedures." Hodge's mind wandered as he smiled slightly at the thought of this class being offered at MIT. All of the personality assessments, IQ tests, polygraph examinations, medical checks, and extensive interviewing that he had undergone over the prior months felt like a surreal dream when he compared them to his life before. Now he was back in his element—in the classroom for his first day of official training. He had the same brand of notebook and pen he had always been partial to, but the pen had suddenly taken on more heft. In the ten weeks in which he had been at the Farm, about a quarter of the operatives had been asked to leave or quit. He knew that there would be a steady rate of attrition as the process continued.

The lecturer began, "Before you can effectively interrogate, you must master human psychology. Psychology is not a discipline that ended with Sigmund Freud or one relegated to basket cases discussing their childhoods on therapists' couches. Understanding human psychology is a critical component to intelligence work and success in the field." He hit the clicker. A slide of a Middle Eastern man in his early twenties with sallow skin, a thick beard, and oversized Western-style clothing appeared on the projector. "This is Ahmed. Ahmed was bullied throughout his school years for being smaller than the other boys. To gather intelligence from Ahmed, you need to become his friend." The lecturer jabbed at the button on the remote again. The slide changed to another Middle Eastern man, but one with an altogether different countenance. His arms were crossed and powerful. His chin strode upward. Like Ahmed, his clothes were also Western, but it was clear he had an eye for how to present himself in a masculine manner despite his relative youth. The coup de grâce? His beard was twice as thick as Ahmed's. "This is Muhammad. Muhammad was his school's alpha. He had his pick of the prettiest hijabis, a loyal group of suck-ups, and the respect of all his peers. To gather intelligence from Muhammad, you need to challenge his position."

Hodge scribbled the words "challenge Muhammad." At that moment, he wished that he could show this notebook to Mirele. Tattoos never appealed to him, but he might have to get that one, if for no other reason than to mess with Mirele whenever he was cleared to head back to Cambridge. If he went through with the gag, Hodge knew what would occur. Mirele would call him all manner of names, criticize his understanding of issues of substance with her baseless arguments, and then head to bed with him. Among her many other exceptional talents, Hodge considered Mirele an unparalleled lover. After months at the Farm without a woman's touch, Hodge relished what lay in wait for him when his training had concluded.

At first, Hodge viewed the daily physical and mental tests at Camp Peary to be formidable challenges. The exclusivity inherent in the demands lent them an air of excitement. That feeling was fleeting. In short measure, Hodge began to exceed expectations for recruits. The days started to blend together into a peaceful monotony. Scout Sniper school at 1400. Learn to assemble a sniper rifle by hand in under thirty seconds? Easy as pie. Tactical exercises at 0500. Construct a ghillie suit and evade simulated enemy combatants in Camp Peary's acres of unimproved land? No sweat. Range at 2200. Dope your scope and score a grouping on a target 800 yards out? Piece of cake.

After several months at the Farm, the water-based exercises were the only type of training that elicited even the slightest reaction from Hodge. Swimming came easily to him, as most things did, but the tranquility of the water belied hidden depths better left unexplored. About half of the recruits that had entered with Hodge were still powering through the rigorous training out of some combination of pride, adventure, patriotism, and their own innate exceptionalism. The other half had returned to a life where regardless of whatever deeds they chose to pursue, they could speak of them without betraying national secrets, the tightrope that is the global world order, and their own free existence outside of prison. Hodge expected that many more of his peers would be asked to leave or choose to do so of their own volition in the coming weeks as the intensity continued to escalate. It was understood that every recruit possessed unparalleled ability across a wide array of fields, but Hodge and his peers still failed on a continuous basis at the Farm. This failure was part of the process; what mattered was how a recruit dealt with falling short. Those who could power through were the survivors. Regardless of the circumstances, Hodge would not allow himself to wash out. He had been given this opportunity and would do whatever was necessary to see it to the end.

The torture was the part of training for which Hodge had the deepest appreciation in preparing him for any possible contingency. He and three other recruits had been locked in a tiny containment room for five days. Hodge was deliriously tired from a one hour per night sleeping schedule, physically broken down from sporadic assaults for which no defense was expected, and on the verge of starvation from a diet of water. To defecate, a tin can lined with a plastic bag was placed in the corner. It had been well used the first two days, but Hodge learned through his experience that fecal matter was difficult to produce without ingestion of edible matter. The cell was often enveloped in an eerie silence, as neither Hodge nor any of his fellow "prisoners" had the strength to speak, but external speakers occasionally piped jarring noise into the cell at an ear-splitting volume. Wildly off-key saxophone music was one of the recurring favorites. A scratchy recording of Rudyard Kipling reading his poem *Boots* was another. Hodge had memorized every cadence of Kipling's voice as he proceeded through the poem. "We're foot-slog-slog-slog-sloggin' over Africa! Foot-foot-foot-foot-sloggin' over Africa. Boots-boots-boots-boots-movin' up and down again! There's no discharge in the war!" Difficult as the experience was to endure, Hodge felt a certain level of resignation when the exercise was completed.

After every manner of test had been passed and almost eighty percent of his recruiting class had left the program, Hodge was sent to Langley. Due to his expert marksmanship, proficiency in Arabic, and knowledge of the core issues related to Islamic extremism, he was selected to operate out of hotspots in the Middle East and North Africa. Hodge was seated in a classroom with a group of men who were also selected to work as contractors in the region. A four-star general with the Air Force addressed the group, beginning without any introduction. "1983, the U.S. Embassy bombing in Beirut. 1983, the Beirut barracks bombings." Hodge steeled himself at the mention of the apparent place of his father's demise. "1984, the U.S. Embassy annex bombing in Beirut. 1993, the shooting at CIA headquarters, right here at Langley. 1993, the World Trade Center bombing in New York. 1998, the U.S. Embassy bombings in Kenya and Tanzania. 2000, the attack on the USS Cole in Yemen." The instructor took a breath, then continued. "2001, the destruction of the World Trade Center and the deaths of thousands of American lives. Are you getting the picture? These people do not like us. Furthermore, our intelligence indicates that Islamist terrorist cells are not only continuously plotting to attack U.S. interests abroad, but to also score another decisive attack on our soil. The potential for terrorist attacks in the near future is extremely high. Since President Ronald Reagan's departure, President George H.W. Bush, President Bill Clinton, and President George W. Bush have abandoned President Reagan's muscular approach to leadership and adopted a far more reactive approach. They have sought to develop peace through the proliferation of McDonald's and other Western products into Muslim-majority nations. Unfortunately, I am not yet aware of a way to stop an IED with a Big Mac." Hodge smirked at the line, agreeing with the sentiment. *We have to be right all the time; they only have to be right once.* Hodge had always been a master of control, but eight months of training had instilled in him a new level of discipline. He surmised that at the beginning of the year, he would have laughed.

6

MOGADISHU, SOMALIA

DECEMBER 2002

Guuce Duale was welcomed home with a peck on the cheek from his wife Jamilah. The fragrant aroma of her sambusas, pastries that resembled samosas filled with spicy minced meat and vegetables and seasoned with cardamom, wafted throughout their one-room home.

"I hope you worked up quite an appetite, zizou." Like most young men in Somalia, her husband enjoyed playing soccer, teaching their son the basics of the game at every chance. He was no Zinedine Zidane, but Jamilah was happy to see her husband and son grow even closer through the beautiful game.

"Oh indeed I did, walal." The couple were extraordinarily loving for Somali standards. While Guuce knew that many other men did not use terms of endearment for their wives or even kiss them on the mouth, he was never ashamed to show his affection for Jamilah in private, or when around his brother and son. She always returned his affection in equal measure.

Guuce's brother Erasto lived with the family. He entered the home with Sharmaarke, who had a soccer ball tucked under his twiggy young arm. "Walaalka, I have a story for you." Erasto was a man of moderate temperament and a controlled countenance, yet he was barely able to contain his laughter. Guuce was surprised to see his brother in such an excited state.

"Oh. What is this story?"

"Abdullahi had a customer, a rich man, an engineer in the Hodan District, who needed to have his VCR fixed. When I arrived, a man was at the door. The man had tears in his eyes, brother. I asked him what had happened and he told me that he had come to ask for a beautiful woman's father's blessing and she had closed the door on his ugly face." Unable to control himself any longer, Erasto burst out in laughter.

"The poor man. Erasto, that is a terrible story. Everyone deserves to be loved," Jamilah replied.

"May Allah be merciful for this transgression, but the man who was crying, he was so ugly. He was missing an arm. And the woman was beautiful."

"Mashallah," Guuce exclaimed as he tried to stifle his laughter.

"Why was he missing an arm?" Sharmaarke asked as he tried to head the soccer ball through the open door. Not quite an expert on the pitch just yet, Sharmaarke's ball spilled over towards the charcoal of the side-feed stove. Jamilah deftly kept the ball away from the flame with her foot.

"Manchester United has a contract waiting for you, walal," Guuce joked.

"Do they pay in shillings?" Jamilah remarked, a smile on her face.

"They pay enough that my brother can have his own bed. They pay enough that you can give him some money to take to marry that girl."

Erasto laughed. "She was beautiful, subhanallah."

"You are getting old, big brother. You are twenty-three. Soon you will be gray and crippled. Is that the time you will find a wife?"

"Inshallah, I will marry soon when I find a suitable woman."

"Love is a great gift," Jamilah said. "When you find love, like I found love with your brother when I was thirteen, you don't wait."

Erasto adopted a mockingly serious tone. "It is not a difficult problem to find love. I do have an arm." The brothers both laughed. Jamilah served the sambusas on the plates that had been fashioned out of scrap metal. Sharmaarke tried again and expertly headed the ball out of the door. It was a blissful evening for the entire Duale family.

7

SOUTH AMBOY, NEW JERSEY, U.S.A.

DECEMBER 2002

Hodge had completed nine months at The Farm, but his training was far from finished. Instead, it had merely been put on ice for the next three weeks during the holiday season. Mazuski had informed him that he would be proceeding to team leadership training, a program with an expected duration of ten weeks, or, as Hodge translated it, another two and a half months away from Mirele. Afterwards, Hodge would be deployed to an as-yet-unknown location. Until then, Hodge was free to do as he pleased, with the one exception being that he could not mention where he had been for the bulk of 2002. Mazuski had primed him on his cover story: He had been working with a nonprofit based out of Uganda setting up health clinics in rural villages. It was a hell of a left turn, but Hodge was instructed to say that he'd had an existential crisis after graduation. He'd recognized that the academic career he had been pursuing was meaningless and impotent. Upon realizing that he wouldn't save the world writing policy papers from an ivory tower, he had struck out to make some sort of difference. Mazuski said to make sure that he phrased his decision in those exact words. Both men smiled at that remark, but only Mazuski coughed.

After his experiences at the Farm, driving to South Amboy from Cambridge was a breeze. He made it into town in just under four hours, a record time for the twenty or so trips he had made between his university and hometown. Hodge knew that his mother would continue to be despondent and his brother would continue to be bothersome. It had never been difficult for Hodge to handle this reality.

Hodge met his mother and brother at a playful fifties-style diner just off Exit 11 on the Turnpike. The ex-military recruits had unanimously said that the food at Camp Peary was better than the barely-fit-for-consumption MREs they had grown accustomed to in combat. Hodge was halfway between a gourmand and a health nut, eating small meals every few hours that he prepared on his own. He reveled in picking out fresh vegetables for a large protein-filled salad with chickpeas and pine nuts that he would often season with exotic spices, or finding the leanest swordfish fresh from the day's catch at The Waterfront on Atlantic Avenue. However, this diner in Woodbridge brought back memories. Coach Hays would take him and the guys on the team here after every win. Hodge was convinced they had the best burgers in the Northeast, a judgment only somewhat clouded by nostalgia.

Dennis dipped his burger into the pool of ketchup smothering the fries and the iceberg lettuce and solitary cherry tomato that passed as a side salad in diners like these. He took a bite, then wiped the excess sauce off his lips with the back of his hand, leaving a streak that resembled a wound. Donna tapped her nails against her plate. It was almost a rhythm, but not quite. Was she trying to tap the Bee Gees? Maybe subconsciously. There was something apt about Donna tapping the rhythm to a song that paramedics use to remember the correct rhythm of CPR. She was alive, but just barely. She hadn't taken a bite. Chris Hodge checked his watch. It had been over seven minutes since their food arrived. He and his brother were almost done with their burgers and Dennis had already finished his french fries.

"How's your burger?" Chris asked Donna.

She looked at her youngest, then at the plate. "I'm not hungry," she whispered.

Dennis dipped the last bits of his burger into the ketchup and licked his fingers with such disregard that his side of the booth was beginning to resemble a full-blown crime scene. With his mouth full, he decided to point out the elephant in the room. Bits of pieces of hamburger and bread flew across the table into his brother's dish. "So now you're going off on some, what, aid mission? Where the hell did that come from anyway?"

"I realized I couldn't save the world writing policy papers from an ivory tower," Chris deadpanned.

"Where the hell is Uganda anyway?"

"East Africa," Hodge wouldn't give his brother the benefit of getting a rise out of him.

"I didn't forget about what happened the last time you came here. What the hell is wrong with you? All those questions about Dad? You know how much it upsets her. Are you trying to kill Mom, asshole?"

Donna's eyes teared up. Hodge finished the last of his burger and daydreamed of tin cans and the scratchy voice of Rudyard Kipling.

8

CAMBRIDGE, MASSACHUSETTS, U.S.A.

JANUARY 2003

Mazuski had called Hodge the night before and told him to be in front of his apartment building at 0800 hours. Hodge did a double take when he saw a vintage coupe parked in front of his building. Mazuski was in the driver's seat. He rolled down the window and beckoned Hodge to come inside.

"Should I even ask?" Hodge said, a smile on his face.

Mazuski beamed with pride. "If you were wondering, it's a Lancia Beta 1800. One of the best handling cars ever made. I put in Pirelli tires, an ANSA exhaust, and dual Weber carbs."

Hodge nodded his head and entered the vehicle. "I fulfilled my end of our bargain, why don't you fulfill yours? Were you there with him? Were you in Lebanon?"

Mazuski had long relied on his innate verbal dexterity to manipulate events and individuals. In this situation, Mazuski judged that a firm approach rather than the clever tongue that was his normal weapon of choice was the right tool for the job. "If your mind is not on your mission, you are a dead asset. A dead asset cannot lead a team. A dead asset is irrelevant." The car hit a red light and Mazuski started coughing. He wiped the blood off his mouth with his left hand and kept his right hand on the wheel.

"Then I better not be a dead asset," Hodge replied.

9

VIRGINIA, U.S.A.

MARCH 2003

Hodge had completed his first two months of team leadership training without a hitch. After almost a year of this intensive grind, he was a transformed man. His ambitions of becoming a prominent intellectual figure now seemed far removed. While discovering the truth about his father remained a driving goal, Hodge had embraced "the suck." If Mazuski revealed the truth of what happened to his father right now, Hodge would still proceed with his work as a contractor. To Hodge, this role was such an extreme break from the tedium of an ordinary life. The risks were exceptional, but Hodge knew that without risk there was little value in a reward. Without risk, growth was impossible. Without risk, there could only be stagnation. In a way, Hodge figured that he was fortunate to have the opportunity to live this life, even if he could never speak about his experiences.

"Are you aware of the Geneva convention?" Chris Hodge asked, his voice dripping malice at Rich Kempton, a burly blond contractor who was playing the part of a captured insurgent. Hodge had cuffed Kempton's hands together, tied him to a chair, and taped his mouth closed. Kempton muffled out wild indecipherable sounds as he desperately attempted to break free, an effort that was to no avail. "I am not a soldier. I am a private contractor. The Geneva Convention? Not applicable." Hodge screamed his words in Kempton's face as if his tone could melt skin. Surprisingly, it couldn't. There were other substances for that, Hodge had learned.

When Hodge ripped the tape off the faux insurgent's mouth, Kempton pleaded for mercy. "Please! Please!" He begged, adopting a poorly imitated Middle Eastern accent of unspecified origin. Hodge had never seen an Islamic extremist who looked like a 19th century painting of Thor and sounded like Tim McGraw impersonating the Soup Nazi from Seinfeld. He knew that the real targets he would have to face were far from caricatures.

"I need information. You love your family. You wouldn't want anything to happen to your family. To your little sister Zaynab. To your mother. I need information," Hodge demanded. The exercise reached an abrupt conclusion when an instructor nodded his head, an unspoken approval of Hodge's performance.

Team leadership training offered Hodge and his fellow future team leaders the opportunity to simulate a variety of situations that they were likely to experience in the field. It was instilled in the men that the one predictable aspect of their job was its unpredictability. They were expected to operate intelligently, not as automatons, but to stick as close to mission orders as possible. One such eventuality that Hodge and the others were prepared for was the certainty that one of their team members would be injured in battle. Hodge learned basic Tactical Combat Casualty Care. He learned how to correctly apply a tourniquet or apply pressure to stem the bleeding from a wound, and how to check the pulse of an injured limb. He learned to use the Glasgow Scale to check for concussions and to assess soft tissue damage using DCAP-BTLS (deformities, contusions, abrasions, punctures/penetrations, burns, tenderness, lacerations, and swelling) after a traumatic injury. He would learn to run his hands along the wounded man's arms and legs and ring them almost like a rag, then squeeze and push down on the pelvis. He learned that if a team member lost consciousness, to rub his sternum or pinch under his arms. Mostly, Hodge learned that the best medicine is to lay down the most rounds down range. If unable to drag the wounded out of the line of fire, the best tourniquet in the world would be useless.

Preparation for combat was extensive. Hodge's weapons training was as a sniper and CQB. For a week, they had flown him and several other team leaders to an installation in Maine's Longfellow Mountains. At seven thousand feet above sea level and with blizzard conditions obscuring his vision, Hodge scored near-perfect hits on lifelike models of enemy combatants at distances of over one thousand yards. His instructors told him to treat the bitter cold and rocky terrain as a vacation. If he were stationed somewhere among Afghanistan's impossible landscapes, he would remember this exercise as a cakewalk.

One of the foremost components of team leadership training was brushing up on his Arabic. Hodge and other team leaders practiced perfecting their inflection and accent with the help of native speakers who exchanged assistance as U.S. assets for citizenship. Hodge thought that these teachers had a hell of a deal. Live amongst the mullahs or embrace freedom. It was an easy choice.

On the last week of training, it was revealed to Hodge that he would be deployed on three separate missions as a primary sniper, secondary interrogator, and tertiary medic. Afterwards, if he performed to expectations, he would assume the role of team leader on various ops. His first destination was Iran.

10

LANGLEY, VIRGINIA, U.S.A.

AUGUST 2003

Chris Hodge returned to Langley after his third and final deployment as a rank and file team member. In his first few tastes of action, Hodge's teams had amassed a total of twelve high-value kills in Iran, Syria, and Yemen. Hodge sniped a respectable five kills between the three locations.

Hodge's final task before he could become a team leader was to assemble a team of five other contractors to eliminate two local warlords who had obtained control over large swaths of the city of Mogadishu. These men had plunged the city even further into chaos. Hodge found humor in the futility of the mission. The goal itself was not difficult in comparison to some of the missions that other team leaders had been given. Maybe Mazuski had put in a word to go easy on him because he thought Hodge was a soft college boy. If that were the case, it would be a horrible error in judgment. Hodge once aimed for the life of an elite, if not iconoclastic, academic. That goal was no longer relevant. His priorities had shifted.

Hodge stood in front of a whiteboard with a marker in his hand. He had already slotted himself in on the chart as team leader with a secondary function of sniper and tertiary function as interrogator, but still needed two snipers, an interrogator, a medic, and a language specialist to round out his team. Every contractor was expected to be versatile and at a minimum be able to fulfill three of these roles. Hodge's goal was simple. Choose the best contractors.

Jake Cantrell was Hodge's first interviewee. He had graduated from Johns Hopkins University with a Pre-Med degree and served as a 68W (Army combat medic specialist) on the ground in Kosovo. He was an operator by history, but his outward appearance did not reflect that of a meat eater. Cantrell was a light-skinned biracial African-American with poofy auburn hair and a Pacific Northwest Zen vibe to him. Despite being six years older than Hodge, he had retained his babyface.

"You know we don't work for the military. We don't have anything to do with the Geneva convention, nor do we wear a flag. Do you have an issue with that?" Hodge's words were less a question than an accusation.

"No." Cantrell knew that Hodge was testing him. He had been used to it throughout his military service and much of his life. It was one of the reasons he had joined the Army in the first place. Cantrell was proof that books should not be judged by their covers given that his performance during counterterrorist operations had earned enough notice for him to be at Langley meeting Hodge for this assignment. Through the hour-long interview, Cantrell had earned Hodge's trust. Hodge was ready to place his life in his hands. He had many criteria for admission to the team and could forgive a number of eccentricities, but trust was paramount and non-negotiable. Cantrell did not look like a soldier, but Hodge was a contractor set to run a team, not a director poring over talent at Central Casting. Hodge knew that Cantrell would work out just fine.

11

MOGADISHU, SOMALIA

SEPTEMBER 2003

Camp Mogadishu was a small base camp behind wire a few kilometers outside of the city. Some of the larger forward operating bases, or FOBs, were shared with official U.S. military personnel, although the contractors had their own separate quarters and were officially discouraged from interacting with others on the base. It had been years since the United States had any official involvement in Somalia, but the threat of Islamic radicalization in Somalia spilling over to neighboring countries and the anarchic conditions of a country without a functional government necessitated that threats be monitored and, when appropriate, eliminated. Hodge understood the importance of addressing the problems in Somalia and other hotbeds of Islamic extremism. The doves at MIT who would occupy the halls of power in a few decades were not the only ones who obstructed efforts to improve these countries. Even many of his fellow Americans supported the hasty retreat from Somalia and remained suspicious of most foreign entanglements. The majority paid heed to sound bites and propaganda that served to keep these countries unstable. Hodge conceded that a few innocents would always be collateral damage when targeting the bad guys. That was the nature of war. What always seemed to be unspoken was that the scale of death in countries given over to Islamic extremism would be far greater if left unchecked, and the spillover effects could never be confined to "somewhere else" in a globalized world. Eventually, the car bombs would be targeting the cute little coffee shops and yoga studios of suburban America if terrorism was not contained.

Chris Hodge and Whiskey Team had been flown onto the base the night before. As Hodge entered the welfare and recreation center, he observed his men unwinding. Language specialist Anthony Latone, known as Bozo, and sniper Louis Tabbedtikosin, known as Rain Man, were playing *Halo: Combat Evolved* on an Xbox that Rain Man had brought to the FOB. Bozo and Rain Man shared a bunk bed in one of the rooms on base. When Bozo observed Rain Man placing the video game console into his storage locker, he joked that "None of us are thieves here, brother, but some of us are gamers. Keep that out for tomorrow." Rain Man was more than happy to comply with that request.

Cantrell, known to his teammates as Hippie, lived up to his moniker, flawlessly strumming *Baba O'Riley* on his acoustic guitar. His bunkmate Kirk McClung, known as Steam, was counting off push-ups. Even in the midst of physical exertion or sleep, Steam never removed his Oakley sunglasses or West Virginia Mountaineers baseball cap. In his initial interview, Hodge had found out that Steam would in fact remove them on mission, but never on base. Steam asked Hodge if that would be a problem. Hodge couldn't see why it would be for someone who was an even better shot than he was. Despite his roughneck ways, Steam had been working as a contractor longer than any of the other men assembled and had an excellent record as an interrogator when on mission. For Hodge, the results were all that mattered.

When not on mission, the contractors more or less had free reign to pursue whatever activities they chose. There was a gym on the FOB and a small library inside the welfare and recreation center with a handful of books that the men could check out, as well as a collection of movies that the men could watch on the television. While Hodge did not care how the men chose to spend their time under most situations, he wanted to counter the perception of the team as six separate units with little cohesion. Steam was off doing his push-ups, Hippie played his guitar, and Bozo and Rain Man played Xbox without any communication beyond the occasional grunt or "oh shit," always from the far more communicative Bozo. Bling was not even in the rec center with the rest of Whiskey Team. He had made it clear to Hodge from their initial meeting that he preferred his privacy and did not view the job as a social club. There were only two reasons why Bling worked as a contractor: he was an ace at the job and it paid extremely well. He told Hodge that he would do this for only a few more years and then he planned to retire to the mountains of Colombia and live like a king. His track record of more confirmed kills than any other current contractor allowed Hodge to overlook his antisocial tendencies. Regarding the men who did choose to interact, Hodge found their conduct left much to be desired. Hodge left the rec room and headed for the generator outside. He switched off the power.

When Hodge reentered the rec room, he was carrying a camping lantern. He placed it down in the center of the room.

"Thank you, Jesus. I thought he'd never stop. You gonna smash Hippie's guitar, too?" Steam asked.

"I play it, I get to smash it, man. Like Pete Townshend."

Hippie lifted the guitar above his head and swooped it down, doing his best Pete Townshend impersonation. His reflexes were on point; the guitar was mere inches from a floor-based demolition.

"I ain't never met a spade who liked *The Who* before. You're OK, Hippie." Steam was a contemporary Archie Bunker in military drag. Although he was the furthest thing from politically correct, Steam was hardly a racist. Steam believed that every man he served with-be they spade, spic, or whatever-was his brother, which to Steam meant granting automatic license to hassle them on any grounds.

"My white side, Steam." Hippie was the youngest of Michael and Stacy Cantrell's six children. They had married in 1965, when it was still taboo for a nerdy white physicist like Michael and a free-spirited black artist like Stacy to join together in holy matrimony. Hippie grew up in the sleepy town of Bremerton in Washington State, and although he and his family had dealt with some tension over the years, people accepted him and his kin. There had never been a need to develop a protective shield because of his background.

"You gonna put the power back on, Wild Man?" Bozo asked. Hodge shook his head. It was a negative on that request. Hodge wanted the guys to wait it out in the dark for a bit longer. He clocked an idea in his head. He might have to break this trick out the next time he visited South Amboy.

Hodge pointed the lantern at Rain Man. "I thought I was quiet."

"Focused," Rain Man responded. Louis Tabbedtikosin had been raised by a single mother, though she was a mother in little more than name. She had been a mean and violent alcoholic. His older sister seemed to suffer the brunt of the abuse and soon turned to alcohol herself. Louis learned quickly to stay out of their way, retreating to the sanctity of the nearby woods and the quiet recesses of his own mind. When his sister snapped, he was the one to discover the work of her violent retribution. He could still feel the texture of his mother's congealed blood gluing his rubber soles to the cracked linoleum as she lay lifeless on the kitchen floor, a carving knife protruding from her carotid. He wouldn't speak at all for a month following the incident and joined up a month after that, preferring the clarity of purpose and discipline of military life to one dictated by the fraught complexities of human relationships.

Bozo slapped Rain Man on the back. "This guy may not say another word for the next month, but damn if he doesn't end up smoking more skinnies than any of us."

"More'n you, at least," Steam interjected. "Wild Man, don't you know dumb I-ties like Bozo can't shoot straight?"

"I think I'll be all right," Hodge smiled.

"You're shitting me. You too? Hodge ain't a guinea dago wop name."

"My father was half-Scotch Irish and half-Italian. Northern Italian. My mother is full Sicilian." The glib smile never left Hodge's face as he explained his background to Steam.

Steam turned to Rain Man and punched him in the shoulder. "We the only Americans here?"

"Ho-Chunk." Rain Man did not smile or betray any emotion whatsoever. He was a man after Joe Friday's own heart.

Bozo jumped in. "Guess you're the head of the Klan by default." Bozo's father had been a degenerate gambler, blowing through his paychecks on horses that were supposed can't misses, yet always seemed to fail to live up to such lofty expectations. His father's habits kept his family poor, too poor to live anywhere but Boston's notorious Southie community. Southie was a neighborhood where if you did not have relatives in the IRA, you were a target for all manner of working-class rage - especially if you were of Italian descent. It had been hell growing up, but Bozo's experience as an outsider in Southie made him both tough and well-acquainted with gallows humor, a trait that had been amplified once he joined the Navy and became a SEAL.

"Yep," Steam responded, a devilish smile on his face.

"Good. That's what I like to see. You're a unit. Act like one." The point made, Hodge left the rec room. The only question on his mind was whether he should turn the generator back on or let the gamers wait it out a bit longer.

At 1400, Hodge entered the small intel trailer that was on the FOB. There, Jackson Powell, the official CIA military liaison for Hodge's mission, sat behind a desk in this cramped space. There was only room for a metal folding chair on the other side of the desk, computing equipment, and an endless pile of files inside the trailer.

"Welcome to the biggest shithole in Africa," Powell remarked as a greeting.

"Happy we're here."

"Your target is Diric Khalif Barre, a local warlord. He's one of our Tangos who has made half of Mogadishu a dysfunctional warzone."

"Kill mission?" Hodge's testosterone had started to flow. It was a quiet first night. He took care of the preliminaries with his team, then read through over one hundred pages of *The Satanic Verses* before he went to sleep. Maybe if he played his cards right, Hodge would have a fatwa issued against him, just like Salman Rushdie.

"No. Snatch mission. Find out what he knows and use this information to infiltrate his direct superiors. They're to be eliminated."

"Location intel?"

"Our intel confirms that he's holed up in a shit shack about thirty klicks north of Mogadishu."

"Hot?" Hodge asked.

"You look educated. Are you familiar with *Dante's Inferno*? Cause you're stepping into it."

Hodge turned to leave the trailer. He knew that he would have to walk through the fire and maybe even the deepest layer of hell. Unlike Dante, he could never write the tale.

Almost as an afterthought, Powell remarked, "Oh, and you'll have an asset. Name is Gucci or something." Powell held out a file without looking up.

Hodge skimmed the document. *American asset...one brother Erasto, mother died in childbirth, father deceased, Lebanon 1983. Lebanon in 1983? How about that for a coincidence?* "Thanks." Hodge placed the asset's file back on top of Powell's tower, then walked out.

Hodge had been growing a beard for a month. Officers had advised him that in order to blend in with the population, the beard would help. Hodge found the statement funny. Even having dyed his beard black, he would have had a hard time blending in with the crowd in Italy. The aim was for him to portray himself as a Levantine Arab or coastal North African to the local population, but any cover other than a Viking was hardly believable for Hodge. Still, covert agents were expected to be incredible actors, but this wasn't a movie set. They wouldn't get endless takes if they didn't quite nail the part.

Chris Hodge was set to meet Guuce Duale at one of Mogadishu's many souks. The largest souk in the city and country, the Bakaara Market, was in a no-go area and entrance was strictly controlled by Mohamed Qanyare Afrah, a faction leader in Mogadishu who had set up a security checkpoint outside the souk. Afrah was officially the Minister of National Security for the internationally recognized government of Somalia, but his record was hardly squeaky clean.

The entire city of Mogadishu buzzed with life, but the souk in which Hodge entered in one of the calmer areas of Mogadishu—calm being a relative word when it came to Somalia—was particularly crowded. Hodge walked down the narrow street past men and veiled women who hawked all manner of daily essentials. Shouts in Somali, Oromo, and occasionally Arabic for maize, sorghum, beans, peanuts, sesame, wheat, rice, medicine, and petrol assaulted Hodge's ears. Somalis were starving while the price of food was wildly inflated. Revolution was near.

Hodge had done his best to blend in with the crowds. He had donned his pajamas, or local Muslim attire, to draw as little attention to himself as possible. It had been years since Somalia had been a tourist hotspot for Arabs or any other group of people, and Hodge's light complexion stood out. A few children ran over to him. Some older men pointed at him. One young man cursed at him. That guy was a gem. He was trying to sell a whole collection of counterfeit wares: Ethiopian and

Kenyan passports, forged birth certificates, even a fake Master's Degree in Medicine and Surgery from the University of Bologna written in such poor Italian that it would shame a four-year-old from the boot.

Hodge continued through the souk, assessing the area for any threats. Powell had told him that the area had been cleared, but he had also told him that he would be a fool if he didn't take his .40 Glock semi-automatic pistol with him. Hodge did as instructed, having taped the weapon to his leg under his macawii, a long piece of white cloth that Hodge had wrapped around his waist in his attempt to go native. He reached his destination and hid himself behind a row of pashminas. The middle-aged Somali selling counterfeit currency to the locals was a friendly who supplemented his payouts from the CIA with his daily trade. The friendly ignored Hodge as he haggled over the price of the fake dollars with an elderly man.

Guuce Duale hurried towards the pashminas. He knew that he was running late and felt guilty. The Americans had been paying for his son's education at the local madrasa. They even paid in full for his books and bought him multiple uniforms. Guuce had barely any schooling, but hoped for a better life, perhaps one day in America, for his son. The last thing that Guuce wished was to jeopardize this excellent arrangement. All he had to do was translate, drive, and act as a general guide to the area. Guuce hoped that the new American he was to meet would forgive his tardiness and not assume that he was a threat.

"Good afternoon. I apologize for being late." Guuce said in a hushed tone in Arabic. He had been told that the American he was to meet could communicate in the language.

"Don't make a habit of this," Hodge said in a voice barely above a whisper. This haphazard and out-of-breath asset had not left a positive first impression on Hodge. He seemed sloppy. Sloppy errors could get Hodge or his team members killed.

"My brother, he borrowed my shoes to go to the masjid and then he left them there. I apologize. My brother gets distracted at times," Guuce explained, hoping to convince the American of the truth of his story, unbelievable as it may appear.

Hodge smirked and nodded his head. *Yeah, if that's one thing I know, it's how brothers are. Maybe this guy isn't so bad.* "You and him get along?"

"Yes. He lives with us, with my wife, my son."

"What's your son's name?"

"Sharmaarke."

"Shamaarke?" Hodge's mother's maiden name was De Luca. People in New Jersey, both non-Italians and Italians who had melted into America's pot, had a hard time with that one. He wondered how they would fare with Sharmaarke.

"Sharmaarke is a name we give to protect our sons from evil. Inshallah, my son will be protected." Like many Somalis, sweeping hand gestures animated his every word. While Guuce, knowing the privacy this meeting required, tried to control his voice, the protection of his son raised it to the standard high decibel levels of Somali speech. He could not help it. Sharmaarke was his flesh and blood, God's gift to him and his family.

"That's why we're here," Hodge replied. *It really was*. Hodge believed that Whiskey Team could do far more good for the Somali people than any policy paper.

"Yes. And we are grateful," Guuce knew that many of the local warlords and imams, including his own, considered the United States to be a great evil and had persuaded many of his people to the same line of thinking; however, politics was beyond his concerns. To Guuce, the Americans had cared for his son and paid his living expenses every month. Any greater discussions about national or world affairs was a matter for men with the power to resolve the issues amongst themselves.

"I need a driver." That was the point of the meeting. Hodge and his team needed a driver to get them around Mogadishu and the surrounding areas. Guuce was already working with another team before Hodge and his men had been deployed. Powell had told Hodge that their asset could lead them to safe locals to act in the role.

"My friend Cabdi has much experience."

"No incidents?" Hodge asked.

"None." Cabdi had introduced Guuce to the life of a driver. From a young age, as a boy without a father, Guuce had plied his trade on the streets of Mogadishu selling water bottles. Cabdi had opened a new world for Guuce of driving Western tourists throughout the city. It was excellent work for an eight-year-old and it made Guuce feel good to be able to contribute more fully to supporting his family, even if it only lasted three months until the war. His brother Erasto had joined him in the trade and while his family were far from wealthy, the two young boys were able to meet all their own material needs from the income they earned.

"I need to meet him." In his line of work, Hodge had to be skeptical of all assertions of character. Hodge had read in the file that Guuce's father died in Lebanon. If he was part-Lebanese, that would explain his light skin and eyes. Powell told him Guuce was clean. Interviews with those close to him had indicated that he did not know anything about his father. Maybe he had an older brother who died too, though if he did it was more likely to have been from malaria than at the hands of an asshole with three DWI's who was driving with a fake license and identification. Hodge's only consolation was that the asshole's body was destroyed beyond recognition, whereas his brother's was intact for an open casket.

"I can arrange a meeting at my home. Afterwards, I would very much like you to meet my wife, my son, and my brother." Hodge had been briefed on the hospitality of the Somali people. They were just as renowned for their generosity of spirit as for their absence of government and prevalence of extremism. The Somali character knew no moderation, Hodge supposed.

Hodge nodded. "Alright, Gucci." Hodge said, pronouncing his asset's name like the fashionable Italian brand. He had a good feeling about this guy, his initial impression aside. There was a warmth to his personality and an innocence to him.

"Guuce," Duale pleasantly corrected Hodge. He had long been used to Westerners being unable to pronounce his name.

Hodge switched to English, lowering his voice even further, "Ehh...I'll call you Blackbeard." The moniker worked on so many levels. Guuce would only understand the surface observation of his thick black beard. Hodge imagined there was no way that lore of the fearsome pirate had traveled this way.

Blackbeard smiled. "I call you Baseball, great American pastime." His English was good despite the heavy accent. He had picked it up from an early age via his trade, before the situation on the ground put him out of business. His recent work as an asset had supplemented his typical form of practice over the last decade of watching the handful of VHS bootlegs of American movies with his friends at one of the few electronics shops in Mogadishu.

What could Hodge do, but laugh. From now on, as far as these two men were concerned, he was Baseball and Guuce Duale was Blackbeard.

Two days later, Hodge had taken up Blackbeard's invitation. Hodge sat down for tea, his rucksack at his feet, with Blackbeard, his brother Erasto, and his son Sharmaarke in Blackbeard's modest home in the Hamar Weyne District near Via Roma. Blackbeard's wife Jamilah was in hijab, but a few strands of her long loose curls were exposed. Hodge was observant, but her hair was not particularly difficult to spot. He surmised that the family's relationship to Islam was moderate, perhaps only cultural.

"Have you ever seen a cheetah?" Sharmaarke asked Hodge in perfect Arabic.

"I've seen a cheetah." Hodge, his ex-girlfriend Kendra, and Spencer had spent two weeks in South Africa after junior year. They had stayed a week in Cape Town seeing the sights and taking in the nightlife. Their plan was to spend the entire two weeks in Cape Town, but even the best laid plans have a way of unraveling when a young single gentleman abroad meets a spritely coed from Stellenbosch University. Melisse drove her American fling and his friends across the country. Their first stop was at a farm outside of Pretoria. The kooky lady who operated the place grew the best mushrooms that Hodge had ever tasted. The next day after their stop in Pretoria, Melisse and Kendra shopped in Sandton's upscale boutiques while Hodge and Spencer may have somewhat overdone the shots at a whiskey and cigar bar. The final leg of their trip was at Kruger National Park, where among many other wild animals, Hodge saw several cheetahs. Hodge had an amazing time in South Africa, but he was aware of the potential for danger that lurked all around while he was in that beautiful country. After his training at the Farm, Hodge knew that if he ever headed back to South Africa and was stopped by carjackers at a streetlight—or as they call it, a robot—he would be more than prepared to deal with the situation.

"An elephant?" Sharmaarke inquired.

"Them too."

"But you haven't seen a zebra?"

"I have seen a zebra." *Kruger was a hell of an experience*, Hodge remembered. "What's your favorite animal?"

"Giraffes. They're so tall. Do they have them where you're from?"

"I'm afraid not," Hodge replied. "But we have bears. They do this." Hodge performed his best imitation of a bear's deep and menacing growl, which sent Sharmaarke running into his mother's arms.

"Don't get scared," Jamilah reassured her son in her native Somali, stroking his shorn head, "Baseball's just kidding."

"Thank you for the tea, Jamilah. And the hospitality."

"You are very welcome."

"What do they say in America?" Blackbeard asked in Arabic, then switched to English, "You are my brother?"

"Some people say that," Hodge responded in English as he pointed to his milk-white face. He switched back to Arabic, "Though I don't exactly have the right look for a brother."

Hodge and Blackbeard laughed. "You're here in Somalia. We are all black here, my brother."

"That's true. But you and your brother are more of a sandy brown though. What's the deal?"

"Our father was Lebanese," Blackbeard explained.

"Lebanon? What the hell was he doing here?" Hodge asked.

"Making us." For a man of few words, Erasto's comic timing was brilliant.

Hodge turned his attention to Jamilah. "I hope I didn't scare your son."

"He's a good boy," Jamilah responded with typical Somali politeness.

"He gets frightened. But the things he sees here in Somalia, it can make a young boy nervous. Life was easier before '91." Erasto longed for a return to the Somalia of his youth. Under the leadership of Major General Mohamed Siad Barre, fighting between clans had been eliminated and the country was a just land that consistently progressed. Erasto had mythologized the Somalia of his childhood into a paradise.

Blackbeard chimed in, "What we have seen can make anyone nervous, Baseball."

"It's going to get better." Hodge didn't believe it, but these were good people. He hoped that he was wrong. Maybe he and his team and the many other teams operating out of Somalia might turn the tide. Maybe the Somali people would reject extremist forms of Islam and demand good governance. Maybe the U.S. and its allies would engage in more formal combat against the tyrannical despots and terrorists. Maybe, but probably not. The U.S. and the West at large had adopted appeasement and called it diplomacy. This policy necessitated the glossing over of all but the most overt and threatening acts of Islamic terrorism, ensuring its survival here and throughout the Muslim world.

Jamilah clutched Sharmaarke close to her. "Inshallah!" Hodge liked that expression. If God wills it. There was a fatalism tied to its religiosity. It seemed an appropriate expression for a place like Somalia.

"We're working to make this place safer for you, for your family." Hodge switched to his best blaxploitation accent, "My brother." Blackbeard and his family had proved themselves to be good people to Hodge. No experience as a contractor could ever be perceived as one hundred percent secure, but Blackbeard was so innocent, almost goofy in his manner. Hodge sensed Blackbeard was the kind of guy who could take a joke. From time to time, he may even throw a few gibes back at him.

There hadn't been many African-American students at Hodge's private school, but some of the few who did attend were on the football team. Marcus Dawkins, one of Hodge's favorite targets at wide receiver because of his lengthy wingspan and exceptional footwork, had taught him a homie handshake his sophomore year. It had been a few years since his gridiron days, but he still remembered the handshake. Hodge

did play a little football after high school. He had been a backup
quarterback on the Engineers football team freshman year, but decided
to pursue other endeavors after it had become clear that he would not get
much burn on the field. Duncan Rogers was deceptively athletic for an
Ivy Leaguer and a year ahead of Hodge. Hodge's career path took him to
Somalia, while Rogers was now a second-year starter for the Düsseldorf
Panther of the German Football League. Hodge was not one for spiritual
mumbo-jumbo, but if there was such a thing as a sixth sense, he knew in
his bones that there was no way that Duncan Rogers ever learned a
homie handshake.

Hodge busted out Marcus' handshake on Blackbeard.
Blackbeard could not keep up with the motions. Hodge had heard
theories that Horn Africans, despite their complexions, were Caucasoids
who had adapted to the intense heat of the land by developing darker
skin. It was the usual pseudo-scientific horseshit that Hodge sometimes
liked to amuse himself with when browsing the World Wide Web, but
Blackbeard's awkward and delayed reactions seemed to prove the point.
Even Duncan Rogers could do better. "Looks like I'm more of a brother
than you," Hodge's smirk was wide.

"I don't understand," Blackbeard replied. Some things were
lost in translation.

"When all this is over, I'll explain."

"That's a promise?"

"It's a promise." Hodge reached into his rucksack. After fishing
around for a second, he took out a new pair of shoes that he had
retrieved from the post exchange, or PX. He handed them to Blackbeard.
"A gift for your hospitality." Hodge's stoic face matched his deadpan

delivery, but Blackbeard and Erasto both caught on to the joke, bursting out in full-belly laughter.

Blackbeard had initiated a meeting between Hodge and Cabdi and everything was good to go with their new driver. Whiskey Team had acclimated to their surroundings and, after five days on base, were itching to make their move. At the FOB, everything proceeded the way Hodge planned. The team, sans Bling, had started to gel into a unified force through the usual off-field clowning and horseplay that was common to all the military branches and as contrasting a behavior from their action in combat as possible. It was one part *Animal House* and one part *Black Hawk Down*. Hodge expected it no other way.

Cabdi owned a beat-up Toyota Land Cruiser. Personal transport of the four-wheeled variety was not common in Somalia, but Hodge swore that nearly every vehicle that he had seen on the road was a Land Cruiser. Maybe the skinnies did not have as much of a grudge against the Japanese as they did with people from Detroit.

Hodge insisted that, despite the sweltering heat, Cabdi keep the windows rolled up. This was not a request that Cabdi had any problem fulfilling. Cabdi had a nervous disposition. Despite taking their money without reservations, he distrusted the Americans because of the information that Guuce's father and his imam had shared with him about how the United States sought to conquer the Islamic world and ban Islam. Cabdi did not hold his own people in the highest esteem either, living in fear that potential for homegrown violence and chaos would grip his family.

Hodge's entire team was inside the Land Cruiser, all dressed in the local pajamas. None of them, even Hippie, could pass as native to the area. It felt like a suicide mission, but Powell had assured Hodge as to the team's safety, a promise that Hodge found rather dubious. *Who the hell else will go in and do their dirty work? Promise everything and give almost nothing.* One day, Hodge might be far from these hot spots and give the orders from safety, or in Powell's case, relative safety, but for now he felt a growing anger at the risks that he and his men had to face. That anger was balanced with his rational belief that he could have walked away from Mazuski's still unfulfilled promise, but what kind of life would that have been other than a coward's?

To Hodge, everything on the road was a potential danger. The Toyota Noah–shockingly not a Land Cruiser–in front of their vehicle that was driving just a bit too slowly could be a threat. The crumbled buildings that may have fallen from a suicide bomber might house any number of threats. The malnourished Somali in a turban walking behind the car, yet another possible threat. The intact building with obvious remnants of past shelling, perhaps that was a hideout for Islamists. The Land Cruiser passed an empty apartment complex with about twenty young Somali men milling about, AK-47s in hand. They ignored the Land Cruiser and continued joking around with each other. Their actions reminded Hodge of the antics of his own men. Horseplay was horseplay for martial men worldwide, a necessary relief to the constant specter of death.

Hodge and his team were surprised by their first assault. Two young boys had pelted their Land Cruiser with rocks. Cabdi drove as fast as he could, but one of the side windows cracked from the force of impact. Hodge thought that if the kid who launched that rock had been born stateside he could have grown up to be the next Roger Clemens.

Cabdi had driven Whiskey Team north out of Mogadishu about half of the distance to the target's location, stopping at the end of a dirt road in the middle of the Somalian savanna. There was nothing for miles upon miles other than the grasslands and the acacia trees that formed the bulk of the landscape. The land abounded with wildlife. Hodge had seen an array of foxes and antelopes, hundreds of birds of different varieties, and even a leopard. Cabdi had explained during the ride that poachers had destroyed the elephant, zebra, and giraffe populations. It seemed clear to Chris Hodge that the people weren't the only ones in this land being embraced by the hand of death.

Cabdi popped the trunk as the team exited the Land Cruiser. Hodge walked to the back, taking out six camouflage uniforms without any identifying national markers or nametags. Until their missions were completed, the team would remain nameless men without a country, both symbolically and literally.

Hodge slammed the trunk shut and walked over to the driver's side window. He counted off twenty five-dollar bills. To Hodge, the payout seemed like a pittance, but for Cabdi this was almost a half year's salary for one day's work. He knew that the warlords and the Islamists paid well for certain unspeakable deeds, but not this extravagantly. Cabdi had known of the wealth of the West, but its limitlessness astonished him. Once he received his payment, he sped off. Whatever became of the Americans was not his problem any longer.

Hodge led his men north through the savanna. His map showed that their target was a little over sixteen klicks away. The men humped through the savanna for almost three hours, covering about eleven klicks without any greater incident than seeing a terrified warthog that sped past the team after they had come upon its hidey-hole. East Africans always seemed to win every marathon. *Even their animals are fast*, Hodge thought to himself, after Steam raised the point in a far less PC fashion.

Hodge signaled for his team to halt their movements. "Skinny." He had noticed in the distance movement from someone or something and didn't want Whiskey Team to take any chances.

Rain Man observed the figure with his Steiner military-grade binoculars. "Skinny. Sixty to seventy years old. Western clothes. Turban. Walking with a camel. Radio in hand."

"Let's rack out for four hours," Hodge ordered. Even though Whiskey Team was only five klicks outside of their destination, there was no use in proceeding when there was a possibility of engagement with a non-target. Hodge had been ordered to ensure that he and his men follow all mission directives. Going John Wayne was not only bad policy, but an easy way to alert unsavory elements to their presence. Recklessness was to be avoided at all costs.

The current terrain did not offer a wealth of choices for an effective spot to disguise themselves. Hodge started the night on standby, his M4 at the ready for any disturbances. His men slept in a circle around an acacia tree. Before turning in, everyone, even Steam, shut their mouths for all but the most essential communication. At 0100, Hodge woke Rain Man up to relieve him. There had been no signs of any enemy activity and whoever that skinny was, he had long left the area, heading in the opposite direction of Whiskey Team's destination. "Spell me until 0300 and monitor the perimeter." Rain Man nodded in assent and took up his post, M4 in hand.

After two uneventful hours marked by nothing more remarkable than the symphony of sounds from the savanna's nocturnal population, Rain Man woke Hodge up.

Hodge wiped the gunk from his eyes. "Anything?"

Rain Man moved his head sideways. "Negative."

"Binoculars."

Rain Man passed the Steiner binoculars to Hodge. Hodge scanned the landscape. Rain Man was right. All quiet on this front, other than the birds.

The team was awake and getting their kit together. "Let's move in ten mikes," he commanded. Through the dead of night, Whiskey Team humped the final few klicks to the target, over the vast plains, a few light hills, and through a shallow river. The worst obstacle the men had to face were the squadrons of mosquitoes. When they were six hundred yards out, the men changed out of their pajamas and into their field dress. The bright whites of the pajamas were easy targets and their enemies knew they were not here for the Muezzin's call to Fajr prayers.

The team cloaked themselves in the grass and vegetation, while Hodge observed the location from which the terrorists were operating. It was a conspicuous lone shack that appeared to have been made from cement, but which Hodge knew was a typical Somali mud and grass-based structure. As Hodge stared through the binoculars, the Muezzin exited the location. He was right on time to signal the faithful.

It was an easy siege. *Almost too easy*, Hodge thought. When the Muezzin began his adhan, reciting in a musical voice, "Allahu akbar, allahu akbar, allahu akbar, allahu akbar," an older insurgent and a young boy with a familial resemblance entered the shack from outside to fulfill their religious obligations. After the Muezzin finished his recitation, he too entered. It was at that point that Hodge and his team made their move. They moved through the fatal funnel, armed to take on the cavalry. The event was anticlimactic. No one, including their target Diric Khalif Barre, a distant relative of Siad Barre, former leader of the Somali Democratic Republic that toppled in 1991, was armed. "Any movement and you're dead," Hodge shouted in Arabic. Caught off guard, they offered no resistance. Hodge and the team bound Barre and his three associates' hands and ankles with zip ties, then radioed back to base that they had succeeded in their objective.

The base confirmed exfiltration back to Camp Whiskey. The terrain outside of the shack was wide open for the heli to land. With their targets neutralized and no other enemies or civilians in sight, it would be a simple process. The heli arrived twenty mikes later. Barre was thrown into a six by six by six containment room on the base. Hodge was never made aware of the fate of the Muezzin, the old man, or the young boy. Whatever had befallen them, it was not his concern.

Barre's containment area resembled the one that Hodge himself had endured during his training. Barre had been here for three days. As expected, the room overflowed with feces and urine. Despite being a fan of the kings of thrash metal, Metallica's album *Ride the Lightning* played at beyond maximum volume was painful to listen to, even with Hodge's noise-cancelling headphones. The interrogators had played that album on repeat for the last seventy-two hours. Hodge would have preferred to hear Rudyard for old times' sake.

Barre was slumped on the concrete floor. He looked exhausted and disoriented. Some of the guys must have had some fun with him already. Hodge assumed that being the new guy, there were some activities to which he was not yet privy. When Barre finally noticed Hodge, he summoned every bit of energy and shot up towards the bars, shaking them with a preternatural force. "Prayer mine. Duty Allah. Geneva," Barre pleaded in barely intelligible English.

Hodge stood in front of the cell. "There are bigger concerns for you than your religious obligations."

"Islam. No Mecca. No Mecca. Geneva."

"Nor are we concerned about Geneva. We do not represent any sovereign state or flag." Barre did not fully understand what Hodge had communicated to him, but he did understand the tone and his situation. The last of his energy expunged, he collapsed in the cell, saving Hodge the trouble of getting in on the action. He was a tough nut to crack, but after eight days, on the verge of death from starvation, Barre decided to talk. This was helped in no small measure by the administration of several drugs that had a questionable long-term impact on the health of their subjects, but were excellent for extracting information. Hodge had been informed that the drugs Barre had been given made sodium thiopental seem primitive by comparison. After that, Hodge never saw Barre again either. He knew better than to ask about a captured skinny terrorist's whereabouts after his purpose was served.

It had been almost two weeks since Hodge had seen Blackbeard. He welcomed the opportunity to meet with his new friend and asset at one of Mogadishu's few remaining upscale restaurants. The place was near the airport, outside the city, in one of the few safe zones. It had been hit with a terrorist attack six months ago. An Austrian diplomat, Chinese oil mogul, Assyrian Christian aid worker, and ten locals were casualties. The restaurant had a perfect track record of safety since that incident, which was about as good as could be expected in Somalia. It still attracted the moneyed set, and many of the patrons were foreigners as evident by the variety of tongues overheard. Fried fish and goat were the restaurant's specialties. Blackbeard dined on tandoori chicken and shrimp. Hodge had his grilled goat steak medium and a side of goat cheese. The food was edible, but inclusion on a future Zagat's guide to Mogadishu was doubtful at best.

"Is he on point?" Hodge asked.

"He is a truthful man, mashallah." Gurey Hoodo Abdullahi had been both a surrogate father and close friend to Guuce. Abdullahi had taught him Shax, his favorite game, one which they played every Friday after visiting the masjid. He also welcomed Guuce to watch movies in his electronics store on a regular basis. Guuce must have watched Abdullahi's bootleg copy of *Superman IV: The Quest for Peace* over a hundred times. Even Abdullahi could recite much of the movie when Guuce or one of his other friends put the film in his VCR.

"What's our in?"

"Safety." Like most Somalis, family was paramount in Abdullahi's life. He had lost his eldest son to a respiratory infection ten years ago. Abdullahi was desperate for a payout of American dollars.

With even one of their payouts, he could be assured that his wife would receive treatment equal to one of the warlords' own family. For that reason and that reason alone, he would do whatever the Westerners asked.

Hodge nodded. *Promising safety? Not a problem.*

Abdullahi and his family lived well by Somali standards. His home was small, but clean and modern. For years, he had supplemented the paltry income he received from running his electronics shop with occasional work for his imam. Just like he planned to now do with the Americans, Abdullahi did not question why he had to drive someone somewhere or bring a package to a certain location. He just did as he was told and took the money so that he could sustain his family's lifestyle. Now, with his wife having noticed a large lump on one of her breasts four weeks ago, it was even more critical to have the ability to provide for his family.

Upon entering Abdullahi's home, Chris Hodge and his entire team shook hands with Abdullahi. Much like in the U.S., handshakes served as a sign of respect between men upon meeting or when bidding farewell in Somalia. Hippie was a leftie, but made sure to use his right hand to avoid any undue offense to the asset. Somalis believed that the left hand was unclean. When Hodge had briefed his men on the Somali people's customs before the visit, Steam seized the opportunity to crack a joke at his bunkmate's expense. One tradition veered off dramatically from what the men were used to as native-born sons of the shining beacon of liberty. Unlike in the States, Somali men, as a sign of friendship, greeted each other with a hug and a kiss on the cheek. Hodge and his team were far from that point with Abdullahi. The team had no qualms with skipping that custom.

After the customary handshakes were completed, Rain Man took up his position providing watch by the front door, Bling guarded the rear, and Hippie moved near the window. All three team members were armed with M4 carbine assault rifles. It never hurt to be prepared in this country.

Hodge, Steam, and Bozo sat down with their legs folded on a large Persian rug arrayed over the center of the floor in the main room of Abdullahi's house. Abdullahi sat in the same fashion opposite the three contractors, further away than Somali custom dictated. He had heard from Guuce that Westerners had issues with space. "Mr. Abdullahi, it is a pleasure to see you on this fine day," Hodge began in Arabic, opening with small talk, as custom dictated, and making sure to look Abdullahi in the eyes as he spoke.

"It is a pleasure to see you as well, and your friends. Thank you for visiting my home."

"It is beautiful weather."

"Our country is a beautiful land. It was once a paradise. How I wish for the days before '91 to return to my country."

Hodge took out a stock photo of a smiling all-American family, white picket fence and all, and passed it to Abdullahi. "My family. They are back in America."

"You have a wonderful family." Abdullahi passed the photograph back to Hodge.

"Mr. Abdullahi, if it is not too rude to begin, may we discuss the matter at hand?" Hodge asked.

"Certainly. How may I be of assistance?"

"Do you have intelligence on Sheikh Darwish Ali Warsame's location?"

"I do not know," Abdullahi stonewalled. He had helped the sheikh before and was prepared to do so again if the Americans did not bestow a generous offer.

Steam whispered in Bozo's ear. "Tell him this. Tell him we can guarantee you and your family will be protected. We want to take care of you." Bozo translated Steam's message into Arabic. As skilled as Hodge was in Arabic, Bozo had a quicker mind for direct translations on the fly, the core reason why Hodge had selected him as his language expert in the first place.

The three men had discussed the framework for the interaction beforehand. This was Hodge's cue to reel him in. "If you can recall this information, we are prepared to extend a gift of twenty thousand dollars."

Hook, line, and sinker. If he accepted the job, Abdullahi would not only be set up for life, but could afford treatment for his wife's illness by the best doctors in Kenya or Egypt. Not only did Abdullahi inform them of Warsame's location and his knowledge of the warlord's operations, but agreed to drive the team during their mission to eliminate this highest of high-value targets. It was dangerous, and he felt like a traitor, but with twenty thousand dollars he could close the electronics shop and leave Somalia behind. Abdullahi could relocate his family to Canada, Australia, or somewhere in the EU and never live in fear again. Most importantly, he could save his wife's life. Of course, if the Americans botched their mission or word ever spread, he and his family were all at risk, but Guuce had vouched for these men. It was a calculated risk. Though not entirely comfortable, Abdullahi rolled the dice.

After Abdullahi had met with Powell and Hodge to relay the intricacies of the information, he was told that the operation was to be executed in two days. He tried to stay calm and go about the ordinary business of opening his shop, caring for his family, and interacting with his friends, but his mind was preoccupied with fear. He was afraid of being found out as an ally of the Westerners. He was afraid of not receiving the money after the completion of the operation. He was afraid of Warsame and his men killing not only the Americans, but him on this foolish mission. He wondered if his greed had overtaken his sensibility. It was moronic to imagine a future with his wife and children in a large home in Melbourne or Toronto or Berlin. Twenty thousand dollars American was a rich man's bounty for Somalia, but what would Somalia have in store for him after he completed this task for the Western devils?

Hodge entered the trunk of Abdullahi's Toyota Land Cruiser. Hippie followed behind. "I've got your back." After Hodge nodded, Hippie slammed the trunk shut and returned to the front seat of the Land Cruiser. Steam, Bozo, Bling, and Rain Man were crouched low to the ground in the back seat. Even in their pajamas, their light skin was a dead giveaway. With the mission about to begin, they needed to avoid any firefights beforehand that could put anyone at risk or delay the completion of the objective, and so they did their best to stay out of view.

Abdullahi's hands were on the wheel, shaking like someone with Parkinson's. He drove the men to an abandoned building one klick away from Warsame's location. The Americans had placed another stipulation on his contract. He had to drive Hodge and the associate with a complexion similar to his own to the building the night before, presumably to ensure its safety for one of their operations. After fifteen minutes, the men returned to his vehicle and once he dropped them back on their base, Abdullahi was able to return home. Gripped with anxiety, he was unable to sleep that night, despite his wife's consoling words and her promises of how their lives would be transformed after today's deeds. Abdullahi hoped that he would be able to return to her, and that she and their children would not suffer retribution for his grasping nature and betrayal of his people.

Abdullahi had transported most of the members of the team, sans their leader and the member with the darker complexion, to the abandoned building. The street was not crowded by Somali standards, but there were onlookers. Whiskey Team wore headdresses and flowing beards. Their assault weapons-none of which were Kalashnikovs–made them conspicuous. A lone teenage boy darted in the opposite direction at a speed incongruous with the somnific pace that marked all movement in this city. The people of Mogadishu had endured many strange attacks from Somalis and their foreign associates. Even the foolhardiest of residents knew better than to interfere with these types unless prepared to suffer martyrdom. Luckily for Whiskey Team, ordinary life in Mogadishu must have had a hidden pull greater than death for most of the onlookers. As to what that appeal may be, none of the men in Whiskey Team had the slightest idea.

The team had reached the top of the abandoned building without any trouble. They had climbed up the four floors through the stairwell, their weapons ready with plenty of ammunition, alert for the slightest threat. When the men reached the top, they assembled into the pre-planned formation. Rain Man and Bling were on sniper rifles. Bozo spotted for Rain Man at the south corner of the building's roof. Steam worked with Bling's acquisition on the north corner.

As Bozo spotted, Rain Man was struck by how similar the cacophony of neighborhood sounds resembled swarming bees. He could tell that Bozo's assessment of the wind being at about twelve miles per hour and heading in a northwestern direction was accurate. Through his scope, Rain Man could see that the faint lines of the mirage were almost stick straight. The intelligence report that Hodge had briefed them on advised the team to have one sniper locked in on the front door and Rain Man on the back door. His target was 580 yards away. He and Bozo gathered that using a constant of thirteen, they would have to have an MOA, or minutes of angle, of about 5.38. Rain Man broke his usual silence. "This is going to get kinetic."

Bling was low to the ground, his rifle on the front door of the shelled building in the middle of the crowded slum that Warsame had chosen to utilize as a hideout. Steam had double—really triple—duty, assisting Bling on windage range and windspeed, being responsible for staying on comms with Hodge, and taking over on the sniper rifle for Bling if he was hit or any other situation were to arise that left his partner incapable of taking the shot. Steam could see a white Land Cruiser creep down Warsame's street, but had no idea if Hodge was inside or not. *There has to be some damn diversity to the vehicles*, Steam thought. *Almost all of them are white or black and fuck if any of them aren't a damn Land Cruiser.*

Steam's walkie crackled. "Overwatch Whiskey, this is Mogadishu Main. Wild Man approaching HVT. What are your atmospherics?"

"Multiple skinnies everywhere, Mogadishu Main. No visible threats. No eyes on HVT. Over." Everything was going as rehearsed. All Whiskey Team could do was execute as planned and be ready to move off script if anything unpredictable happened. Steam had been a contractor for seven years, working in Bosnia, Kosovo, and Yemen, among other locations. He knew that he would not have many more combat opportunities as a contractor. At thirty-one, he was aging out. Steam would return to West Virginia when he officially aged out, but he didn't have the slightest idea what he would do there besides catch Mountaineers games, start drinking at Coyote Joe's again, and see if he could hustle some of the college kids at pool.

The Land Cruiser had reached the end of Warsame's street. His hands still shaking uncontrollably, Abdullahi circled around the block at a faster speed. Hodge had told him that he would bang on the trunk when it was a go. He had just received word that it was on from Steam. As Abdullahi drove the Land Cruiser up the block again, Hodge started to bang on the trunk. Unknowingly, Hodge had committed a grievous error. He hadn't just alerted Abdullahi, but had also raised the suspicions of a Somali boy who stood across the street from Warsame's complex. The boy screamed for help, shouting in Arabic, "Trouble! Trouble!"

Hippie ordered Abdullahi to speed off instead of popping the trunk. The element of surprise had been lost and there was no telling how many of Warsame's associates were with him. He and Hodge could pop a few, but the overwatch team had their back and the odds were against them winning a firefight even with their superior skill and training. Hippie stayed low and had his .40 Glock at the ready if trouble could not be avoided.

Abdullahi was terrified that the twenty thousand dollars would never be delivered if he or either of the Americans died. With a courage that he never imagined he could possess, Abdullahi drove the Land Cruiser through a hail of bullets and rocks that had been pelted by Warsame's junior soldiers, boys of no more than thirteen years of age. Abdullahi and the Americans had survived, but the Land Cruiser was worse for wear. A rock had shattered the vehicle's back window and one of the back wheels had been destroyed after taking fire. No less menacing was the fact that bullets decorated his front windshield. If Warsame's men were slightly more accurate in their shot and not distracted by the other members of the team's assault from above, Abdullahi would have been a dead man. He thanked Allah for sparing his life and mouthed a silent prayer. Abdullahi hoped that The Most Merciful would spare him from the flames of Jahannam and that his actions from now on would be weighed on the side of righteousness, not on the side of the evildoers, no matter the riches they might be able to offer.

Abdullahi pulled into an empty lot in a vacant area about ten blocks from the war zone. He stripped the registration plates from his Land Cruiser. The vehicle was useless. He needed to drive and cross the border into Kenya in order to leave the country. A large portion of the twenty thousand American dollars would have to be spent on a replacement vehicle. Abdullahi wouldn't dare set foot in his car again. He could not fathom an explanation that would placate any of his former employers.

"Forgot about me?" Hodge had popped the trunk from the inside and exited. "Try riding in the trunk sometime, Hippie. The sunlight looks beautiful through the bullet holes," Hodge said with a smile.

"Sure thing, Wild Man," Hippie replied.

Abdullahi moved in so close that Hodge could smell what he ate for his last three meals. "I demand reimbursement. My vehicle is useless. I cannot drive anywhere in Somalia anymore without being killed."

"I hear Ethiopia's nice. How's your Amharic?"

"Very funny, Dan Aykroyd." One of the movies Abdullahi had seen more times than he could remember was *Trading Places*, one of the few VHS tapes that he had in his shop. Hodge wondered where the reference came from, being that Aykroyd was Canadian and looked and acted nothing like him. Maybe Abdullahi thought that all North Americans looked alike.

"Twenty thousand's what we agreed on. Thanks for not getting me killed. One last thing. If you still want that twenty thousand, get us to our rendezvous point."

It was almost too easy for Whiskey Team's supporting unit. When the skinny across the street had started to raise a fuss, Warsame shot out of the building via the front entrance. Warsame resembled a caricature of a petty dictator. The Somali warlord "costume" seemed to be a bizarre mix of Muslim cleric, military general, and tacky third-world oligarch. Warsame wore his white-tipped beard long and covered his bald head with a military-style beret with various insignias and gold pins that he paired with designer sunglasses. While he sported the traditional Muslim long white khamiis, he covered it with a camo utility vest and a loud, colorful silk scarf.

Warsame was flanked by two of his cronies. They all toted AK-47's, but everyone and their mother had a Kalashnikov in this part of Africa thanks to the Russians. Bling had Warsame in his crosshairs and the idiot was staying stationary as he fired at the Land Cruiser. There was no reason he would assume his attackers were American contractors. To Warsame, the attack was most likely a power play against a scout from another would-be warlord or some useless official from the government. Warsame was brutal, but not a particularly creative thinker. Bling's bullet sailed into Warsame's chest. It was a perfect hit. Warsame clutched at his chest, initially oblivious to the fact that he had been shot. He grasped and flailed as a look of panic and confusion came over his face. As he pulled his hand away from the wound, he observed that his hand and khamiis were soaked with blood. Before Warsame had time to react, he collapsed. His cronies swarmed around him, searching for signs of life where there were none. Whiskey Team's target was eliminated.

Bling kept his rifle locked on the front entrance as one of Warsame's henchmen ran inside. The other at first was a moving target, ducking and dodging as he fired on the Land Cruiser. Bling wondered what the hell had alerted Warsame and his goons. He was in it for the money and preferred to keep his distance from any social club type of environment, but Bling was loyal to the men he worked with, even if he did not care for their company on his own time. He said a silent prayer for Wild Man and Hippie's safety and hoped for the best.

The henchman's idiotic rage as he stopped moving and just started firing on the Land Cruiser must have been God's way of speaking to him at this moment. Bling's shot was another perfect hit, sailing right into Warsame's henchman's upper torso. It was almost too easy. If everything continued in this way, all he had to do was lock onto the front door again and the next one would walk right into his bullet.

Steam radioed Hodge. "Three total targets. Two eliminated, including HVT. Remaining target locked in compound. What are your orders? Over."

Hodge spoke into his walkie as discreetly as possible while Abdullahi drove down the streets of Mogadishu like a lunatic or a New Yorker, screaming every Somali profanity and a few of his own invention. "Put a few .50 rounds through the wall to stir up the target."

"Roger," Steam replied.

Steam had relayed Hodge's command to the team. He thought that Wild Man was a clever son of a bitch. IR thermal wouldn't pick up where the body was behind the walls. Best to just blast through the structure and watch the target and any of his associates scramble like rats caught out of their nest.

Rain Man delivered the round. It sailed through the mud-based structure, demolishing it, but Hodge's tactic had backfired. Inside, there were over twenty skinnies. Steam ordered his team to move.

The overwatch team had just sniped a warlord. They had also sniped one of his associates. They had destroyed their complex and unleashed a new unit of additional combatants. If either faction of

Whiskey Team was expected to have a difficult time reaching the rendezvous point, all probability would point to the group without a vehicle, but Steam led the team to their location with relative ease. Warsame's other men had scrambled and panicked. The bravest of the lot fired aimlessly in the direction of the overwatch unit, but most of the skinnies bunkered down near what remained of their base. After Hodge gave the order to move, Whiskey Team made their way down the building and headed to the hospital to wait for Hodge and Hippie. According to Powell, it was the most secure location. The problem was the absolute lack of security in the ten-mike hump between the abandoned building and the rendezvous point. The men agreed that Powell's description of the hospital, or any place in Somalia, as "secure" was farcical.

While Abdullahi was becoming crazed behind the wheel, his respect for human life remained. It had been almost ten years since the city of Mogadishu had any working traffic lights. Driving was a constant obstacle course of human, animal, and vehicular traffic. Despite the failure of the state and the unending violence and chaos, the Somali people, in a mercurial fashion, were adamant about upholding respectful behavior. Pedestrians were to be allowed the right of way. Abdullahi hit the brakes when he saw a twelve-year-old boy standing in the middle of the road.

The boy had an AK-47 in his hands and a faraway narcotic-induced expression in his empty, frantic eyes. Khat, a stimulant roughly akin to cocaine, was widespread in Somalia; to Hodge, the boy looked soulless. He also looked like a killer. Hodge stealthily drew his .40

caliber Glock and made sure it was out of sight. If necessary, he would use it. He knew that Hippie would do the same.

The boy's Kalashnikov was pressed against Hodge's window. If he made it out of this situation alive, he would have to talk to Powell about the CIA springing for bulletproof glass for every one of their assets' Land Cruisers. Despite the situation, Hodge maintained his composure. He stared into the boy's eyes and addressed him in Arabic. "Go back to your warlord. We're not a part of your plan."

"Leave now." The boy didn't move. His AK-47 remained pressed against the window. Hodge's finger remained on the .40's trigger.

"Go," Hodge commanded. Abdullahi hit the gas. Hodge did not look back. His finger remained on the trigger until they reached the hospital. *Why didn't he shoot? Maybe his reaction time was slowed by the drugs. Maybe he didn't want to waste a bullet.*

Abdullahi, Hodge, and Hippie waited outside the hospital in silence. *You would think he was used to it*, Hodge thought. Maybe not two near-death experiences in one day though. That struck him as more of a weekly occurrence in Mogadishu. Still, it was a welcome respite from his incessant babbling about money, broken promises, and his anxieties. *Abdullahi was nothing but a punk. If you can't do a job, don't take it.*

Hodge broke the silence. "Pat them down, Abdullahi." Abdullahi popped the locks and the rest of Whiskey Team entered the vehicle. Abdullahi went to exit, still in a daze, only able to carry out whatever Hodge ordered. Hodge froze him with a hand on his shoulder. "That's sarcasm." Much was lost in translation in this hellhole.

Abdullahi was quiet throughout the entire trip back to the savanna. The first time he opened his mouth was after he dropped Whiskey Team off where the dirt roads ended and travel by vehicle became impossible. "I should receive more. It was not agreed upon to travel out here after you were done. There were many additional requests. I will have to purchase a new vehicle."

Hodge brandished his M4. "Bill us."

Abdullahi sped off in the Land Cruiser. He had been informed by Hodge that he would be paid tonight on their base outside of the city. If he arrived at the base, received his lucre, and returned home with the twenty thousand American as promised, then he believed that Allah was truly The Most Gracious and The Most Merciful. If he did not, then he believed that Allah was The Judge, The Ultimate Arbiter, The Reckoner.

"How much longer, goddamnit?" Steam snapped. Whiskey Team had been humping through the savanna for almost five hours. Their exfil point was thirty klicks west of where the road ended.

Hodge checked his map. "Four more klicks."

Bozo chimed in, "Now I know how Moses felt."

Whiskey Team reached the exfil point one hour later. When Steam heard the first faint sounds of the heli in the distance, he decided to crack wise, "I'm glad they took so long; gave me a chance to work on my tan." Hodge appreciated Steam for more than just the skills he brought to the team. He viewed Steam as the living embodiment of the group's unrestrained id.

At 2150, Hodge left his quarters to head to Powell's trailer. He hoped that this would be the last time he would see Gurey Hoodo

Abdullahi. *Hoodo. African black magic. The little shit must have sacrificed some chickens or goats under a full moon to whip up twenty thousand dollars from us.* Hodge was a man of his word, and beyond his own personal honor, he had to follow all necessary dictates from above; however, if it was up to him, he would have stiffed that fearful punk.

Hodge waited with Powell outside. Powell was wearing dark sunglasses and stared directly inside the trailer. Abdullahi arrived five minutes late, out of breath and disheveled. "Well? My money. I want my money," he demanded.

Powell remained facing the inside of the trailer. He passed Hodge a briefcase. Hodge passed it to Abdullahi, who immediately opened it and began to count the stacks of twenty-dollar bills.

"Steam doesn't think that brothers can count," Hodge quipped. "He's staring at the bills. Thinks they're fakes," Hodge noted after Abdullahi scrutinized both sides of one of the bills.

"Your money's all in there." Powell also spoke excellent Arabic. It had replaced Russian as, if not a prerequisite, a preferred skill for work in the field.

Hodge glared at Abdullahi. If eyes could speak, Hodge's would say "I am going to smoke your motherfucking ass if you do not leave the premises right now." Abdullahi picked up on the signal. He stopped his count and closed the briefcase, then shuttled off the FOB without another word.

"He'd do the same for them too," Powell explained. "Our assets are all pieces of shit. Don't ever think any of these skinnies are choirboys."

As Powell turned around and faced him, Hodge nodded in agreement. *Why was he telling me something that obvious?* Hodge wondered.

The Dhagax Tuur monument was only a five-minute walk from Abdullahi's electronics shop on Makkah El Mokarramh Avenue near the city's police headquarters. The monument had been an installation meant to commemorate the Somali people's uprising against the Italian colonial government. For Abdullahi, the monument's nearby park was a place where he and his friends would meet to play Shax. He was in the middle of a heated game with Cabdi. Their local imam stood nearby. He watched the players make their moves.

Guuce Duale had promised Abdullahi a game today. As expected, his friend had arrived, greeting everyone with a round of hugs and kisses on the cheek. "So. Twenty thousand U.S. isn't enough?" Guuce laughed.

"How do you know about that?" Abdullahi did not return his friend's mirth.

"Baseball told me all about it."

"Baseball? The American?" Cabdi asked.

"He said you wouldn't stop complaining. About the money. About the vehicle. About everything. You have twenty thousand; what is there to complain about, saaxiib?"

Cabdi stared at Abdullahi. Abdullahi shook his head. They had both been friends of Guuce's father. Abdullahi and Cabdi had promised him that they would care for his sons to the best of their ability if he were ever martyred. Erasto worked with Abdullahi in the electronics shop. Guuce's brother had a mechanically-oriented mind. Erasto would stay in the back room of the shop and diligently fix the occasional malfunctioning device that one of the wealthier residents of Mogadishu brought into the shop. Abdullahi believed that Guuce did not possess the skill of his brother and had become too dependent on the Americans. It was one thing to do their bidding for a large sum of money, but to enjoy bonds of affection with them was different. At the end of the day, they were still the enemy.

The imam spoke up, "I have your gifts. Come see me at the mosque later."

"Gifts?" Guuce asked.

"My apologies. For them only." The imam hugged Cabdi and Abdullahi tightly and kissed each on the cheek. He hugged Guuce rather loosely and grazed his cheek before he walked away from the group.

"What gifts?" Guuce asked the men who had raised him as surrogate fathers.

"It's nothing," said Cabdi.

"How close have you become with this American?" Abdullahi questioned.

One bright Thursday afternoon twenty-five years prior, when Abdullahi was Guuce Duale's age, he and Cabdi were in the park by the monument playing Shax, a habit that they had cultivated since their youth. It was the first time that they had met Guuce's father, Farid El Hout. His complexion was light, like an American's, and his eyes were a mixture of green and light brown that seemed to alter in composition daily. He was only a few years older than they were, but his demeanor radiated with a masculine maturity. He did not speak to them that first day and his only communication was a curt nod before he left the park. Trust had yet to have been established. Perhaps he did not yet know that most Somalis could converse in Arabic. He dropped the first package that day and was not seen again until months later. In time, he became a warmly regarded friend.

"That for the kid?" Hippie asked. Hodge nodded. Hippie had walked in on Hodge as he used a whittling knife to carve up a block of wood. To Hippie, it looked like Wild Man was trying to make a giraffe. "You really think it's a good idea to get that close to the skinnies, Wild Man?" Hippie had grown concerned about how much time Hodge was spending off base with one of their assets. Contractors, being free of the bureaucracy of the organized military, had a great deal of leeway in terms of operations; however, there was still a chain of command. Hodge was his team leader and Hippie did not want to openly challenge him, but he also did not want to put his team leader, his team, and their missions at risk.

"That family's good people." Hodge knew where Hippie was coming from, but he hadn't even met Blackbeard. He wasn't like the other skinnies. He and his family were good people. Spending time with them gave Hodge a respite from the ever-present chaos.

"None of them are good. My opinion." Hippie knew that Blackbeard was on the payroll. That's the only reason why he was nice to his team leader. If they tightened the purse strings, Blackbeard would turn on Wild Man in a heartbeat, or at least try. If Wild Man was operating with a clear mind, it wouldn't be a fair fight, should it ever come to that.

Hodge playfully jabbed his knife in Hippie's direction. Hippie darted out of the way before it even came close to landing. "What do you think, they're gonna slit my throat? Put me in a white slavery ring? Hey, if they end up doing that to us it wouldn't affect you, right?"

"Hey man, it's your funeral."

Hodge laughed as Hippie headed towards the door. "Shut it." Hippie did as he was told. Chris Hodge had to finish his giraffe. They would be leaving Somalia within the week. There was no time to waste.

The tea room was packed with soldiers. There were no Westerners here today to put his friend at ease, but Blackbeard had told Baseball that this place served the best tea in Mogadishu and he wished for him to try it before he left the country. The waiter, an Oromo-speaking migrant, had brought Blackbeard a samovar filled with strong black tea with hints of ginger and cinnamon. After the waiter served his tea, Blackbeard asked that an additional cup be brought out for his friend.

When Hodge arrived at the tea shop, he had a wooden giraffe in his hand. "A gift for your son." Blackbeard rose from his seat to hug Hodge and kiss him on the cheek. After they sat down, Hodge placed the giraffe in the center of the table near the samovar.

"Thank you, Baseball. I'm terribly sorry. I wish I had known you were bringing a gift. I'm ashamed that I won't have time to present you with one before you leave."

"Don't worry about it."

"So what's new, my friend?"

"We're shipping out in two days."

"Back to America?"

"I wish." Hodge took out the black and white photograph of Mazuski and his father and flicked it across the table.

Blackbeard examined the picture. "Who are they?"

"One's the guy who brought me out here. The other might be my father."

"Might be?"

"He died when I was four, in Lebanon."

Blackbeard passed the photograph across the table. Hodge left it in public display.

"What happened?"

"He died in the Beirut barracks bombings."

"I'm sorry, my brother."

"Your father, he died in Lebanon in '83. What was he doing there?"

"Honestly, my friend, I do not know. My father died before I was born."

"In the bombings?" Hodge had to ask. There was too much circumstantial evidence not to pursue the lead. Mazuski had kept quiet for over a year, always choosing to delay rather than present Hodge with the truth. His mother almost certainly knew nothing. On the off chance she did know something, she had buried it with his father. The kinship that Hodge felt with Blackbeard overrode the entirety of his logic. He knew that Hippie was not the only team member who felt that he should not fraternize with Blackbeard and his family, he was just the only one bold enough to express the sentiment. Hodge suspected that perhaps his draw to kinship with Blackbeard was because of a shared past. Maybe that was why Mazuski had him sent to Somalia to work with a half-Lebanese asset whose father died in 1983, the same year as his own father's death. Even if that was so, Blackbeard might be telling the truth. He might be the missing link, yet be just as ignorant of his father's dealings as Hodge was of his own father's.

"I do not know, Baseball."

"You would tell me if you knew, wouldn't you? Your mother never told you anything about it?" Guuce's mother was distraught when she learned that her husband died. She had been left without a father to raise their three-year-old son and was six months pregnant. Without a husband to provide for their family, she sought to erase his legacy. Their children would take her name, not his. All they would know of their father would be the pieces he shared with others. She knew that he had made a plea to two of his associates to tend to their children if he were to face an untimely death. With no other source of income, she accepted their gifts with the shame of not being able to provide in kind.

A tear formed in Blackbeard's eye. "My mother died bringing me into the world."

"Uncles? Aunts? No one knew?" Hodge felt a guilty knot form in his stomach. Knowing that he would be leaving Somalia and perhaps never see his friend again, a compulsion to press him had overrode his sense of empathy.

"In my clan, we are all family. My brother and I were raised by our friends. But they tell me that they do not know anything."

"Right."

"I hope one day you find out who your father is, Baseball."

Hodge took his first sip of the tea. "It's good. It's a good recommendation. Thank you."

Jamilah peeked through the faded print fabric cloth that covered her home's window. The sun touched down on her mahogany arms. "When will you be home?"

Guuce turned to his wife from the doorway. "It shouldn't be long. The meeting is with a new American. Baseball is leaving Mogadishu."

"Be careful. I worry about you and your dealings with them."

"They are fine people. You like Baseball. And our son has three uniforms and can attend the madrasa. Maybe he will grow up to be an engineer or a doctor. We couldn't do that without them." Guuce kissed his wife. "I will see you later, walal."

Sharmaarke ran over to his father and hugged his legs. "Can we play soccer before you leave?"

Guuce lifted his son high. Maybe he should ask the Americans for help installing a roof on his family's home. A simple one would do, one weighed down with rocks, but he did not want to appear bothersome or ungrateful. They already covered all of his and his family's most pressing needs. "We will play tomorrow. I promise."

When Guuce placed his son down on the ground, Sharmaarke reached for his favorite toy. "This giraffe is my friend."

"Maybe you can make a gift for Mr. Baseball. It is the polite thing to do." Guuce hugged his son and then left to meet with his new handler.

12

LANGLEY, VIRGINIA, U.S.A.

OCTOBER 2003

Mitch Butler's target was a domicile in Mogadishu. The coordinates had been supplied by high-level brass on short notice. He had no idea why this location was the target, but it was not his job to ask questions. Somalia was an interesting location for a strike. Officially, the United States had left Somalia in 1995 when UNOSOM II's mandate had concluded. Butler wondered if there was even authorization to enter Somali airspace. These were not questions for an entry-level subordinate to ask, especially with many of the Agency's bigwigs watching over his shoulder, most with ties to the Five-Sided Puzzle Palace.

"Target in range?" The commander's voice crackled over Butler's headset.

"Target set."

"Engage. 3, 2, 1. Weapons free. Ten seconds."

"Copy that."

From the monitor, Butler could see a young boy holding a toy of some sort in his hand. The child was dead center in the crosshairs as the two missiles hit their target. After that, everything went up in a thick fog of smoke.

13

MOGADISHU, SOMALIA

OCTOBER 2003

Hodge had brought a few of his favorite novels with him to Mogadishu for his downtime. Whenever Hodge wasn't engaged in a mission or discussing logistics with Powell, his favorite pastime was reading. He maintained his rigorous exercise routine every morning, except when in the field, and visited Blackbeard whenever the opportunity presented itself. To vary things up, he occasionally would play *Panzer Dragoon Orta* on the Xbox in the recreation facility. He enjoyed that game far more than *Halo* and wondered why his team members would play a game that sought to encapsulate a military experience when they were in combat day and night. Hodge preferred the fantastic escape of shooting everything in sight from the back of a dragon.

Tonight, Hodge was engrossed in his well-worn copy of Fyodor Dostoevsky's *The House of the Dead.* He had finished *The Satanic Verses* a few nights ago and immediately plunged in to rereading his favorite work of Dostoevsky's. Teddy was a gentleman among the savages in a Russian prison. Hodge was supposed to have been an academic; now, he was among the savages in a third world hellhole. Yet, like Dostoevsky, he too had seen the humanity in some of the Somalis despite the grotesque exterior of their country.

Hodge had read through over eighty pages in the last hour and a half when he was interrupted from his book by an incoming call. He answered his satellite phone. It was Mazuski.

"Chris, tell me, did you enjoy the sands on the shores of Mogadishu?" Mazuski coughed out the city. The way he hacked out the name made his pronunciation mimic the way the locals spoke their capital's name.

It had been weeks since he had been in communication with Mazuski. His patience for his handler's semantic games had worn thin. "You promised answers and you haven't delivered. I had to turn elsewhere."

Mazuski laughed and coughed. Hodge could hear him suck on a lozenge as he spoke. "You're just like your father. Be careful how you go. Mind the company you keep. Your questions might be putting those close to you at risk." Mazuski cut the line.

Hodge slammed his satphone down on his bed.

At 2000 hours, Hodge and the rest of his men from Whiskey Team stood outside the team's housing unit, waiting for their bird to arrive. The mission had been completed and, according to Powell, there was nothing left for these six men to do in Somalia.

"Wish we could have put down more of those skinnies." Steam had found the mission too easy. Only one high-value kill. It was boring. Sudan promised more of the same. That would be his last mission before he had been ordered by his handler to hang up his BDUs and boots. *Old.*

How the hell am I old? I'm only thirty-one. I've got sixty good years ahead of me. Seventy if I lay off the cheap beer and women, although I don't know how good those years would be without them. Steam had seen more action when he wore a flag. Somalia was nothing but a letdown of epic proportions.

"We did our part. Now we have another objective." At Langley, Hodge had learned that keeping the same team for two consecutive missions was a rare occurrence. He wondered if Mazuski had pulled some strings to ensure that he had the same team for his next mission. Hodge had carefully chosen each of his team members. He respected his men and trusted them to complete their missions.

"You ever lighten up, Wild Man?" Bozo asked.

Hodge flashed a dark smile at Bozo. "When I'm with my friends."

Steam slapped Hodge on the back. "So not with us assholes."

Most contractors embraced the jovial horseplay, but Hippie was a more reflective type. Over the last few days, he had been preoccupied on his team leader's relationship with one of the Somali assets. *It's spooky. These people want to kill us. We don't speak their language. Why would someone as intelligent and composed as Wild Man put so much at risk?* Hippie could not come up with any answers. "When he's with his little buddy, I bet he's cool."

"Why have any friends? I'm here for the cash. It's worked for me." A few years ago, shortly after his first few missions, Bling had begun to understand the reality of his line of work. He would never have a legacy. There would be no ribbons. No benefits. Do a job, get shot, get screwed up, and leave. The money could never compensate for all that a PMC gave up in the process, but Bling took it nonetheless. Gladly.

"That's debatable, Bling. And Hippie, the kid's a good kid. His father's a friend." *Hippie didn't understand. How could he understand? Hearts and minds had seemed like a slogan for a political campaign, but he was living it. Blackbeard was putting his life at risk by working with us. He was one of the good guys. Besides, he was a hell of a lot more interesting than his team members for conversation. Rain Man was basically a deaf mute, Steam would be great if you wanted to steer a conversation towards the best titty bars in Wheeling, Bling hated everybody and everything, Bozo was just like his namesake, a clown, and Hippie was the kind of guy who even though he kept his hair buzzed could benefit from a talk with Coach Hays. Blackbeard was like a brother, but he would be gone soon. There was nothing wrong with seeing a friend while the opportunity to do so existed.*

Bozo scoffed. "Friend? You gone off the deep end, Wild Man? These skinnies ain't our friends."

"Point taken." Hodge realized that Bozo, Hippie, and the rest of his men's kickback about Blackbeard came from the shared desire to complete their objectives and ensure the team's safety. These concerns would be justified in almost any other situation. No asset had a spotless record and there was always a level of risk in all of their actions, but it wasn't like he planned to divulge state secrets to him. Blackbeard was a different breed. He was a friend. The rest of the skinnies? They were not friends. Not by a longshot.

Rain Man uttered his first words of the night. "They have agendas." His statement was no different than any of the remarks by the others, but his gravelly voice and infrequent communication added an extra weight to his words. Hodge respected his opinions more than those of the other men on the team.

"Most of them. Not them though." Hodge heard the chinook in the distance. It would be touching down soon. He was glad to be leaving Somalia, if for no other reason than it would likely end the barrage of questions about his social life from the team that he had selected.

The Americans had given Guuce and his family their home, modest as it may have been. Its owner was a local warlord whose objectives were aligned with U.S. interests. The Americans had their agents pay the warlord a monthly sum for their asset and his family to live in this home. They threw in a cache of American manufactured weapons for the men the warlord commanded to sweeten the pot. Until the strike, it was an arrangement that had ensured the happiness of all parties.

Guuce and his family had moved into their home three years ago, when he had first been brought on as a U.S. asset. It was a reward for information that he had supplied which led to the elimination of an Islamist militia. Before that, Guuce and his brother had lived with Abdullahi and occasionally Cabdi. Now, with his home destroyed and his absence from comms with his handler, Guuce Duale had no choice but to move back to his adolescent home with his brother. His wife and son had lived with Abdullahi before. They would have moved back in too, but the strike had left their bodies incinerated.

Abdullahi finally decided to inform the brothers of the secret that he and Cabdi had long guarded. "Your father worked for Allah, not the Americans. He lied to them to free our people." He and Cabdi had made a promise to the boys' mother that they would not reveal the truth of Farid El Hout's objectives to her sons. Honor was important to both men, but Abdullahi believed that the greatest dishonor was to not enact vengeance on those who would murder a defenseless woman and child. There was no need for Abdullahi to persuade Cabdi to his point of view.

"Then why are we not free? What has come from lying to the infidels but mistrust between our culture and theirs? What has come but death for Muslims? Why is my wife dead? My son?" Nothing felt real. Guuce had been in an emotionless daze for the last two days. This state had started when he returned to what was once his home and saw nothing but the remains of the structure. And his son. Baseball's giraffe was in what used to be Sharmaarke's hand. At the site, he found nothing left of his wife.

"We will be free, inshallah," Abdullahi replied.

"Allah has already ordained for you the dissolution of your oaths," Cabdi added. "Your father schemed because peace with the Americans, with the Westerners, is impossible. We are peaceful, but the infidels' intentions are not peaceful. Unfortunately, you have been made aware of that, Guuce."

Abdullahi quoted the Qu'ran, "And they schemed, and Allah schemed, and Allah is the best of schemers."

Erasto had lost his center. Normally, he was composed in word and deed, but wrath had consumed him ever since the attack. Abdullahi and Cabdi had taken jobs with the Americans to develop a better lifestyle for their families. They had no loyalty to the Western devils and would expel them from the Land of Punt if only they had the resources and opportunity. But the Americans and their allies had stripped his people of everything. Once, his people had been the great merchant empire of East Africa. They had been the suppliers of gold to India and Egypt. Now, they were beggars who whored themselves to the West. His brother had foolishly believed that they were trying to restore peace. They had not come to bring peace, but more violence and death. The militias killed like men. The Americans killed you without looking you in the eyes. They were a cowardly people born from the hellfire. Shaytan was known for his deception and his emissaries on Earth had deceived his brother. His brother had acted foolishly. As his older brother, Erasto knew that he had a responsibility to guide his brother into the correct actions, to embark on drawing their blood for shedding his family's own. "Did our father spill the blood of the infidel?" Erasto hoped that his father had killed hundreds, thousands, tens of thousands of Americans and their allies. He hoped that his father acted bravely and resolutely in dealing with these devils.

"Yes. Many infidels, alhamdulillah," Cabdi assured Erasto.

Guuce remained in an unreal state of beatific calm. The worst occurrence had already happened, yet he remained alive. He was now a wanderer on this planet, waiting out the years until Allah called him. "Tell me more about my father."

Twenty-two years ago, the imam at Guuce's masjid was a twenty-eight-year-old clothier who had only the most nominal faith in Islam. It wasn't a desire for truth that brought Xidig Abdiraxman to explore the Qu'ran, but a random encounter with a foreigner. Xidig had met Farid at a restaurant. Being a true son of Somalia, Xidig had a welcoming spirit. He introduced himself to the stranger and inquired as to what he was doing in Mogadishu. Farid did not reveal his purpose that day, but in time, as their friendship grew, he explained how the West sought to desecrate the noble Qu'ran because it was the truth and they, like pigs, wished to stay in the filth of their immorality. If the Americans and the Europeans were against the Qu'ran and they possessed all the power of the world, it stood to reason that there was a truth to Islam that they were desperate to suppress. Xidig returned with him to Lebanon for six months and learned from some of the wisest Sunni teachers matters both spiritual and temporal. When he returned, he introduced his friends Cabdi and Abdullahi to El Hout.

Farid had told him that the Americans trusted him, but that he was engaged in a long game of deception. They had used him as an asset in their mischievous actions in Lebanon. Now, they had a plan for him in Somalia. He was to work with the Western devils to eliminate the rebels who sought to end the dictatorship and bring Somalia to a state of Islamic purity. His actions had given him to a comfortable lifestyle and the information he supplied was minor. While he had the blood of fellow Muslims on his hands, he had a plan to deliver a tenfold response to the Americans.

El Hout put his faith in Xidig. He had been a stalwart friend, inviolable in his trust, and had introduced him to his wife. She was a woman whose delicate features and cinnamon complexion complemented her graceful manner and righteous personality. El Hout made sure never to reveal the specifics of his dealings to her. A Muslim woman was a pearl, to be treasured and protected from blemish, but ill-suited for men's affairs.

When El Hout was martyred, Xidig continued his operations in Somalia with the contacts that he had cultivated. They were brave men who cared little for their lives. They had a righteous cause, to bring Somalia under sharia and purify the nation from the cancer of Western influence. It would be difficult to accomplish, but the men who risked their lives for the cause were rewarded handsomely with foreign money. More importantly, their deeds honored Allah. They would receive their true reward in Jannah.

Xidig brought his childhood friends Abdullahi and Cabdi in on these missions with Farid. They too had once been wayward in their faith, but were amenable to the cause. The money from foreign backers of the jihad had lured Abdullahi, who desired to provide a comfortable life for his three daughters and wife. Cabdi was drawn by the lure of adventure. His chance to be a part of a rebellion, to make history by defeating the infidels, was of great appeal. Both men regularly performed the necessary deeds and communicated the appropriate information. El Hout made the arrangements through Xidig to supply their compensation. Over time, they became even closer to Farid than Xidig himself. One week before he returned to Lebanon to prepare for the event he had been planning for years, El Hout asked Abdullahi and Cabdi to raise his son and future child if the Westerners martyred him. In times of plenty, Cabdi would raise Erasto and Guuce after their mother's death. Most of the time, Abdullahi and his wife cared for the young boys.

14

DARFUR, SUDAN

OCTOBER 2003

Chris Hodge and Whiskey Team had touched down in Darfur the night before. The mission was to be a short one, but no suitable accommodations were available. Hodge did not expect to stay at the Four Seasons of Al-Fashir, but to live for the next couple of weeks in a small cave in the Marrah Mountains with his team was unexpected. There was no light to read Dostoevsky, no electricity to play Xbox, and he had to sleep on the ground in a tiny area with five other people, six when their asset was around. It was a different African experience than his first venture into the continent with the ex, the best friend, and the hippie Afrikaner girl. No one was getting laid here and hopefully his target was the only beast Hodge would meet.

Bilal Nazer was sixty-five years old, but had a young wife and a six-year-old son. Today, they were celebrating Eid al-Adha, the Islamic festival of sacrifice meant to commemorate Ibrahim's willingness to give up his son to follow Allah's command. Bilal was no stranger to sacrifice. His father Basim was an Egyptian from Alexandria who had migrated into Sudan as a young man to fight the British colonial presence. He had married a Sudanese Arab woman soon after he arrived in Khartoum and they had seven children. Bilal was the only one of his four sons who followed in his footsteps, the reason why he had chosen to celebrate Eid with him. In his youth, Basim had arranged the deaths of many British apostates. Now, in the twilight of his years, with little in the way of physical faculties remaining but his record of trust among his contacts still upstanding, he was here to supply his son with arms to kill the abeeds for their apostasy. However, Basim had lived too many years to act with the haste of a young man and preoccupy his mind with tomorrow's affairs. Inshallah, the kaffirs would be wiped clean from Sudan and the country would be free of nonbelievers, but today was Eid, a day of mirth. Today, all Basim had on his mind was the joy of eating the Eid lamb with his family, drinking many cups of Aisha's tea, and basking in the joyful energy and exuberance of his grandson.

Hodge stood watch from 0200 to 0600. He had gotten four hours of sleep earlier while Hippie stood guard outside of the cave. Their location was remote, even by Sudanese standards, and the intel that had been provided asserted that enemy combatants were rarely present in this desolate area. The positive spin was that the men could sleep in peace and would not have to be concerned about car bombs. The negative spin was that it was an almost five-hour hump to the target's location.

Wahid was a Sudanese asset of the Fur tribe. He was twenty-five, spoke passable English and better Arabic and Fur, and was in good enough physical shape to hike the mountains. He was supposed to arrive at 0700, but was about a half hour early. Today, they were heading into

Al-Fashir. Hodge was to gather intel on their objective while the rest of Whiskey Team would pose as Canadian aid workers at a nearby school and be ready to assist Hodge in case of an emergency. There was a good distance between Nazer's compound and the school. Hodge knew that his judgment had to be sound. For this mission, he had to always err on the side of caution because reinforcements would be next to useless if they were already dead.

Wahid drove Africa's favorite vehicle, a steel gray 1997 model of the Toyota Land Cruiser Prado. Hodge sat upfront with him, while the rest of the team was squeezed into the back. Wahid found Whiskey Team's cover story suspect. "I must warn you, it can be a little suspicious to pose as aid workers without a woman amongst you."

"You offering some of your girls? Bozo, you ready to get the HIV?" Steam asked as he punched Bozo in the arm.

"Wahid, hey, you got a sister or ten, right?" Bozo patted Rain Man and Hippie's shoulders. "Boys, don't worry about the virus. I brought enough rubbers for the whole class."

Hodge planned to speak privately with Bozo and Steam. Their behavior continued to cross the line. Wahid would never be confused with Shakespeare, but he knew enough English and body language to understand that he was being treated disrespectfully. The acquisition and timely development of an asset could not be taken for granted. Hodge gauged that Wahid was sensitive and needed to see that the team had his back. For the success of their mission, Hodge had to put a stop to his team's antics. "You two shut it down. We're fortunate to have Wahid with us." Hodge's commanding tone communicated the message. Steam and Bozo fell in line. A wide smile of satisfaction formed on Wahid's face as he drove on through the mountains towards Al-Fashir.

The government-run elementary school had just let out for the day. A chaotic mass of students in uniform, all with shaved heads, exited through the door. Puberty hadn't set in yet. Each student's sex was indistinguishable to the naked eye.

After the last of the students filtered out, Wahid led Hodge's men into the school. Wahid and Hippie carried sacks of rice. Rain Man, Steam, Bling, and Bozo lugged in large containers of clean drinking water. Wahid led the team to one of the classrooms. The room was empty except for a wooden table and a handful of wooden chairs. The oldest and most feeble of the group had sunk into the chairs, while most of the elderly people, women, and children that filled the room paced around. All were anxious for the supplies, desperate to fend off starvation and disease. Many of the people in the room had grotesque injuries and nearly everyone seemed to suffer from extreme malnutrition. They were Wahid's native Fur people.

There had long been tension between the Arabs of the North and the Fur. Some of them had chosen to resist, taking up arms against Khartoum. Their grievances were plentiful. Access to clean water had been blocked, land had been stolen from the Christians and the animists, and racist policies against the Black populations were always present and often codified into law. The Fur had long endured a system of apartheid. Since February, this oppression had turned into a full-on genocide. The Janjaweed would raid Christian and animist settlements, killing any men, women, and children in sight. Some of the attacks had been burned into Wahid's mind. He had seen a smoldering corpse. All the flesh had burned off the skeleton, but some of the woolly African hair remained attached to the skull. Wahid had seen an entire town of wooden huts on fire. The smoke billowed out of these homes like an inferno. He had seen the refugee camps multiply.

Wahid had joined the Justice and Equality Movement soon after the genocide began, but he had yet to participate in any of their formal counterattacks against the Janjaweed and the Sudanese government. Wahid's work in mobilizing his people to resist Khartoum had caught the CIA's attention. At Langley, there was much hope that he could be groomed into a future political leader in the region. The hefty payments offered in exchange for his information and assistance were aimed to ensure his loyalty to American interests in the event that he moved into a future in the halls of power. Wahid's handler had already floated that idea into his head. Wahid was amenable to the idea in the future, but for now his only wish was to end the genocide and liberate his people from Muslim rule.

Al-Fashir was in the far north of Darfur. It occupied a transitional space between the Arab north and the Black south of the country. Over the last decade, Wahid had witnessed the population of Al-Fashir endure a dramatic shift. In his childhood, the city had been about equally divided between Muslim and non-Muslim populations, but since Omar al-Bashir assumed the presidency in 1989, there had been a government-supported policy of Arabization. Through mass migration, disenfranchisement, and at times outright murder, Al-Fashir had become a Muslim-majority city. One of the telltale signs of this change was the growth in the number of madrasas.

Bilal Nazer waited outside of his son's madrasa. For father and son, it had become a daily ritual. None of the other students who attended the madrasa had a family member pick them up after school. For both Zain and Bilal, it was a symbol of a father's love for his son that he would spare his time on such a gesture. Bilal was grateful that Allah had provided for his family's needs. Unlike many others in the region, neither he, nor his son, nor his wife ever suffered for lack of food or drink. His recent dealings in arming the Janjaweed had proved far more lucrative than his previous work as a cattle trader and farmer. Bilal wondered how he could best use his newfound wealth. His first desire was to ensure that his country operated in a godly way and did not succumb to influence from apostates and polytheists. He would provide whatever was needed for the ummah, be it weapons, finances, or his strategic mind. If there was anything left over, he would give it all to Aisha and Zain.

Zain ran into his father's arms after he and his classmates were dismissed from the madrasa. Unlike in the government-run schools, order had been instilled in the boys. It was the right of every child to be disciplined by wise and reasonable parents and elders. This guidance was mandated in the Qu'ran, for without discipline, human beings were vulnerable to wrongdoing. Children, lacking the wisdom and maturity of adults, were especially vulnerable to falling off the straight path. Bilal was satisfied that his son was receiving the finest of Islamic education. Not only was Zain well-versed in the Qu'ran, the hadiths, and the history of Islam's expansion throughout the world, but in his manner he was perfect, never displaying even a hint of an un-Islamic temperament.

This was one of the times Hodge enjoyed the perks of being team leader. While his men posed as hicks from Halifax and handed out bushels of rice, he had the opportunity to play Bond. Hodge was crouched down below the two-foot concrete lips that fenced in the roof of the government-run school. The madrasa that the target sent his son to was kitty-corner from the aid center. This ideal location offered Hodge's team not only a perfect cover, but an excellent opportunity to gather intelligence on Nazer's daily routine. It seemed that the target's segue into AARP membership had caught up with him. Nazer's home was only minutes away from both his son's school and the mosque where he met with leaders in the Janjaweed to supply them with AK-47s and other weapons that accelerated the genocide.

Hodge's handler had supplied him with a state-of-the-art camera with a super-telephoto lens attached. The camera had the ability to capture distant subjects with perfect clarity and split-second speed. His handler had told him that the lens was set up for optimal performance in any situation. Kendra had been a photography buff. Throughout the entirety of their seven-month relationship, she would launch into long wistful monologues about Cindy Sherman, Man Ray, Annie Leibovitz, Ansel Adams, and other less prominent photographers to whom Hodge had never been exposed. He found it a cute personality quirk at first, like how she would always plant one hundred kisses on his lips before they made love, but in time her habits had started to irritate him. Between her erratic mood swings and obsessive tendencies, Hodge knew that she was not the right woman to build a life around and so he ended the relationship. They were still on friendly terms. When he returned stateside, he would send Kendra an email about the camera, omitting the fact that he tested it in Al-Fashir. Hodge knew that she would appreciate the opportunity to indulge in conversation about the topic.

Just as the intelligence reports indicated, all the boys who attended the madrasa were dismissed at 1430. The target's son jumped into his father's arms. It was a sweet moment. Norman Rockwell could have painted it if terrorists had been a source of his artistic inspiration.

Hodge snapped a few photographs of the father and son outside the madrasa, then ducked back down. Discretion was a must in this situation. The Arabs of Sudan were fixated on color. They believed themselves to be lighter than the "Blacks," but to Hodge there was no visible difference. No one in Sudan, be they Arab or Black, would mistake him for a local. If anyone noticed a strange white man taking pictures from a roof it would only end in two ways, a full-on firefight or their target and many of his associates retreating while their foot soldiers took the fall.

After a few mikes, Hodge inched his head to the lip of the fence. He quickly snapped another photograph of Nazer with his son in tow as they entered the home. Bilal Nazer seemed to have done well by Sudanese standards. His home was a long two-story compound-style whitewashed concrete house with an eight-foot high concrete perimeter. The metal gate that led inside was painted an Islamic shade of green. Beyond the compound was a vacant dirt road.

Hodge took a sip from his CamelBak, a water pouch inside what resembled a backpack with a hose that ran forward along its shoulder strap. Dusk was approaching and would provide a welcome respite from the one hundred degree heat. Throughout his childhood,

Hodge's mother had always splurged on air conditioning. She would run the air conditioners in her bedroom and the living room nonstop from the end of April to the beginning of October, despite the temperate climate of northern New Jersey. Heat had never affected Chris Hodge the same way it did his mother. When he was young, he fell asleep on many a summer night without air conditioning only to wake up in the morning with his bedroom's AC on high cool. His mother had talked about moving to Macon, Georgia to reunite with her best friend from high school. She figured that Dennis would move out eventually and Chris had always been a go-getter who would never return to the nest. Her life was already pockmarked by the permanent loneliness of losing a husband and a son. As much as Chris Hodge hoped that his mother might be able to salve her wounds, he knew that Georgia was not the answer. The heat would turn her into a permanent recluse and if she ever made her way out to Al-Fashir, she might question whether hell was a place for the damned after death or before.

At around 1830, Hodge heard the booming echo of the call to prayer. The muezzin gave the invocation from the top of the mosque's minaret. It was a beautiful structure, almost like something out of a cartoon with its rich aquamarine blended amidst the beige that seemed to rise out of the sand and dirt. *Wouldn't it be a laugh*, Hodge thought, *if the mosques were where all the foreign aid was being funneled.*

The intelligence reports had him pinned. He brought his son to these dealings. At least Nazer hadn't yet trained his boy in how to use a Kalashnikov, or if he had, at least he hadn't asked his son to carry one over to the mosque on his back like his old man. Hodge snapped a photograph of the father and son and three other men who entered the mosque. He laid low for a few mikes and then climbed down the two flights of the stairwell to the back entrance. Hodge linked back up with his team outside of the school. While Steam, Bling, and Rain Man had the easier job of handing out a full supply of rice and water, Bozo and Hippie put their medical training to use. The men treated everything from a feverish baby to an elderly woman with Guinea-worm disease. Bozo and Hippie's efforts had saved more than a few lives today. It would all start again tomorrow at 0600, but for now, Wahid and Whiskey Team entered the Toyota for the five-hour trek back to their little mountain home.

Hodge felt that he looked like a fool in his Canadian Red Cross vest. It was one thing to make his teammates wear the outfits. Their experiences together over the past month and a half had made them grow closer than brothers, or at least closer than he had ever been to Dennis. Hodge had learned from his experiences outside his family that it was supposedly an older brother's responsibility to balance being a role model with knocking his kid brothers down a peg from time to time. Still, after he had watched the sun shine into the trunk of a Land Cruiser from an assortment of bullet holes and faced down a drugged-out skinny with a Kalashnikov pointed at his forehead, he could deal with the embarrassment of looking like a goofball. *If I'm going to be a Canadian, why not have some fun with the experience, eh?*

His team entered the school at 1500, the same as the day before; however, Hodge's itinerary had changed. Today, he was to scout out the mosque's minaret. The only obstacle in the way of access to the minaret was a teenage boy whose defiant manner made Hodge wonder if the cocky swagger of American rappers and their music had gained a foothold in Sudan.

Hodge approached the kid. "Hey. Since I got here, I've always wanted to see the view of what it's like down here from up there." At the Farm, Hodge had been trained on how to adopt a Canadian accent. It had been stressed as an important tool for disguising yourself in plain sight when operating in countries hostile to U.S. foreign policy, which covered any place to which he might be deployed. Hodge's natural voice was low, slow, and deep, but for the purposes of this interaction, he changed his vocal patterns. Hodge sounded like a stereotypical middle-class Ontario native who had resisted the standardizing effects of television on North American vocal patterns. His voice was high, fast, nasal, and heavy on the Canadian raising.

The boy responded in English. "It's not for you, infidel." Arsalan received five hundred pounds per week to watch the minaret between Asr and Isha prayers every day after school. He wouldn't even consider allowing a foolish foreigner anywhere near the premises when he had such an easy way to make money.

"What do you do here, eh?" The boy did not respond. "You look tough. I bet you're some sort of guard. When are you here?"

Arsalan just wanted the foreigner to be quiet. One of the things that he enjoyed about guarding the minaret was the peace of the job. The Christians and animists understood not to interfere with holy matters, but the Westerners must have been especially stupid. Arsalan knew not to threaten the aid worker. His boss had been adamant about avoiding drawing undue attention to the mosque unless threatened. This guy was just a tourist. "Until eight. Why do you care?"

"Someone else here after?" The boy glared at him. Maybe in a few years he'd become one of Hodge's objectives and be in the center of a .308s scope. "You must think I talk a lot, don'tcha. I'm a Canuck, eh. We're a friendly people." The boy fixed his eyes on Hodge. He did not remove them until Hodge turned around and left. Hodge understood that this interaction had been a failure. If a hidden camera had observed him, this would not have been a successful or appropriate engagement. Hodge had said too much. His actions had jeopardized the mission.

When Hodge entered the classroom, he found Steam handing out bags of rice to what seemed like an endless procession of people. Al-Fashir was a city of about two hundred thousand residents. Half of the women, children, and elderly people of the city must have passed through this classroom yesterday and today if the current line was any indication. Hodge whispered into Rain Man's ear. "You think you and Bling can handle this by yourselves?"

Rain Man nodded. He immediately began switching between handing out the bags of rice and administering the clean drinking water, bouncing between both tasks like a ping pong ball. Bling did not alter his far more nonchalant pace. He stuck only to handing out the rice.

Hodge pulled Steam aside and walked with him into an empty classroom. "It's a go for tomorrow night."

"Staying on-plan?" Steam asked.

"No. Fence is too short. Easy visibility."

"Where are you taking it from?"

"Minaret."

"Same time?"

"Right."

"Fuckin' A, bad boy." Steam whispered as he pounded fists with Hodge.

Zain dribbled his soccer ball towards his father. He was a natural athlete with a winning combination of power, speed, and agility. Bilal Nazer thought that his son had all the tools to one day play in La Liga or the Premier League. If Allah willed that to happen, he hoped that his son would remain on the straight path. Bilal knew that he was likely to be dead by the time his son reached the age of maturity. He hoped that the virtuous principles he had instilled in his boy remained intact, regardless of whatever his life had in store for him.

Zain ducked and weaved around several imaginary defenders. In his mind, an elaborate fantasy was taking place. He was a superstar in the World Cup on a breakaway. If he netted the ball, Sudan would be the first African nation to take home the FIFA World Cup Trophy. If he missed, the game would drag into extra time and the fate of his country would be unknown. Zain moved in close to his father and then backed up as his father anticipated the shot. With intentions to deceive, he fired an outside kick past his father, who by a miracle of timing was able to get in front of the ball. Father and son embraced before both headed inside for intermission. The muezzin had given the adhan for Asr and they would pray while Africa's hopes had been put on ice for a few more minutes.

Hodge knew that he had almost no margin for error. He lit a Camel Light 100 outside of the school. Every twenty seconds, he took a hesitant puff. Hodge was not a smoker, but he needed a cover from which to observe the muezzin's movements. Once he entered the mosque for prayer, Hodge would have to haul ass to the minaret.

Hodge threw his cigarette down and dashed towards the mosque in the oppressive heat. He scaled the stairs to the top of the minaret in under a minute. Hodge threw his overstuffed Toronto Maple Leafs backpack down and zipped it open, procuring his .308 and a pair of gloves. He slid the gloves on and doped his scope, aiming for the front door of the compound. Any second now, Nazer would exit with his son if his patterns held. Scoring the scratch would be the easy part. Leaving the minaret was where things could become deadly.

The son exited first, hugging the ball against his chest. His father came out behind him. The lines of the mirage were facing northeast. There was almost no wind. Hodge took his shot.

The bullet sailed through Bilal Nazer's upper chest. At first, Zain was too stunned to react. Then, like a switch had been turned in his mind, he began to scream. His mother ran out of their home and cradled him in his arms as she screeched through her tears.

It was pure Isaac Newton. Every action had an equal and opposite reaction. As a trained sniper, Hodge realized that after a public kill in a populated area, there would be a commotion, with everyone scrambling towards the scene. The mosque, the madrasa, and the school buildings had all emptied out as people ran for the compound or to leave the area.

Arsalan had a different idea. His job was to guard the minaret, but he decided to appropriate a different purpose for the structure. The spiral staircase was enclosed. If there was any shooting outside and he remained quiet inside, he could ride out the panic until it dissipated or he found out what was happening. Arsalan rushed into the minaret and headed up a few stairs to what he perceived as safety.

Hodge ran down the spiral staircase until he was about two-thirds of the way to the entrance. He noticed a shadow of a figure had moved into the lighted space at the bottom. Hodge slid against the wall and crept down the stairs. It was the kid.

"Did you see it? They're bombing us!" Arsalan cried out with tears in his eyes.

Hodge wondered if he could play out this situation without resorting to violence. The kid's tough guy act was just that – an act. "Wow. I don't know. What happened, eh?"

Arsalan snapped back to reality. What was the Canadian doing in the minaret? "Why were you up here, infidel?"

"I told you I wanted to go to the top of the minaret." Arsalan stared at him with hatred boiling in his eyes. It was time to act. In one deft motion, Hodge slid behind Arsalan and put the kid in a headlock, making sure to have his muscular arms directly under the kid's jaw. Hodge pushed the guard's head forward and squeezed, pulling his own shoulders back. Hodge flexed his biceps to cut off the boy's arteries and stop the blood from circulating to his brain. After Arsalan passed out, Hodge picked the boy up, bound his hands and ankles, and rested him on the foot of the second stair. He then ran through the minaret's arch towards the school. Hodge made sure to avoid the main road after he saw that a panicked mob had swarmed the passageway.

It had only been three days and nine hours of work, but it was long enough to have convinced Bozo that he made the right career choice. The boy could not have been older than eight years old. All of the skin on his head and hands was patchy. His eyes were red. Worms made these children look like they belonged on an undiscovered Hieronymus Bosch painting. Even when one was treated, another would replace them. While Bozo tended to this boy, Hippie cared for a girl who was likewise afflicted. Rain Man, Bling, and Steam had it easy. All they had to do was look at some of the people who were dying more slowly and hand out rice and water. Steam did not even do that half the time. Right now, he was in the back room as Wild Man attempted to eliminate the target. Whether Hodge wanted him to stay at the ready for comms or not, Steam was eager to get back to something much more kinetic. He would give anything to aim his M4 at an extremist rather than interact face to face with such misery.

Hodge had completed his objective and relayed the information to Steam. Steam rushed into the classroom. He pointed his finger at the door. "Whiskey, let's get the fuck out of here."

Wahid addressed the crowd in Fur while every member of Whiskey Team stopped what they were doing and zipped to the exit. "My apologies. There's an emergency. We'll be back tomorrow." Wahid hated to lie to his people, but the team had to depart before things got ugly.

As Wahid exited the school, he popped his vehicle's locks. Hodge darted past his asset into the Land Cruiser's shotgun seat as the rest of the team jumped into the back. "Move, move, move," Hodge shouted as Wahid rushed into the driver's seat. The Land Cruiser shot off towards the mountains. Not more than fifteen mikes later, the Janjaweed burned the school. Over four hundred people died that day. It was nothing new. The Janjaweed had been raiding villages and killing Black non-Muslim farmers since the 1990s. Whiskey Team made it to their cave intact.

Hodge woke the members of Whiskey Team at 0600. By 0615, the men had started their hump through the mountains. Their exfil point was over forty klicks away in the brushlands. Hodge did not yet know the site of his next deployment. He hoped that he would have at least a few weeks in Boston to enjoy some time with Mirele, learn how Spencer's dissertation was going, and change the filter in his air conditioner.

Bozo tapped Steam on the chest. Steam shoved him aside. "Wild Man, please tell me this asshole isn't actually coming with us next time."

"I'm gone. Gonna miss me?" Steam replied.

Bozo laughed. *Of course I'll miss you, you crazy son of a bitch.*

"What's next?" Hodge asked.

"Back home to Wheeling. The beer's cheap and the girls are pretty. The hell else I need?" Steam's father had been a coal miner for over thirty years, but he was his own man. The oil and gas industry seemed a lot more his speed. The industry had started to dry up when he was a kid, but maybe he'd make a new life for himself out in Wyoming or Colorado. Wherever he ended up didn't matter to him that much. All that mattered to Steam was making sure that he did whatever the hell he had to in order to keep the good times rolling until he had his fill and kicked the bucket.

"How about you, Rain Man?" Rain Man had told him in the cave last night that he needed a change of pace. Hodge had asked him why, but he just shrugged his shoulders and told him it felt right.

"Truck driver. Time to think." Since he was eight years old, Rain Man had always wanted to be a truck driver. He had never felt at home in Monona. His people were scattered, without even a reservation to call their own. Rain Man felt there was no place that was uniquely his. Instead of fighting it, he always tried to embrace that feeling. He joined the Marines out of high school and on base in Afghanistan right after 9/11, he had met a few contractors. It was a brief stint in the private army, but he had enjoyed it. Now, it was time for something else.

"How's that any different from being here, Kemosabe?" Rain Man was the Teller to Bozo's Penn. Bozo liked the guy even though he had a knack for finding cover and fragging him from impossible to reach locations. Bozo wished his real-life skills had translated as well as Rain Man's had to video games.

Seeing Rain Man's smile, Steam felt compelled to break up the mushy shit. They were warriors, not guests on Oprah. "Y'all look like you're about to cry. Hippie, why don't you play Kumbaya on that damn guitar of yours?"

"I would, Steam, but they didn't let me bring that to the cave." Hippie was staying on with Wild Man. His military career was over the day he signed on as a contractor. The years were against him. Soon, he would be unable to continue in this line of work because he was a few years into his thirties. The thought of returning to Bremerton or embarking in any part of civilian life scared Hippie. He would keep doing this until he either died or the powers that be forced him to retire.

Hodge turned to Bling. "I know what you're going to do. Colombia." Hodge hoped that he could remain relevant without becoming bitter and cold towards his fellow man; he was aware that the odds were against those propositions. Bling was right. No one cared about them. They were expendable. Irrelevant after their expiration date.

"That's right. I made my fortune. I don't have to work another damn day in my life."

Hodge placed one hand each on Steam and Rain Man's shoulders. "Steam. Rain Man. Bling. Be careful adapting to home. No one knows what we do, who we are, and there's no retirement plan. You don't get to come back as heroes from this job. We do bad things to bad people, but we only do it for a few years. Leave it where we did it."

Rain Man nodded. Those were the terms to which he had agreed. He already didn't talk with anyone about his experience in the Marines. It would be a cinch for him to remain quiet about the last seven months. Those who had not experienced it with him could never understand anyway. Rain Man believed that even a fellow contractor, even someone on his own team, would have an entirely different experience. Since everything was subjective, what he had been doing this last year did not merit any comment.

Steam turned to Hippie. Wild Man's words, loathe as he was to admit it, had shaken him. For him, this was another of life's grand adventures and he felt that his experiences over the last seven years had ended far too soon. "Dang. Guess you can forget Kumbaya, buddy." Steam removed his Oakleys and West Virginia Mountaineers cap. "Wild Man, if you ever wanna bend some rules and get an old bastard like me back, do it. I'll work for you anytime."

15

EAST COAST, U.S.A.

NOVEMBER 2003

After Sudan, Hodge had twenty days in-country before he had to deploy to Sana'a. Three days into his return, while enjoying a Barolo with Mirele at Landmark, he received a call from Mazuski on his BlackBerry. Mirele was not amused when Hodge excused himself to take the call. After an hour of verbal jousting on the topics of etiquette, politics, and gender roles, they returned to Hodge's apartment. She left the next morning with a satisfied post-coital grin on her face. Hodge left a few hours later for a flight to Washington.

The flight was on Mazuski's dime. He only paid for coach. For the entire hour and a half, Hodge was serenaded by the screams of a distraught baby girl. The aloof mother in the next seat had on her headphones. Hodge could hear a pop singer sing that she was going to be alright. *Maybe yes, maybe no*. Hodge turned his attention back to the skies.

When Hodge exited the gate at Reagan National, he sat outside the terminal as Mazuski had instructed. Hodge placed his traveling bag on the next seat and closed his eyes. In a few minutes, Mazuski would arrive. Until then, he would wait.

Mazuski had made punctuality a habit. Hodge could not recollect a single instance of his handler being even a minute late for a call or meeting. He could not recall a single instance of Mazuski being more than two minutes early either. When Mazuski walked over towards him, Hodge moved his rucksack down to the floor, resting it near his handler's loafers.

"This seat taken?" Mazuski asked.

Hodge motioned towards the seat without looking at Mazuski. He whispered into his handler's ear, "There was some chatter about a strike. I expected some information from my asset in Somalia, but he's been out of comms. Was he involved?" Hodge didn't expect that he and Blackbeard would be pen pals after he left Somalia, but a drone strike in his asset's neighborhood seemed like an appropriate reason to reach out.

Mazuski smiled. "You're doing well, Chris." His latest coughing fit had produced a mass of blood. After Mazuski wiped the blood away with a napkin that he had procured from his shirt pocket, he popped a lozenge. Mazuski folded the paper into eighths and placed the wrapper back inside the bag. "I've been proud." He extended a lozenge to Hodge. Hodge shook his head. Mazuski placed the lozenges back in his pocket. "No need to look elsewhere for your intel. I have what you need."

To Hodge, intelligence agents were leopards. They never changed their spots. They spoke in vague phraseology and avoided making committed statements. They supplied disinformation to guide their assets into performing desired actions. These were essential factors in tradecraft. Hodge expected nothing different from Mazuski. Even if he did reveal the supposed truth of what had happened to his father,

Hodge would need to verify the information. The whole situation was a race against time. Mazuski looked like he would been dead within a year and that was being generous. Hodge knew that stupidity was repeating the same action and expecting a different result, but being unable to deduce a better course, he decided to press Mazuski again. "Who authorized the strike and what was the target? What happened to my father? You never tell me a damn thing. I've succeeded in every mission and yet you still keep me in the dark. What the hell am I doing wrong?"

Mazuski stood up to leave. He looked straight ahead, down the long terminal at its endless passengers and pilots and security and flight attendants, its many restaurants and newsstands. Mazuski looked everywhere other than at his asset or in his asset's direction. "Not here. Soon." It was a weak cough. There was no mucus, no blood. He covered his mouth and then walked into the crowd.

Hodge rented a car and drove to South Amboy. The trip to D.C. had been a waste, a power trip on Mazuski's part. He had planned to visit his mother and brother for a few days before deploying to Yemen, but Mazuski had accelerated his timetable.

Hodge was unsurprised to see that New Jersey had retained its quality of timelessness. His mother had upped her dosage of Klonopin by an additional half milligram. Dennis had somehow earned salesman of the quarter at his job. Donna Hodge told her youngest son that Dennis wasn't thinking of moving out just yet and that he spent the bulk of his paycheck on GameCube games. There was a new guest in the Hodge household. Dennis had met an eighteen-year-old Puerto Rican girl named Glenda. Her mother was in jail. When Dennis wasn't at work, they made the beast with two backs, smoked marijuana, and played GameCube. When he was at work, she smoked marijuana and played GameCube. Donna was happy that her son finally had a girlfriend, but was alarmed by her missing detergent and forks. She told Chris that the next time he visited, the house might be up for sale.

Hodge left the next day for Boston. When he returned, after hours on the road, he found that there was no toilet paper in his apartment. At the supermarket checkout line, a well-dressed woman complained that there were no organic eggs for sale. She railed on about this matter to the bored teenager at the register, demanding justice. She thought her lack of organic eggs was a real problem, one worthy of an immediate solution. Hodge was eager to return to Yemen.

16

SANA'A, YEMEN

NOVEMBER 2003

Yemen's capital was an interesting mix of old and new. The last time Hodge was here, he had been stationed near Al Ghaydah on the other side of the country and never had the chance to visit Sana'a. Hodge had heard that the Old City's architecture was breathtaking. He had heard that the souks were an experience. If not rivaling Dubai or Abu Dhabi, the new hotels were supposed to at least aim for an appeal to the upper echelon. Most importantly, Hodge had heard that amidst all the sights, the most noteworthy was the U.S. Embassy, which had recently been besieged by crowds of armed anti-American protesters who had forced the personnel into lockdown.

Chris Hodge's first order at Camp Sana'a was to visit the head shed on base. Philip Walz worked for the Bureau of Intelligence and Research, reporting directly to the State Department. Walz' job in Yemen was to gather intel to support official and unofficial U.S. foreign policy, coordinate official and unofficial power to maintain security back home and in the Middle East, and utilize any and all diplomatic processes to maintain working relationships with Middle Eastern governments that were not actively hostile. To say that any were friendly was a stretch, but Walz embraced an approach saturated in realpolitik, a trait that had earned him advancement and the respect of his direct superiors.

Walz was not paid for his customer service ability. As soon as Hodge entered the head shed, he began his in-briefing. "Local hostiles have zeroed in on the embassy for redress after two al-Qaeda HVTs were KIA by our drones. Sitreps state that yesterday at 1700 a staff member was dragged out of his vehicle. Bludgeoned to death."

"Savages." If this made the news back home, Hodge would have to add this to his mountain of evidence to persuade Mirele of the facile nature of her arguments. Hodge could not fathom how a Jewish woman, an Israeli no less, couldn't move beyond platitudes like coexistence. If the Nazis ever made a resurgence, he wondered if there would be useful idiots in the Jewish community who would support their beliefs as just another alternate form of expression in a diverse world.

"Since then, the Ambassador, his wife, their teenage daughter, and two members of the staff have hunkered down in the complex. The crowd disperses at night, although approximately ten to fifteen of the most vehement remain at all times. All occupants must be evac'd."

"What's our strategy? Suppressive fire from an overwatch team with TACP to pin them down? QRF on hand?"

"We can't get kinetic. Politics warrants that none of the protesters be harmed."

"Understood. Avoid another Somalia. Maintain status quo." A primal vestige in the lizard part of Chris Hodge's brain wished to throw off the veil of civilization and cover the entirety of the crowd in a hail of machine gun fire. Hodge recognized that in this trait, he was a mirror image of the jihadists he fought. Once, he sought to change the world with policy papers. Now, he had become resigned to doing his small part to eliminate some of the worst of the bad guys. Interacting firsthand with these elements had dampened Hodge's hope for their redemption.

"The Yemeni President cannot officially condemn the protests. These terms are non-negotiable."

"Kalashnikovs?" Hodge asked. No matter the country, agitators always seemed to come equipped with AK-47s. A memo must have circulated among the cretins of the world informing them that if they spent their money on food, clean water, or housing they could only arm themselves with slingshots.

"A lot of Kalashnikovs. Other projectiles too – rocks, bottles. RPG damage to the structure."

"Best approach?"

"Burandanga powder and an infrasound setup, payload via drone."

"Burandanga?" This was where things started to become interesting. Dennis played games of espionage like *Metal Gear Solid*; Hodge lived his brother's fantasy worlds. "Devil's breath, right? The powder made from scopolamine?"

"Correct. At our dosage, the targets will be zombies."

"No free will, hallucinations, seizures—"

Walz cut Hodge off. "They'll forget where they were too. Immediately after the payload's dropped, the drone will order them to disperse."

Hodge scoffed, sensing a missed opportunity. "Just disperse? Burandanga facilitates compliance. Why would we not supply anti-jihadist instruction while they're in that hypnagogic state?"

"Effects are only in the short term. After dusting the targets, LRAD speakers will be dropped via drone. Accurate positioning is to be confirmed by your team."

"You'll blast the LRADs to disperse future protesters?"

"Not blast," Walz corrected. "They won't hear anything, but they'll feel it." Above all, Walz considered himself a professional. He recognized that his actions were essential for the stability of his country and the prevention of the Middle East's further slide into chaos. Still, Walz recognized the internal joy he received from overseeing these types of actions. It almost made him feel like he was a child again on Christmas Eve, filled with the dopamine rush of endless wonder and anticipation.

Hodge was familiar with Devil's breath, but never expected that he would be involved in a mission that depended on the successful dusting of hostiles with the substance. "Muscle contractions, brachycardia, convulsions—"

Once again, Walz interrupted Hodge. This time his excitement had peeked to the surface, breaking his staid veneer. "Yes. Vision loss too. Your eyeballs ever vibrate?"

When he was young, Bozo had wanted to be a stand-up comedian. As a child, his parents allowed him to stay up late on weekend nights to watch *SCTV* and *Saturday Night Live*. In return for their generosity, he entertained them on request with a flawless impersonation of Count Floyd's howl and Transylvanian accent. This unique skill made Bozo quite popular in elementary school, but relegated him to a sadder fate in sixth grade. That year, Bozo sat at lunch with boys with visible orthodontic apparatuses and eyeglasses so thick that they could genocide Southie's ant population if used with ill intent. After Bozo's father retired from the force, his family moved to Shaker Heights to be closer to his maternal grandmother who had been diagnosed with lung cancer. Bozo retired the accent on the drive to Ohio. None of his new friends freshman year obsessed over superhero comics or comedians. No one in Ohio told him to "take his dago ass back to the North End." Bozo welcomed the changes. Any adolescent boy would. Besides, he was self-aware enough to realize that he was not funny on his own. All he could do were impersonations.

Bozo was cognizant of the fact that there was a real possibility that he could be killed in action at any time. The missions that he and his teammates undertook were dangerous. If he died, he would not have his body buried at Arlington. His country would not even acknowledge him. His parents would never be made aware of his fate. Bozo was game for these conditions, but a little bit of comedy to quiet the reality of the situation was his version of therapy. During his downtime, Bozo would, without fail, visit his family in Shaker Heights. The last time that he was in Ohio, Bozo rifled through the stacks of VHS tapes in his bedroom closet and picked out some of his favorites to take with him to Yemen. He left his copy of *SCTV* reruns taped from NBC in his teenage bedroom, but did spend an evening watching the video with his parents. It was the first time in fifteen years that he impersonated Count Floyd. The howl still made his parents laugh, but his accent was rusty. Bozo's father was confused. "What is that? You trying to do Count Floyd or Jackie Mason?" *Maybe some things were better left in the past*, Bozo concluded.

None of Bozo's teammates had ever heard of *Fletch*. That wasn't a surprise. Only Hippie had heard of Chevy Chase; that was a surprise. Bandito, christened Carlos de Jesus Sanchez in Fresnillo, Mexico, had arrived in the United States with his family when he was thirteen. By the 1990s, Chevy Chase had stepped out of the limelight. Bandito's ignorance was understandable. Maybe the *Vacation* movies had never been dubbed into Spanish. Jack "Squire" Squires was only twenty-six. He was practically a baby in comparison. Given his age and the fact that there was nothing even remotely offbeat about him, it made sense that he had never heard of a wacky guy like Chevy Chase. Squire's call sign came partially from the fact that he was almost painfully polite. This refinement had been rigorously instilled in him from birth on his parents' Connecticut estate. At his sister's debutante ball, his grandfather had made a loud off-color joke about fighting "the Japs" in World War II, horrifying his family, but delighting Jack. When his grandfather passed, Squire knew that joining up would be the best way to honor his memory, although he never quite got the hang of those off-color jokes. Anders Wilson, known as Uggo, was from Minneapolis. Bozo had no idea why Uggo had never heard of Chevy Chase. Maybe his parents were Swedish or Norwegian and had a Scandinavian-only entertainment policy in his home. There was no other explanation for why a middle-class Reagan baby would not recognize Chevy Chase.

Bozo had brought his VHS of *Fletch* to the welfare and rec center and, after much effort, persuaded everyone to turn off the video games for a bit to watch. Uggo and Squire were the only ones who did not laugh at Fletch's response to Gail Stanwyck's question: "Are you always this forward?" *Only with wet married women. That line was genuinely funny, even if you're strait-laced or Minnesota morose.* Uggo looked like a pretty boy type to Bozo. Maybe he was worried about laugh lines around his eyes. Bozo figured that might explain why the guy from the Great White North became a contractor instead of a male model.

"Pause it." When Chris Hodge entered, Alpha Team killed their horseplay. Bozo sprang from the floor to the VCR on command like a trained puppy. "We're moving at 0200."

It was only five hours until Alpha Team was to head to the embassy. The drones would do the dirty work of dusting the protesters with Devil's breath and moving the LRAD speakers into place to keep them permanently away. Alpha Team was responsible for overseeing the operation and moving the Ambassador, his family, and their staffers to safety. It would be a small operation. Walz had reported that there were only five Americans stationed in Sana'a who were not military. All non-essential personnel had already been ordered back to the U.S. after the protests had started one month ago. Washington had hoped to ride out the surge of protesters, believing that an official apology for the behavior of two Libertarian-leaning cartoon creators who satirized the Prophet Muhammad on American television was enough to placate the crowds. It was an error in judgment. Terrorist groups operating out of the region had seized on anti-American populist sentiment, rendering the situation a powder keg about ready to burst. When the protests began to turn violent, everyone in the embassy holed up inside. The security presence was low, with only the standard minimal number of members of the Marine Embassy Guard stationed at the compound and no additional reinforcements brought in when the protests had started. With a crowd of hundreds of protesters daily, many of whom remained permanently outside the complex into the dead of night, Washington finally decided to act. The media had yet to catch wind of the situation, and the President and his Cabinet sought to maintain their optics and not spread their official forces too thin. It was decided that the embassy would be evac'd by private contractors through the CIA. Alpha Team knew the plan. No additional preparation was needed. Until then, the men watched *Fletch*. Hodge decided to join them. He needed a good laugh and had heard of the film.

The eighteen protesters who remained outside the U.S. Embassy throwing rocks at the complex and chanting "Allahu Akbar" were hardly rank and file Muslims upset over a perceived slight towards their prophet. They all had official terrorist bonafides, with memberships that spanned a variety of insurgent groups. Some were foreign al-Qaeda operatives who had traveled into Sana'a in the past month with the explicit intention of amplifying anti-U.S. and Western hostilities. The terrorists viewed the situation as a standoff. The numbers among ordinary Yemenis weren't there yet to storm the embassy, but in remaining a constant presence they could voice their opposition and challenge the Americans' ability to interfere in governmental affairs. Walz was confident that his plan would not only break this stalemate, but rescue all personnel. He had not found it difficult to convince Washington to move on his plan.

At 0130, everything was set in motion. A small ultraquiet drone began to atomize the air over the embassy with scopolamine, forming a mist in its wake that rained down on the night owls outside the complex. During the first few seconds, the protesters raged and tried to cover their mouths. A few seconds later, the effects had taken hold. After they had been dusted, the men were zombies, pliant to the command that emanated in Arabic from a robotic voice. "Disperse immediately. Disperse immediately. Disperse immediately." With all free will already vanquished by the large dosage of Devil's breath, the protesters did as they were prompted. They left the compound's perimeter en masse as fast as possible under their condition, with many hindered by vision problems, hallucinations, severe itching, and a complete lack of normal cognitive functions. Even with their physical problems, the slowest of the protesters was gone within a mike.

The threat of the protesters had been neutralized for the present moment. Phase two of the plan commenced. Four different drones, all with large LRAD speakers affixed to hooks, hovered over the complex. The movements of the drones were coordinated through an operative at Centcom. Within two mikes, the LRAD speakers had been secured in place as a protective shield around the embassy. Two LRADs were on each edge of the back of the complex and another two LRADs were on each edge of the front. The LRAD speakers would not be able to ensure that future protesters wouldn't arrive in front of the embassy, but they would be able to ensure that without special noise cancelling earphones, they would never wish to return.

At 0205, the bird touched down in the back of the complex. Alpha Team split into three factions after they exited the bird. Hodge and Bandito entered the compound through the embassy's back entrance to secure and transport the personnel. Bozo and Hippie examined the two LRADs at the front of the complex to ensure that they were in position. Uggo and Squire checked the two LRADs at the back of the complex.

"Who are you? You're not the Marines." Gretchen Wallis was fifty, but she had not hit the wall just yet. She had the blonde hair and big smile of a prototypical all-American beauty. Her teenage daughter Aimee could have passed as her younger sister. The only difference between mother and daughter was in the matter of temperament. Mother Wallis was a frazzled bundle of nerves, but her daughter was composed. Aimee's incredible demeanor given the circumstances made Hodge conclude that she might be a good fit for the IC or military, but Hodge knew that was not her path to take. He had known girls like this in high school and university. They always had someone to do their dirty work.

"No ma'am, we're not."

Ambassador Wallis chimed in with an explanation. "They're here to help us."

Before the conversation could continue, Hodge and Bandito prodded the family towards their escape. "We cannot guarantee your safety in this location. You need to exit immediately," Hodge did not need to provide any further instructions to receive their acquiescence.

After Hodge and Bandito evacuated the Wallis family and two members of the U.S. Foreign Service who had stayed behind in Sana'a, they linked back up with the other members of the team. "LRADs in position?" Hodge asked.

"Roger," said Squire.

"Roger that," Hippie replied. Those devices were sturdy. Even if the drones were misguided, it would be impossible to get the LRADs to budge by human effort. Bullets would hardly make an impact on them either. Hippie surmised that you would need to have some serious weaponry to take out the speakers, but expected that the embassy would need more than the normal Marine detachment to prevent a mob from trying. Hippie was shocked that his orders did not include a plan to evac the Marines, but figured that they had their own exfiltration plan to avoid the worst of possible situations.

"Move." At Hodge's command, his team entered their bird. Five mikes later, Alpha Team was back at Camp Sana'a. The Ambassador and his family and staff stayed on board, landing in Saudi airspace later that night. The next day, the Wallises were back home in Falls Church. Gretchen Wallis' husband was fifty-eight years old. After three difficult years in Yemen, Martin Wallis finally listened to his wife's advice. On his first full day back on American soil, he turned in his resignation and made a few calls to some friends. Life as an influence peddler on the Beltway could not be any worse than living under siege for a month.

Hodge entered his quarters after the return to Camp Sana'a. His adrenaline had been kicked in full gear by the rescue mission, so an attempt to sleep would have been a futile effort until his nervous system stabilized. Hodge reached for his copy of Albert Camus' *The Plague*. Rats infesting a Muslim city. The irony was not lost on him as he started to read the first chapter. Five pages in, Hodge was interrupted by his satellite phone's ringtone. It was only 1925 in Washington and naturally Mazuski had been made aware of what had been on Hodge's itinerary for the night. "The last time we spoke you said that you had information," Hodge barked out.

"Check your email, Chris." Before Hodge could respond to Mazuski, the line went dead. Hodge opened his laptop and logged into his email account. There was an email from a person listed as "Unknown Sender" with a subject titled "Link." The weblink led Hodge to a site written in Arabic. There were two videos embedded on the homepage. Perhaps Mazuski had fed him a clue as to his father's disappearance or maybe it was just another mind game. Hodge clicked the first video, desperate to end the enigma.

17

MOGADISHU, SOMALIA

OCTOBER 2003

The Duale family was beloved in their community, but Guuce could not have predicted the outpouring of support that he would receive after the drone strike. Hundreds of people, many of whom he recognized only in the vaguest possible fashion, had shown up to comfort him and his brother at the funeral rites. Guuce and Erasto had searched for the remnants of Jamilah and Sharmaarke, eventually finding their bones amidst the wreckage. They judged which remains belonged to which family member by their size. Sharmaarke's hand, clutching the giraffe at the time of the attack, was a useful guide for the bones that were more difficult to determine.

Guuce and Erasto wrapped the remains of mother and son in green linen cloth. The cloths were embroidered with gold Arabic letters that spelled out the name of Allah. Guuce spoke the first words of the funeral prayer over the haphazard remains of his wife and son's skeletons. Soon, they would be buried, the fragments of their heads facing towards Mecca.

After Guuce had finished the funeral prayer, Erasto turned to the crowd that had assembled. He knew that his grief was expected to be dignified and that it was un-Islamic to wail, break objects, or say anything that would cause a Muslim to lose faith in the glorious revelation of the Prophet Muhammad. As he began his plea, Erasto put forth his best effort to summon his brother's composure, yet by his own standard fell far short. "All Western infidels need to be killed. They come to our land and kill our families. My brother's wife is no warlord. My brother's son is no warlord. I am no warlord and he is no warlord. We are peace-loving Muslims who only desire to please Allah, peace be upon him. But the infidel is not peaceful. The infidel has murder in his heart and we must fight to defend our families and our land from the infidel. It is our jihad."

After they were buried, Guuce did not utter a single word for the next fifteen days. He did not leave Abdullahi's home during that period. He ate only the smallest portions of the food that his surrogate father and brother brought him. Guuce performed all his prayers during this period of grief, but he brought every other function to a standstill. This was not a time for action. This was a time that served only two purposes: to remember the family members he had lost and to contemplate the appropriate response to this tragedy.

18

SANA'A, YEMEN

NOVEMBER 2003

The second video had just ended. Chris Hodge stared at his laptop, barely able to comprehend what he had just seen. He was snapped out of his daze by an incoming call on his satellite phone. "What happened?"

"A mistake. A costly one." Mazuski's voice conveyed no empathy. It remained as devoid of emotion as it had been in all of their conversations.

"How did this happen? Was this you?"

"A low-level making a chain of events into a tragedy."

Hodge's throat trembled with anxiety. "This wasn't you?" Regardless of the answer, Hodge could not be certain either way. His mind raced through the possible scenarios that may have led Mazuski to call in the drone strike. It could have been some sort of loyalty test. Would he remain amenable to orders afterwards? It could have been a power play, Mazuski's way of signaling to Hodge that he controlled life and death. It could have been justified. Blackbeard or his brother may have gone rogue. *They trained us to be perfect actors. Maybe the entirety of our friendship was a ruse from his end.*

"Mistakes may have been made, but the fallout, that's your job. Situational intel is forthcoming." Mazuski was concerned about his asset's emotional state. *Death happened in this line of business; fragility never should be present.*

Hodge killed the line, then hit the lights. Sleep would have to be his form of escape tonight.

When Hodge woke up, he did not visit the gym. It was the first time since he had become a contractor that he chose to forgo that aspect of his morning routine without a valid reason. Hodge tried to read *The Plague*, but found that he had to reread every sentence three or four times to comprehend its meaning. He put the book down after two pages. His mind could only focus on the business at hand.

Hodge entered the welfare and recreation center. His team was huddled around the television playing *Call of Duty*. Insults flew around the room as fast as kills happened on the screen. Hodge stared at the game and its players until Bozo hit the pause button on his controller.

"There a ghost here, Wild Man?" Bozo snapped his fingers, trying to loosen Hodge up. It didn't work. Some of Bozo's previous team leaders, like Hodge, had maintained a professional degree of distance from their men, but this was different. Bozo assessed that his team leader's mind had gone off-center. Wild Man was not weak-willed. If something had affected him, it must be something bad, something that would merit such a reaction.

"No." Hodge paused. *They could sense it. They could sense that his mind wasn't on his mission. An asset whose mind is not on his mission is a dead asset. An asset whose mind is not on his mission is not worthy of command. Embrace the suck. Shit happens. Your brother died. Your father died. Your friend's wife and son died. It happens. It doesn't affect your job. It doesn't affect your performance. If it does, you're not relevant, and if you're not relevant, you die and other people die. Fear is the mind killer. Do your job.* "Intel confirms an HVT in Khamr. We move at 1400."

"We got a haji cab driver to get us all the way out there?" Not that he had a choice in the matter, but for Uggo a two-hour ride cramped in the back of a Japanese-made vehicle was preferable to recreating the Book of Exodus.

"Yes." Hodge had already in-briefed his men on their first day in Yemen about Mohamed bin Ali and the village from which he was believed to be operating. Nothing had changed so nothing more needed to be shared.

As soon as Hodge left, Bandito spoke up. "Unpause that shit. I'm gonna frag all you mother—"

"Try it, dude," Hippie responded.

"You're not gonna do nothing except cry like a little bitch after I smoke your ass." Bozo unpaused the game and the four-player competition recommenced.

Uggo's soldier used a large rock formation as cover to snipe Bandito's soldier. "You're down, bitch!" Uggo thumped his chest in triumph.

"You're the bitch, pendejo." Bandito screamed. "That was a punk ass shot. Hiding behind rocks and shit."

"Yo," Bozo handed his controller to Squire. "Sure you don't want to get in on the action?"

"I'm good, Bozo. Thank you."

"Yeah, whatever, mister manners. Bandito, I'm gonna smoke your ass again."

Alpha Team, sans their leader, played for another two hours before everyone went to the DFAC for lunch. Plenty of meat was on the grill and the lunch bar had Indian that day.

Ahmed Khan was one of their assets in Sana'a. He would serve as Alpha Team's driver whenever one was required for a mission. Ahmed was young, but with a light complexion aged by the unyielding desert sun and an onset of male pattern baldness that began early in his teenage years, he looked closer to forty-nine than twenty-nine. After Somalia and Sudan, Hodge was relieved that in Yemen there was some variety in the vehicles. Ahmed owned a Toyota, but at least it was a Hilux.

Ahmed turned to the team squeezed in the back of his pickup and addressed them in broken English. "We about half hour now."

"Keep your eyes on the road." The venom dripped from his voice. There were millions of potential pitfalls on the job, and Alpha Team would not die because of an unfocused driver.

Ahmed turned his attention back to the road and kept it there until the team neared Khamr. He was studying computer engineering at the university. Ahmed gauged that the skills that he was developing and his partnership with the Americans could be parlayed into a job in the United States. He did not mind being the recipient of a gruff command or having to undertake a dangerous assignment. Ahmed viewed the exchange as favorable. These tasks put him in a better position to obtain the life that he hoped to lead.

Hodge ordered Ahmed to pull his Hilux to a stop when they were five klicks outside of Khamr. Ahmed did as told, letting Alpha Team out near a rocky outcropping amidst the arid landscape.

"Ahmed. Tomorrow at 1900, be here." There wasn't even the slightest hint of equality in Hodge's command. Ahmed was his asset. He would do as told. *Hippie was right. You don't become friends with these people. If you become friends with them, you make mistakes, become unfocused, and end up in a box.*

"What if it all goes wrong?" It was Ahmed's first time being utilized in this role. He had no idea what was expected of him if the team met with misfortune. Would he be asked to transport a dead body through the countryside? Should he wait indefinitely even if he was not contacted by Hodge?

"Then you wait." His asset's choice of words had irritated Hodge. Their operation would not go badly. Ahmed's people would be the ones to get messed up, not Alpha Team.

"How long I wait?"

"Until we're back." Hodge lightly slapped Ahmed a few times on each cheek. "You understand that?"

"OK. I understand. I leave now." Ahmed could sense that he had done or said something to make his handler upset, but he did not know the affront. He assumed that Hodge was a man who did not enjoy conversation. Ahmed resolved to speak less and give more of himself to the tasks that he was asked to perform.

"1900 tomorrow."

"Yes. I understand."

"Good boy. Go now." Hodge disdained breaking protocol, but Ahmed had a subservient manner and an apparent need to be micromanaged. It was a near impossibility that a sap like that would turn. Hodge allowed himself the luxury of coopting Ahmed into a metaphorical punching bag. Better that than make him into a friend. That would be pure ignorance.

"We'll camp out three klicks west from here." The nearest village going south was Raydah, which was thirty-five klicks away. Going west was Alsoodah, forty-nine klicks out and devoid of a straight route. Going east was Al-Harajah, which was more than an hour away by vehicle. In the unlikely chance that any sand-dwelling nomads came their way and did not feel like extending a welcome to their foreign guests, Hodge knew that Alpha Team was more than equipped to take out a few hotheaded stragglers.

"Any signs of life? Who owns this piece of shit land anyway?" Uggo asked.

"No one."

Hippie grinned. "Allah's very own land."

Bandito surveyed the area. "Napping in the dirt."

Bozo decided to test out a new impersonation. He adopted Steam's West Virginia drawl. "You're used to that, yep? Sleeping in shit?"

Bandito snapped back, "Fuck your ass, Christopher Columbus."

Hodge iced Bozo and Bandito down with a death stare. "Save it for the Xbox unless you want to meet Allah yourselves."

"Roger, Wild Man," Bozo apologized.

"My bad, Wild Man."

After a pregnant pause, Hippie broke the silence. "I like it. Sleeping under the stars. When I get too old for this, I want to buy an RV and travel. Drink brews and play guitar wherever the road goes."

Uggo rolled his eyes. "Permission to call Hippie a pussy, Wild Man?"

Hodge stared at Uggo with disdain. Uggo broke his gaze after five seconds. It was a tactic that Hodge had employed on Millie when he was a teenager. You stare until they look away in order to establish dominance. She was a defiant cat by nature, but always became submissive when Hodge showed her that he had a backbone. Once the team's behavior was in line with Hodge's expectations, they headed west towards their personal oasis.

"You were an asset." Hodge had sacked out two hours ago, yet his mind was not at rest. "My asset. Are you civilized? Civilized?"

Squire shook his team leader awake. "You good, Wild Man?"

"I'm fine. Go to sleep. I'll take over lookout."

Hodge had been back at his quarters in Camp Mogadishu, whittling the boy's giraffe from the block of wood. Like a jump cut, the dream shifted to him presenting a headless giraffe to Sharmaarke. The boy received the gift with glee. Blackbeard patted him on the back in appreciation. Then, he wasn't in Somalia anymore. He was in the Longfellow Mountains in Maine. Sharmaarke's head was on a target 800 yards out. Direct hit. Jamilah's head was on a target 850 yards out. Direct hit. Erasto's head was on a target 900 yards out. Direct hit. Blackbeard's head was on a target 1,000 yards out. Squire had interceded at that point. Hodge's dream had concluded without a satisfying resolution.

Squire rested his head on his bag and fell asleep in a matter of minutes. Hodge pointed his M4 towards the faint outline of the road in the distance. There were no shadows in that direction.

Hodge checked his digital wristwatch to confirm. It was 0700. Hodge knew he had to get his head straight. "Get up. We're moving." He shook Bozo and Uggo awake earlier than planned. Bandito and Hippie were already awake. Within ten mikes, Alpha Team had started humping back to the road. They were only five klicks away from Khamr once they drew near to the path. Even with three Arabic speakers, pajamas over their bodies, and the privilege of being in a land where the complexions varied from the darkest ebony to a sallow olive, Hodge made sure that Alpha Team did not attract any unnecessary attention. The team would stay one klick west of the road as they moved north towards Khamr.

The plan was to move as a unified front, inspecting each room of the three domiciles that intelligence had narrowed the location down to until they found Mohamed bin Ali. There was the possibility that bin Ali would be alerted to the disturbance and evacuate. If that happened, Alpha Team would be on their own to complete the mission, but intel could not conclusively determine from which home their target was operating. It was not even assured with greater than seventy percent probability that bin Ali was still utilizing Khamr as the base from which he and his fellow terrorists were directing their attacks against Americans and other Westerners. The last time he was in Yemen, Hodge had taken out two of bin Ali's associates in Al Mukalla. Maybe bin Ali had left Khamr to pay his belated respects.

Hippie, Bozo, and Squire were on one side of the entrance. Hodge stood in front of Uggo and Bandito on the other side. Everyone had their M4s at the ready. Hodge gave the order to move. Alpha Team breached the doorway of their first location. Inside they were met with an old woman who collapsed to the ground in terror. Hodge called out in Arabic, "Stay down. Move and you will be killed. Where is Mohamed bin Ali?"

Paralyzed by fear, the woman did not respond. The chattering of the remnants of her deteriorated teeth was the only sound emitted from her mouth. Hodge and Bozo remained in the main room. They zipped the woman's wrists and covered the entry. Hippie, Squire, Uggo, and Bandito paired off and searched the other two rooms. This location not only did not appear to be bin Ali's base, but it was almost devoid of any signs of life. The kitchen area had a handful of pots, pans, and utensils, but no food other than the smattering of vegetables housed inside a woven basket. Besides for an unexpectedly nice bed with a rainbow-patterned sheet draped over it, the old woman's bedroom was also Spartan. There was a calendar affixed to the wall, a rust-stained fan, a handful of eye droppers, and a bottle of aspirin. Alpha Team did not extend any explanation for their actions. The less she knew, the less she could share with bin Ali or other hostiles. The team could hear her teeth still chattering as they released her and rushed out of her home.

The next location to inspect was two mikes from the local government office in the center of town. Despite their efforts at discretion, Alpha Team's movements had caught the attention of a handful of locals. Hodge and Bozo aimed their M4s at the crowd, while Bozo called on them in Arabic to disperse. Some complied, heading to unknown locations. Perhaps they would alert bin Ali. A few followed Alpha Team to their next location. The villagers did not appear to be armed. They could be contained if their numbers didn't increase.

Alpha Team breached the domicile after Hodge motioned for his team to advance. Hodge and Bozo guarded the entrance, their M4s halting the threat of any obstruction from the onlookers during the search. Hippie, Squire, Uggo, and Bandito searched the empty home. The place appeared to have recently housed a family. The bedroom had a stuffed rabbit and a red soccer ball on the floor. There were no Kalashnikovs or any Islamic effects inside, other than a Qu'ran. If bin Ali used this location as his base, Hodge's intel must have forgotten to mention that his cover was to play the Yemeni version of Ward Cleaver. Hodge warned his team as they exited the location, "Our target could be in any of these domiciles. Intel is off sometimes. Stay frosty."

The team tried to disperse the crowd as they advanced towards the intel report's final potential hideout of bin Ali, a home further down the dirt road away from the government office. Alpha Team tried to bat the crowd off, swatting at them with the butts of their firearms. Some of the members of the mob dispersed, but others continued to follow Alpha Team. Their shouts attracted additional attention along the way.

A middle-aged father, his infant son in his hands, stood in the doorway of the final house. When the team pointed their M4s at his skull, he instantly stepped aside. Hodge had thought he'd seen him. Not bin Ali, but Blackbeard. Most likely, it was a hallucination. Hodge could concede that he had not been himself since he clicked on Mazuski's email. At the Farm, he had undergone all manner of psychological testing to determine if he was mentally sound enough to handle the stressors inherent in this line of employment. Hodge recognized that his current mindset, if expressed at Langley, would have led to an immediate rejection of his candidacy. He would have been forced back into academia and ended up in some college town. Maybe he would have published a book on the topic of Islamic extremism. Maybe his book would have been successful. He could have become a public intellectual. His path would have been different. That was a distant memory.

It was like he was in a trance. Hodge went AWOL on his team, pushed off the crowds that encircled him, and rushed towards the nearby courtyard where he could have sworn he saw the shadow moving. Ahead of him, the dark shadow brushed past the linens that hung on a clothesline in the courtyard. Hodge pushed through a series of alleys and chased the shadow. Women screamed in his face. Children ran away from him. Old men cursed him in Arabic. Young men eyed him suspiciously. By the time Hodge reached the linens, the shadow was gone. As he moved through the courtyard in a mad dash, a woman clad in a burqa tripped him. Hodge fell flat on his face, but he saw the shadow again as it ran off into the distance. He had to chase it. He had to chase him. Hodge sprang back up. The woman tried to kick him in the face, but he caught her foot and shoved her to the ground. He had to keep moving. Villagers and natural obstacles were ever present, but Hodge kept chasing the shadow through the village's homes, roads, and into a bazaar. There, behind a row of pashminas, Hodge caught his shadow.

"What are you doing here?" Maybe his screws weren't all the way loose just yet. He was right. It was Blackbeard.

Blackbeard stared at Hodge. He didn't say a word. His eyes were devoid of emotion.

"Why haven't you been on comms?" Hodge's voice began to falter. "W-where did, did you go?" Hodge pointed his M4 at Blackbeard. The shadow was not armed. It was not a fair fight. Hodge's hands had started to shake like Abdullahi's on the wheel. He couldn't believe it. Blackbeard had flipped. *It made sense to those of a certain antiquated mindset. If Americans killed your wife and son, you kill them. Pure barbarism. And no amount of money could make something like that go away. It's a worldview in which everything is perceived as a matter of honor.* Still, Hodge felt Blackbeard's actions to be a personal betrayal. *Does he think I had something to do with it?* "You're working with them? You know how many innocent lives they've taken?"

"Innocent lives? Like my wife and son? That was you and your government."

Mazuski's words echoed through Hodge's mind. "Your questions might be putting those close to you at risk." *Who? Who was at risk? My team? My family? Blackbeard? Which questions?* The man spoke in riddles. They were often easy enough for Hodge to discern. Not now. Not in this situation.

Hodge stabbed at the air in front of Blackbeard with his M4. "Is this what you want?" *Is that what Mazuski wanted? Was that the right thing to do? What had he done? Nothing. He was not even armed. His brother made a call to jihad. But here he is in Khamr. Why? Was he an operative of bin Ali? What the hell was going on?*

Guuce turned his back to Hodge. His mind was clear. If Hodge shot him in the back, he would join his wife and son in paradise. If he did not shoot, perhaps his new associates would notify him of Hodge's location once again and he could enact his vengeance, if that was Allah's will. Guuce had realized that Erasto, Cabdi, and Abdullahi were correct. The Americans were murderers. Not just of his family, but of Muslims worldwide. They would not bring peace to Somalia. Bringing peace was not their agenda. Their agenda was to amass money and subvert Islam. America glorified shirk. They glorified everything that was haram and worked against everything that was halal. They were like their master Shaytan, a nation with forked tongues desirous only of leading innocent Muslims astray. He would honor his father. He would honor his family. He would honor the ummah, fight the unbelievers, and spare them no mercy.

Hodge's hands eased off the grip as Blackbeard walked away. The shadow's back remained turned to him. He wasn't on the list. He didn't draw a weapon. There was no choice but to watch the shadow disappear.

When Blackbeard left, a mob of villagers had replaced him, swarming around Chris Hodge. All he heard were screams. He did not react. He could not understand anything. Hodge heard M4 fire above the crowd. The crowd dispersed. It was his team. Everything had begun to restore to reality.

Bozo pulled Hodge up from the ground. "One Tango down. The hell happened to you, Wild Man?"

"I thought I saw our target."

"Let's move, Wild Man." Bozo did not understand what had happened, but he understood that the longer that they remained in Khamr, the greater the likelihood a major clusterfuck would occur. As the team lead in Hodge's absence or otherwise inability to perform the task, Bozo took charge in leading the team to escape from the village. Alpha Team's M4s had kept the villagers at bay. Bozo was not an especially religious man, but he vowed to himself that the next time he returned to Ohio, instead of searching through his VHS tapes, he would go to mass at St. Anthony's with his parents and light a candle. He had witnessed a genuine miracle. Alpha Team had entered a village in one of the most radicalized of Islamic states, a village where a major terrorist operated within its borders, and yet there had been no team or civilian casualties. Sure, they killed the man and his son in the doorway. The man had charged the team after Hippie and Bandito found bin Ali cowering in the back room, but Bozo counted the man amongst the hostiles. Alpha Team had gathered the DNA samples in their kits for each and departed. Regarding the son, Steam had always joked with him that I-ties have bad aim.

Alpha Team was on their way back to the hideout. It was only a little after 1100 and they were already halfway to their rally point. Ahmed would not arrive by the road for almost eight hours. The team had time to kill and Uggo had made sure they were safe. Some of the more courageous villagers had tried to follow the men out of town. As soon as a few teenagers had started to pelt Alpha Team with stones, Uggo went apeshit. He fired on their legs. The ones who still possessed the ability to move did not.

He thought he saw the target. Bullshit. Bandito decided he would have to be the one to speak up and expose the elephant in the room because the rest of Alpha Team seemed unwilling to confront their team leader on this insane lie. "What the hell happened back there, Wild Man?"

"Nothing." There was no way that Hodge would delve into this again. Hippie had already clocked him for being soft with Blackbeard. If he admitted anything to his men, it would end his career as a contractor. Mazuski would disappear, he'd never even have the slightest possibility of learning the truth of his father's story, and he might be tracked down by international terrorists. He would also have to maintain absolute confidentiality or answer to Mazuski and his ilk. Honesty would have to give way to expediency.

Uggo smirked. "Nothing?" *Even Bandito isn't buying Wild Man's cover story.*

"Can't believe you missed it, dude. It was beautiful." Hippie punched Bandito in the arm. "This crazy dude popped two slugs in the back of that bastard's head. It was so freakin' sweet."

"Next time," Hodge said. His body trekked through this wasteland with his team, but his mind remained fixated on the shadow in Khamr.

The first thing that Chris Hodge did when he returned to Camp Sana'a was confer with Walz about the op. Hodge hoped that this would be the only time that Bozo or any team member had to be on hand to sketch in missing facts. The second thing that Chris Hodge did was shower. He was drained. Everything might not be better in the morning, but he would be reequipped to handle himself in a professional fashion and move forward. Before he could turn in, Hodge received an incoming call on his satphone. *Mazuski knew. Of course he would know*. Hodge answered the call. "Next time I won't hesitate."

"We normally don't extend a next time, Chris."

"So that's it?" *If it was over, it was over. The events had already elapsed.*

Mazuski coughed into the receiver. After his fit died down, he continued, "There are." The coughs had started to come on with greater frequency. "Individuals." This time, blood poured out of his mouth. "Who have taken a keen interest in your abilities. They have deemed you relevant."

"Who?" The public face of the hidden hand that steered his entire life was Mazuski. Hodge wondered which individuals or organizations were at the bottom of the rabbit hole.

Mazuski deflected, "A question."

Hodge had a begrudging respect for Mazuski. Without him, he would have never embarked on this path. Mazuski and whoever he received orders from had steered him into an exceptional life. They had opened doors for him that were, if not impossible, improbable to be opened for a child from a single parent household in a working-class New Jersey town. They had set him up for success in every endeavor. By his own merits, Hodge had been able to rise to the challenge in every aspect of his life, including in his present duties as a contractor. But there was a price to pay. Hodge had been strung along for almost two years without learning any new information about his father. Blackbeard's wife and son were possibly targeted as a loyalty test. He was indebted to Mazuski, but his evasive ways were a source of consistent frustration. "You didn't—"

"If one of your men were to aid an enemy combatant, would you alleviate the threat?"

"Of course," Hodge could see where Mazuski planned to steer the conversation. Yes, he would have no qualms about shooting or otherwise neutralizing one of his team members if they had decided to aid the enemy; however, this was something that did not happen in the operator community. Hodge's father had been killed by Islamic militants. If someone that he trusted and respected and chose for his team were to flip, it would be the ultimate betrayal. They had relative freedom, more than in any branch of the military. They were compensated extraordinarily well. They were exposed to a life of secrets and action that most people could not even fathom. Most importantly, they were afforded the opportunity to make things just a little bit safer for their loved ones and the world at large. If a man on his team flipped, impossible a likelihood as that was, Hodge would put him down.

"How close are you to your men, Chris?"

Hodge cupped his face in his hands. Guuce Duale. Blackbeard. The shadow. He did not shoot him. Blackbeard had gone rogue. Erasto called for jihad. Hodge knew that a homie handshake was not equivalent to a wife and son's love. If he were in Blackbeard's position, tragic as it was, he would not even consider going vigilante. Hodge believed that if one were placed in that position, there's a civilized response and a Stone Age response. Hodge did not have to choose between those options. He was in an altogether different position.

Mazuski coughed into the receiver. Twenty seconds later, he continued. Hodge could hear him suck on a lozenge as he spoke. "Intel confirms that your friend has been aiding al-Qaeda militants in Yemen. We have coordinates on his location, a desert complex in the Rub' al Khali." Mazuski had tested Chris Hodge his entire life. The student had always passed. Mazuski had known that he would pass. This was the first test for which Mazuski had serious doubts. If Hodge failed, he would no longer be relevant. If the nature of the failure was grievous, Hodge might have to be subject to a greater punishment than just receiving his walking papers. Mazuski had a certain pride in Chris Hodge. He viewed him as a willful son, but his head was always in check and he was always amped. Regardless, to Mazuski, his duties and his obligations came first. Chris Hodge would receive the same treatment as any other asset.

"Nothing survives there." The name of the desert translated as "The Empty Quarter." Somehow, a few of the nomads did not receive the message and inhabited this hyper-arid region. In July and August, temperatures exceeded 124 degrees. Hodge did not expect a November frost in the Rub' al Khali.

"Exactly." Mazuski cut the line.

Walz had arranged the meeting with Abdur ibn Musa, Yemen's current Head of State. He and Chris Hodge had been escorted by the Yemeni President's personal armed bodyguards to the location ibn Musa reserved for his clandestine dealings. It was a calculated risk to go along with the bodyguards. Intel had confirmed that ibn Musa was amenable to U.S. interests, but there was no guarantee that his bodyguards held such views. The fact that ibn Musa was a despot who had a record of launching attacks on his own people and had the backing of Yemen's Army quelled any personal misgivings the bodyguards may have felt about dealing with Americans. Their own cultural biases notwithstanding, the bodyguards did their job and escorted Hodge and Walz to the location without a hitch. Hodge and Walz had complied with the bodyguards' only demand, that they be blindfolded throughout the route.

Hodge could tell that ibn Musa was tense. Even though Yemen's President attempted to portray himself with the dignity appropriate for a world leader, his body had betrayed him. At Langley, Hodge had learned the typical signs that a person was nervous. Throughout the course of their conversation, ibn Musa displayed most of the symptoms. Ibn Musa rubbed his forehead, he blinked frequently, he compressed his lips, he interlaced his fingers and squeezed them together, and he rubbed the skin on his hands together so much that Hodge assumed he moonlit as the before in a hand model advertisement for Eucerin.

Ibn Musa addressed the men in Arabic, "We cannot have any additional drone strikes. Your government has created a troublesome situation."

Walz responded in an Arabic so perfect that it would have befitted an erudite Saudi, "With all due respect, we can't allow al-Qaeda to operate with impunity out of your country."

Ibn Musa perceived Walz' response as an affront. Al-Qaeda was a threat to upholding his own legitimate power in his country. The perception that he would sanction terrorism galled him. "We are doing our part to suppress militancy." Above all, ibn Musa was a politician. He had mastered the art of sublimating his irritation, regardless of his personal feelings on a matter.

Hodge had picked up on ibn Musa's slight shift in tonality and the increased rapidity of his nervous ticks. This entire op could fall apart if he did not adjust the course of this conversation. "Sir, you have done an exceptional job keeping your country safe and limiting jihadism." Hodge could see ibn Musa ease into relaxation and begin the process of dropping his guard. All these third world dictators needed was a bit of flattery to appeal to their overinflated egos. Then, you could meet your objective while they could maintain their pride. Walz picked up on Hodge's tactic. He briefly turned his head towards Hodge and gave a tiny nod of assent, before he refocused his attention on ibn Musa.

"Thank you, Mr. Morton."

Chase Morton was Chris Hodge's alias for this op. In all his covert actions, he used aliases. It made sense to him. As a contractor, he was a man without country, history, or even a name. Externally, he could be asked to be anything. Internally, there was nothing but a blank slate. "You're welcome, sir. And please rest assured that we understand your position. You have seen your country, the country which you love, your home, your family's home, the home of your ancestors, more fully reach its potential under your stewardship."

Walz had clocked Hodge's approach and mirrored it. Butter ibn Musa up with flattery. The power that he turned on his people betrayed his inner weakness. He wanted to be admired. When the gushing admiration waned, so did his susceptibility to manipulation. "Of course, it's not our goal to interfere in your country's affairs, sir, but we do share your concerns and laud your exceptional efforts to date."

"Thank you, Mr. Walz. Mr. Morton. Of course, you understand my position. We are a traditional culture, an insular one. I must limit the perception that the United States is interfering in our affairs. If that perception becomes widespread, it will be my life. The lives of my family. The downfall of my country, our culture being seized by the forces of Shaytan, those who disgrace the glorious revelation of Allah, the Exalted, the Majestic, the Sublime, and his Prophet, peace and blessings be upon him."

Walz wondered how much of ibn Musa's exhortation to Islam was genuine and how much of it was posturing. Either way, his religious beliefs did not matter. All that mattered was that ibn Musa not support terrorism financially or offer terrorists safe harbor in Yemen and that he not interfere in any ops designed to take out the bad guys. Beyond that, ibn Musa could do whatever he wanted and believe whatever he wanted and there would be no problems. "Sir, we understand your need to limit perceptions that the United States is interfering in your nation's affairs. We also understand the imperative to balance active suppression without alienating patriotic Yemenis who may misunderstand your government's approach or who may have distorted perceptions about al-Qaeda and other insurgent groups-"

Walz had made a blunder. Hodge had to jump back into the conversation. Ibn Musa's body language signified that he had interpreted Walz's comment as an indication that he had failed on two fronts. "Or who may misunderstand their beautiful religion. We, like all sane and intelligent individuals, know that Islam is a religion of peace.

Unfortunately, jihadists are quite skilled at public relations and have disseminated their distorted perspective widely. Your efforts to protect your country and the noble religion of Islam are recognized. We applaud you, sir." If Mirele had been privy to this conversation, she would have been proud of Hodge's words, but ridicule him for their absolute lack of sincerity. His politics frustrated her. Her politics frustrated him. Conversation with Mirele was useless, but at least they had found a perfect way to channel their frustrations while burning more than a few calories in the process.

"Thank you, Mr. Morton."

Walz delivered the payload, "Sir, we respectfully ask your permission to supply local anti-jihadists loyal to your government with weapons and intelligence. We also respectfully ask for your help, when possible, in providing the locations of our mutual enemies."

Ibn Musa nodded. He agreed to work with the Americans. The insurgents demanded sharia and sought to topple his government. The Americans could topple his government in a matter of hours. He had no desire to extend them an invitation to place a new figurehead in power. The presidency was his and he would do whatever he needed to do to maintain his position.

When not on specific missions, Chris Hodge and his men spent much of their time at black sites, small bases that were usually walled up and always devoid of an official paper trail. The black sites were where Hodge and his men gathered their intel. Alpha Team was one of many groups of contractors operating in-country to eliminate terrorist cells. Ibn Musa was not the most forthcoming with information and he did not intend to supply Yemeni troops unless his interests were directly threatened, but he was comfortable with allowing contractors to operate with impunity. Once the nameless men had completed their objectives, it would presumably be safe for a new ambassador to return to Sana'a.

Alpha Team had returned to the Embassy to follow up on their mission. It had been three days since the LRADs were installed as a protective shield around the embassy. The Marines and Alpha Team all wore specialty headphones to protect themselves from the emitted frequencies. Hodge had observed a terrorist that had returned with headphones in his ears to cancel out the frequencies. Though he was wearing noise-cancelling headphones, they were ineffective against the ultra-low vibration that was being used to guard the embassy. Like the other terrorists, he doubled over, vomited, and then scrambled away from the complex. This already had happened numerous times. The Marines would take turns cleaning the front of the embassy. Hodge joked with them about how mopping up terrorist vomit still beat a week in Gitmo.

"I can't see! My heart! My heart!" A few hours later, another terrorist had sought to brave the barrier. Instead, like the rest, he doubled over and vomited profusely. Al-Qaeda and the other insurgent groups must not have invested their money in appropriate technology to facilitate effective coordination. Hodge thought that smoke signals might be a good place for them to start.

"Take him," Hodge spoke into his walkie.

Uggo's usual sneer was on his face as he exited the embassy. He carried the immobilized protester off the facility and threw him into the back seat of an unmarked vehicle parked outside. Uggo slammed the door. The car sped off. Uggo had never been briefed on where the jihadis were taken to, but he supposed that wherever they were sent they would be "encouraged" to provide intel and information. One of the main reasons that Uggo left the USMC's ANGLICO unit after his tour of duty was because of the irritating amount of bureaucratic nonsense with which every soldier, even in an elite unit, had to contend. In the Marines, everything was compartmentalized. Uggo viewed the process as wasteful, but protocol was protocol, so he followed Wild Man's orders.

Hodge and Uggo had donned their pajamas. Most Yemeni men wore a jambiya, a type of traditional dagger, on their person. Hodge thought that was not only an interesting fashion accessory, but a practical measure; however, a jambiya did not pack the same punch as a .40 Glock or an M4, so its potential uses were less apparent to his team, other than providing a slight degree of cover. Everyone on Alpha Team had full beards. Hodge's own was thick and flowing, somewhere between bin Laden and ZZ Top. He was the only natural blond on the team. Hodge had dyed his hair, eyebrows, and beard shoe polish black on his first day at Camp Sana'a.

Yasser Khayat was an active figure in the anti-jihadi resistance. He was British-educated and from what Walz had told Hodge, a know-it-all with a snooty persona. Walz had been in contact with Yasser about coordination between his freedom fighters and various teams of contractors. Hodge and Alpha Team were brought in to seal the deal on the partnership.

Hodge and Uggo had traveled to the Old City, an area where the more well-to-do and modern citizens of Sana'a lived. Yasser's block was full of ornate homes in the traditional architecture of the Arabian Peninsula. A few residents were around that morning, but the area appeared tranquil. If jihadists were present, they were advertising their presence even less conspicuously than typical.

Hodge and Uggo removed their pajamas, slinging them on their shoulders when they arrived in Yasser's home. Afterwards, Yasser shook hands with Hodge and Uggo.

"Where are your men?" Hodge asked Yasser.

Yasser winked, aware of the farcical nature of the proceedings. "I should ask you the same question, Mr. Gray." His English was as flawless as the Queen's.

As usual, Hodge was operating under an alias. Yasser was sharp as a tack and hungry with political ambitions. His wealth afforded him a measure of influence and had attracted the attention of ibn Musa. At present, Yasser's relationship with Yemen's leader was positive and mutually beneficial, despite their unspoken mutual distaste for each other. In this part of the world, there was no guarantee that today's friend would continue to align with you tomorrow. No native could be trusted beyond their joint interests at that specific moment in time. Yasser was no exception. "My associate, Mr. Beilein."

Uggo extended his hand again. It was a gut instinct in response to an introduction, but Uggo immediately realized he had made a faux pas. Hodge had brought him around as backup and extra muscle on the off chance that the meeting did not move according to plan.

Yasser grinned. He shook Uggo's hand for a second time. Yasser hoped that the American contractors had more grace in the battlefield than in social situations.

"He's Polish." Hodge had grown up in the United States' multiethnic Northeast Corridor. There, almost everyone seemed to have some sort of recent immigrant identity if you went a few generations back. Wop, mick, polack, kike, wetback. To Hodge and his friends in middle school, these slurs were not meant to exclude, but were a way for him and the other boys to show each other that they belonged through a playful dig on their ancestry. "Part Polish. It's not a question of etiquette, but of innate intelligence." Uggo was not even Polish. He was a Minnesota Dane with some Bavarian ancestry, but his recent gaffe helped lend believability to the role that Hodge had chosen for him to play.

"Forgive me, Mr. Beilein." Yasser flashed a false smile at Uggo and then turned his eyes back on Hodge. "I know of American perceptions of Poles. To us, the American Polish joke is our Turkish joke." Hodge nodded in understanding. Uggo remained as neutral as a stone. "Right. Well, Mr. Gray, we've established that you're a man with warm regard for efficiency. Let's begin our conversation, shall we? To what do I owe the pleasure of this visit?" Walz had tried to keep Yasser in the dark. To get him to budge on the meeting, Walz had to slip in that he sought to forge a partnership.

"Our mutual friend, your President-"

Yasser interrupted, desperate to clarify the point. "He is no friend of mine. I do not associate with cowards, with religious bigots, with Al-Qaeda-backed stooges-"

Hodge knew all about ibn Musa's backstory. He was a typical politician, one who played to the poll numbers. When Yemeni sentiment was against the terrorists, he enacted tougher policies. When anti-U.S., anti-Israeli, and anti-Western sentiment grew beyond its usual intensity, he made veiled references to the defense of Islam and culture that served as a dog whistle to Islamists. His true feelings might forever remain unknown, but it had been made clear to him that he would be deposed if he actively supported terrorist actions. The fact that he was seen as a moderate traitor to Islam by the extremists made his decision to play ball even easier. "He's started to associate with a better class of people."

Yasser scoffed. "Do you truly believe that? You don't appear as simple as your friend; my apologies, Mr. Beilein."

Hodge put his cards on the table. It wasn't a royal flush, but he believed it would be a winning hand. "We're offering our help. Weapons. Intelligence. Cooperation on the wet work. Making Yemen unfriendly for our shared enemies."

Yasser had already made his decision. "OK." He had surmised what type of partnership the Americans and their covert agents desired. The meeting had only been a formality designed to test their willingness to act in good faith.

"That easy for you to decide?" Hodge asked.

Yasser's smile was tinged with an underlayer of contempt. He could work with them, but that did not mean he had to like them. *Sometimes the enemy of my enemy is my friend*, he thought. "I look forward to a mutually beneficial relationship. A pleasure to meet you, Mr. Gray." Yasser and Hodge shook hands. "Mr. Beilein, a pleasure."

Yasser and Uggo shook for the third time. "Mr. Beilein, one question: Are you mute?"

"No." Uggo put his pajamas back on, ran his hand over his jambiya, and headed towards the door.

The Rub' al Khali Desert was an endless sea of sand. The dunes were sand. The hills were sand. The roads were sand. The rocks were sand. The clouds became sand behind the Land Cruiser. Hell was not eternal fire but eternal sand.

Yasser had supplied three of his men. Naturally, he was a scholar rather than a fighter; he did not come along for the ride. Hodge wondered how many ivory towers there were in Yemen. Junaid was behind the wheel. Beefy and mustachioed, Junaid's son had been abducted into terrorist training at the age of eight. Hamed was taller and lanky. His father had worked by an American military base in Saudi Arabia. The Americans had always treated his father well, and compensated Hamed after his father was killed when the base was attacked. Ayoob was older with a heavy beard. He had to flee his village and lived, for a time, in a refugee camp where an international NGO exposed him to western education and philosophy. Yasser's three men and the six members of Alpha Team had squeezed into one Land Cruiser for a two-day trip through the desert to eliminate a special target – Blackbeard.

Hodge had choked when Blackbeard caught him by surprise in Khamr. This would not happen again. He had run the reasons through his head for why he had broken with common sense and allowed Blackbeard to escape. He was a friend. Bull. He was a terrorist. Did

Mazuski kill his family? Maybe. Or maybe it was an error. His response, however, was to collaborate with a murderous organization bent on the subjugation at best—more realistically the murder—of all non-Muslims. The concept was alien. If a terrorist had killed him and his mother, Hodge's father wouldn't blow up a mosque in Dearborn. And everyone has a backstory. Losing a wife and a son. That's hard, but there are other reactions that are far more appropriate than going full jihad. But he had gone full jihad. He was now an enemy. The fact that he had the inclination to radicalize meant that he had always been an enemy. In a matter of minutes, he would be dead. Hodge hoped that he would have a chance at redemption. He wanted to be the one to fire the kill shot.

The Land Cruiser had stopped two klicks outside of the complex. Yasser's team and Alpha Team walked through the sand towards Blackbeard's complex. The heat was unbearable. Alpha Team chugged water from their CamelBaks. Yasser's men sipped from theirs.

Amidst the endless sea of sand was a traditional Arabic house with a small white gate around the complex. The gate did not cover the entrance. It was almost like an invitation to enter.

Hodge had coordinated with Junaid on the tactics. Alpha Team would stand back and provide overwatch while Yasser's men stormed the complex and shot anyone on sight, including the target. Everything quickly became a shitshow. When Junaid, Hamed, and Ayoob stormed through the door they were assailed by a hail of UZI submachine gun fire.

An insurgent emerged from the complex, his UZI in hand. Bandito had him in the crosshairs. He fired a kill shot into the terrorist's upper torso, sending him collapsing down to the ground; however, the shot was a second too late. The terrorist had sprayed bullets in Hippie's direction, nailing him in the arm.

Hippie's arm was a waterfall of blood. The terrorist had caught his brachial artery. Even through the pain, Hippie maintained his calm. "Aw damn, dude. Am I gonna die?"

"Bozo, medical attention ASAP." Hodge did not want his man to die on him. Hippie was tough. Tough enough to take a shot and not whine. Tough enough to call him out when he befriended a skinny.

"Damn. It hurts like hell."

The door of the complex was wide open, but there were no sounds, no movement. Bozo raced towards Hippie, his M4 in hand in case any other terrorists were in the residence. He threw his rucksack down on the sand and detached the field kit, then opened it and reached in to grab antiseptic, an "Israeli" bandage, and a combat tourniquet.

Bozo had been trained for this situation. His actions were automatic. Solution in the wound. Bandage tight around the arm and tourniquet in place if needed. Fingers on the neck. Check the pulse. Bozo would do everything possible to save his brother on the battlefield. "Pulse is weak and thready," he called out.

"Pumping fluids?" Hodge fired back.

Squire kept his rifle pointed at the front entrance. Bandito had his long gun covering the rear exit. Everyone else on Alpha Team was equipped with M4s to eliminate the objective, if he was actually inside the complex and the snipers could not get a clear shot or scored a miss. There was nowhere for the target to run. If he exited the complex, he would be dead. The only potential pitfall for Hodge and his men was if he had holed up inside and called for backup. Hodge would normally have his men wait it out, but Hippie had been hit. Not only did Hippie's injury force the action, if there was any action to force, but it meant that they would need a bird to exfil the team. Hodge doubted that Hippie could make it another two days.

Bozo grabbed the saline bag from his rucksack and held it up high for inspection. Uggo, being tertiary medic on Alpha Team, had joined Bozo. Uggo grabbed Hippie's good arm and searched for a strong vein. He flicked his line to make sure that it was running and then inserted it into Hippie's vein.

Bozo checked Hippie's pulse. He hoped for a better result. Hippie had been through hell and back with him. Bozo had been a contractor for three years and had seen five of his men die, two in one night on an ambush. There was no way he would allow Hippie to become number six. "Pulse is slightly better. We need to get him somewhere."

"Can he survive five hours without permanent damage?" Hodge needed to balance three priorities. At the end of the day, he had to make sure that the shadow was dead, Hippie was alive, and everyone on his team remained safe and hydrated until they were back on base.

"Yes," *With that wound, he could probably last twice that without any permanent damage*, Bozo thought.

"Then he'll have to. Return to position," Hodge commanded.

Bozo and Uggo returned to their strategic placements. Bozo was ready for the order to move through the fatal funnel. His mind was entirely on seizing the complex and eliminating the target and anyone else inside. While his focus was elsewhere, a scorpion stung Bozo's lower leg. "Ah! Goddamn it!" Bozo brushed the scorpion off his leg and crushed it under his boot. "Scorpion got me."

"Stop living in the past." *Does a scorpion hurt? Yeah. Does it hurt as much as your own or a teammate's death? No.* Hodge would not allow his men to get distracted from their mission for such trivial concerns as Yemen's local fauna. Despite the tremendous pain, Bozo returned his focus to where it belonged.

"Time to advance, Wild Man?" One teammate had been shot and another had been stung. Squire did not view the situation as particularly auspicious. If there was no one inside, Hodge could radio to Sana'a Main and get his teammates the care that they deserved. If the target or any of his accomplices were inside, they could be eliminated and then Hodge could radio back. Squire had assessed that the only bad move to make was no move, but he did not wish to embarrass Wild Man in front of the team. As long as there was a skillful way to persuade him to take action without the loss of face, Squire would utilize that approach. It was basic professionalism.

"Hold off." It didn't make sense to Hodge that one lone terrorist, a nobody, would be inside the complex all by himself. The Yemenis had tried to seize the compound and died. Rushing into the situation could produce disastrous results. Hippie had time. Bozo was a big boy. None of his men would die on Hodge's watch because of haste.

Squire accepted the order. He would press again if necessary, but would wait it out for a bit first. Fifteen mikes seemed like an appropriate amount of time to ask again if Wild Man had not made a move.

Squire did not need those fifteen mikes. Three minutes later, a woman wearing a burqa emerged from the complex to break up the impasse. She held a baby in front of her head, wore a vest packed with explosives, and was armed with a detonator. The bomber charged towards Alpha Team in a straight line from the door. It was Bandito's shot.

A woman with a baby. She was not who he had signed up to fight. His father had abandoned him and his mother as a baby. Bandito would never admit it, but he was a mama's boy at heart. She had his back through the hard years in the barrio, working two jobs to make sure that he had something to eat and clean clothes to wear. She had sacrificed for him. That's what mothers do. That's what his wife did for their two daughters.

In a split second, Hodge had clocked Bandito's reticence. There was less than a minute before the woman would be in range to detonate. Depending on her range, all six men could die or at best be deformed for life. The M4s were useless. A bad shot could detonate the bomb. The team needed the precision of a sniper and Bandito had the shot. Hodge shoved him aside and took the shot himself.

Everything slowed down at that moment for Chris Hodge. The bullet sailed through the air for an eternity until it hit the terrorist in her shoulder. It was a miss. Hodge would have hit the nerve base of her skull if he was on the long gun at the beginning. He did not imagine that one of his men would have a meltdown.

Uggo called out the obvious, "It's a miss."

The wounded suicide bomber grabbed her shoulder and wailed in pain. Then, she released the trigger. The bomb detonated. She and her baby were dead. Instantly. Smoke and shrapnel scattered all around. A few more yards and it would have been ugly.

"A fuckin' baby, man! That's sick shit, man! I can't understand that shit! It's fuckin' sick! It's inhuman, man! What the fuck are they doing, man? Where the fuck are we?"

Hodge ran over to Bandito. It was time to advance. Bandito was in no shape to join them on the mission. "Bozo, Uggo, Squire, we're moving. Carlos, stay here. Be ready." Hodge knew Bandito wouldn't be ready. *Guys like that, guys who break down, they're not relevant. They become dead assets. Worse, they turn other assets into dead assets.* Hodge figured the best thing for Bandito to do was let his tears fall in the sand and provide some drinking water for the scorpions. At this point, he needed to stay out of the way.

The four members of Alpha Team who remained both physically and psychologically intact had already advanced inside the complex. Bandito called out to Hippie, desperate for someone to acknowledge the unspeakable nature of that woman's actions. "Fuck, man! My fuckin' God! It's crazy! That bitch killed her own fuckin' baby, man!"

Hippie did not acknowledge Bandito. His actions had placed the entire team at risk. There was one less able-bodied man available if the target or any other terrorists were in the complex. It was horrible that a woman would kill a baby, most likely her own, in the name of her religion. But horrible things happened all the time in this line of work. If Bandito could not handle that, he should have taught sixth grade Spanish.

Bandito stood over Hippie. "Fuck! What the fuck?" Did his teammate not realize the awful nature of what just happened? How could he not respond?

Hippie averted his eyes. He said a silent prayer for his teammates who chose to do their jobs and not break down.

The complex's door had been wide open. Hodge had entered first and scanned the front room. No action. "Let's move." Hodge and Squire paired up and Bozo and Uggo did likewise. The units checked each room. The shadow was not there. No one was there. Nothing was there. The place was empty of all the creature comforts. It had only the barest of clean water and food. There was one bed. Everything had been skimped on except the weapons. There was a stockpile of AK-47s that covered the corner of the back room. Hodge scanned through them. Behind the firearms, on the wall in red spray paint, was a message in Arabic. See you soon. The shadow was one step ahead. Hodge assumed that he would have to wait for his chance at vindication.

Alpha Team linked back up in the front room after the building had been secured. "Now what?" Bozo asked.

Hodge spoke into his walkie, "This is Alpha 4. Requesting exfil. Hippie requires immediate medical attention. Bozo needs antivenom treatment. Bandito is unstable. John Doe, Papa Bear, and Paul Bunyan all KIA. Bitch with explosives and one Muj down. HVT not at the complex. Over."

"Roger that Alpha 4. Exfiltration in 150 mikes."

"150 mikes? We have a man down with a potentially fatal wound." Alpha Team were way out in the desert, about four hundred klicks from the base, but their birds could reach a top speed of over 160 knots. Hodge knew that the bird should be able to reach their location in about ninety mikes.

"Sorry Alpha 4. Not enough available units to initiate exfiltration before 150 mikes. Over." That was the price to pay for being spread too thin. Yemen was a hotbed of terrorism and there were innumerable units operating within the country. Throw in a tight-fisted approach to funding and situations like this were bound to occur. There was nothing for Hodge to do but wait the situation out and hope for the best.

Bandito was treated like a ghost after Alpha Team had returned to Camp Sana'a that night. None of his teammates talked to him. None of his teammates looked at him. None of his teammates responded to him. They didn't know what to say and couldn't console him. Bandito knew that his actions were wildly inappropriate. He understood that there would be consequences. Bandito waited inside the room for Hodge. The hammer would be dropped. It was nothing to kill a man. He had seen that all the time growing up in his neighborhood. Kids shot other kids to gain an advantage in the crack slinging game. It was nothing for the gangbangers in his neighborhood to drop one of their fellow wolves if it meant some actual or potential gain. A woman was a different story. In his two years of work as a contractor, Bandito had never faced this situation before and neither had any other operator he had ever worked with. A mother and a baby. Sure, other members of his team had scored a scratch on women. Bandito assumed that he would be alright if he ever had to pull the trigger on a woman. But that mother could have been his mother. Or his wife. She had the same complexion.

She looked like she was the same age as his mother was when she had him, the same age as his wife when she had their eldest daughter. The baby looked like his youngest. Same complexion and hair texture. It was too much for him to process.

Hodge entered the tiny room and sat opposite of Bandito. He exchanged no pleasantries. He exchanged no recognition of any kind.

"I'm sorry, brother," Bandito cried out.

This wasn't baseball. No three strikes. Only one. "This place isn't for you. More importantly, this job isn't for you. You need to go home and see your wife and your two daughters."

Bandito cupped his head in his hands. "I'm sorry, brother. I'm sorry." Bandito recognized the pleas were only making his case worse. His days as a contractor were over, but Bandito hoped to convince Hodge that he was sorry for how his actions had placed the team at risk.

"We do bad things to bad people. It's not for everyone. Go home to your daughters."

"I'm good, Wild Man. I'm good, Wild Man. It threw me off, Wild Man. A baby. I didn't want to kill no baby."

"If you hesitate, more die." Hodge's words were stained with emotion. Walz had confirmed the approach that was best to utilize in this type of situation. Be supportive. Be managerial. It wasn't that easy though. Not after Blackbeard. He had put his own team at risk to chase after the shadow and when he found him, he didn't finish the job. His teammates completed the objective and he shot a bullet into the ground in a delirious haze. Somehow, he had escaped with only a reprimand from Mazuski. Now, he had to pull the hammer on Bandito. Sometimes justice wasn't blind. Sometimes there were favorite sons.

19

EAST COAST, U.S.A.

DECEMBER 2003

.   For the last twenty months, Chris Hodge had spent the bulk of his time either in training at the Farm or performing missions as a private military contractor in some of the worst locations in the world. One of the hardest things about the new life that had been chosen for him was the boredom that marked the time away from his work. Hodge was to be deployed to Iraq after the new year. Until then, he needed to ride out more than three weeks back in a civilian world that had become unreal.

Hodge had never had a week like this before. Day in and day out, all he did was work out and read. Hodge had phoned Mirele on his first full day back. She had a boyfriend. That was a quick call. Spencer treated him to a few drinks at Landmark. They were only out for two hours. He had to get back to work on his dissertation. His faculty adviser was a hawk with a neoconservative outlook, but one not given to Spencer's skepticism regarding Islam. Spencer told Hodge that she was giving him a hard time on his research. He intended to prove that democratic elections in Muslim-majority nations facilitated the rise and consolidation of power by Islamist parties. Spencer had to send in a draft of a section of his dissertation with major revisions by the first week of

January. If unchanged, she would vote to reject it in its current form and most of the other faculty members on the committee would as well. After Spencer left, Hodge had another drink, and another. John was not behind the bar and Hodge did not feel the desire to strike up a conversation tonight.

The day before Christmas Eve, Hodge drove down to South Amboy. Dennis and Glenda had moved out. It was a miracle. Donna Hodge had upped her Klonopin by another half milligram. Uncle Joe came over for Christmas dinner. Dennis and Glenda came by for the free meal. Everything went as Hodge expected. Uncle Joe made some jokes about how he should be the one buzzing what was left of his hair. Dennis only addressed him in passive-aggressive remarks. His mother barely said anything.

Hodge left New Jersey for Washington after Christmas. He had booked a hotel room for the week. Hodge could not fathom the idea of returning to Boston. The city had become emblematic of all that he had left behind. He was no longer a student at MIT. He was no longer heading towards a career in academia. He was no longer sharing a bed with Mirele. After Spencer completed his dissertation, he would leave to take his first academic job, presumably at a mid-tier university in some backwater of a college town away from the coasts. A Ph.D. from MIT would mitigate some of the blowback for his destruction of sacred cows, but not all of it. Hodge knew that well. He knew that it would be difficult to obtain anything beyond a lecturer position at an Ivy or Stanford even with his credentials because academia blackballed conservative intellectuals. Now, it all seemed like a joke. Some faculty chair in a tweed jacket pooh-poohing someone for the "wrong" political beliefs. Everything that he used to perceive now seemed meaningless since he met Mazuski that night at Landmark. Boston itself seemed meaningless since that night. Maybe he would get an apartment in Washington. His lease was up in March. He wasn't a packrat. It would be an easy move, and he had more than enough money from his work. There was no reason why he couldn't do better than a studio apartment fit for an undergrad. He was a man now.

After his first night in Washington, Hodge contacted Mazuski to arrange a meeting at Langley. It had been almost two years. Perhaps Mazuski would show a little sympathy for him and share his father's story. Maybe it could be a belated Christmas gift. Hodge wasn't holding his breath on that one, but he thought it was worth a shot.

Mazuski had a copy of Sun Tzu's *The Art of War* on his desk. The book looked like it had survived every war that China had been a part of since Sun Tzu had penned it five centuries before Christ. "Your friend wasn't at the complex."

"No. He wasn't."

"Intel has your friend responsible for the deaths of ten American servicemen in Fallujah."

"Ten servicemen?" Hodge could not believe that the man he had called Blackbeard had killed ten American soldiers. When they were friends, Blackbeard seemed like a goofball, an innocent. He did not look like a killer. He was a family man, a good father, a loving husband. But that was the past. Hodge was all too aware of how fate could dictate a radical change in the direction of one's life.

"Innocent lives, Chris." Mazuski coughed. Phlegm this time. There was no blood. The treatments were not working and any positive change was a good sign. The doctors gave him six months. Some people when given a death sentence would travel the world or make apologies or visit Wembley and see the Rolling Stones. Mazuski would go on in the same fashion until his time was over. Others strived for what they wanted. He had it.

"Innocent lives." Hodge had blown his chance. Ten Americans, American soldiers, paid for his mistake. Never again would he allow such weakness.

Mazuski reached into his desk drawer for a bag of lozenges. He popped one into his mouth and folded the wrapper into eighths, disposing of it in the garbage can on the side of his desk. "A gift." Mazuski reached for the copy of Sun Tzu's treatise on military tactics and held it aloft, the cover facing Chris Hodge. "He does not strive to ally himself with all and sundry, nor does he foster the power of other states. He carries out his own secret designs, keeping his antagonists in awe. Thus he is able to capture their cities and overthrow their kingdoms." Mazuski could recite the entirety of the book from memory. Sun Tzu's words had been seared into his mind. He had voluntarily enlisted in the Marine Corps at the outbreak of the Vietnam War. One of the only possessions he brought to Parris Island was his copy of *The Art of War*. Mazuski had found it in a secondhand book store on a visit to New York with the grandparents who had raised him. They found it acceptable reading for a fourteen-year-old boy and purchased it without comment. On the ride back to Erie, their grandson did not waver in his attention. He read the book cover to cover twice before they stopped for dinner in Lewisburg. His grandfather was convinced that the boy would read it a third time if the moon was just a bit brighter.

His grandparents, if they had still been alive at that point, would have been stunned to learn that Mazuski gave that book to Chris Hodge. Twice. Mazuski slid the book across the desk into Hodge's hands. The spine had fallen off. Hodge was careful to avoid any further deterioration. When he opened the book, he saw a faded red stamp on the flyleaf. It read: "From the library of Christopher Hodge."

"My dad's? Why do you have this?" Hodge's face went pale and his pupils dilated to twice their normal size. When he was three, he used to enjoy spinning around on the desk chair in his father's office. After his father died, he never went into that office again. His mother had locked the room and would not allow her boys access. Hodge felt as dizzy as when he used to spin himself around in his father's chair until he was on the verge of throwing up.

"Your country needed you. I volunteered my guidance. For him. For Chris. To keep you safe."

Chris Hodge judged that the situation was no longer tenable. There was simply no way that he would leave this room without an answer. He had been schooled on all measures of psychological and physical methods to garner information. If he had to use them on Mazuski, it might be the end of his career and possibly a lot more than that. But this could not go on any longer. Mazuski could not dangle the truth of his father's story in his face like that. Hodge would not allow it any longer. He was ready to face whatever consequences were deemed appropriate if Mazuski was not willing to give up the information. His life had already taken one left turn. It could take another. Hodge screamed into Mazuski's face, the spittle painting his weathered skin, "You need to tell me right now what happened to my father in Lebanon.

I'm done with your obfuscation. I'm done with your lies. What does this have to do with Blackbeard and his father?"

"Your friend's father was an asset." Mazuski coughed. The blood had come back. It rained out of his mouth. "At one point."

Mazuski took a measure of solace in the fact that although his body had failed him, his mind had never deserted him. He remembered his dealings with Farid El Hout as clearly as if they had been recorded for posterity. The hookah lounge in Beirut. The sweet smell of apple. The slurping bubble sound. His perfect French diction. The way that he thought to use his wife's pregnancy as a reason for backing out. The way that he spoke with such confidence as to assume an assent to the breaking of his commitment. Mazuski viewed him as a waste of talent. He had deceived the deceiver.

Hodge had not budged since moving so close to Mazuski that even a Somali would have viewed the spacing as an invasion of privacy. "An asset? That's insane. This is insane. He worked for us?"

"Why do you think his son worked for us?" It was peculiar to recruit two assets who were legacies. That kind of thing was frowned upon at Langley. He had developed Chris' son from a young age. It was his way to make amends. He had ignored Farid's son until 1991. Their dictator had fled the country. Turmoil would grip Somalia, but he was not sure for how long. Mazuski resolved that if the chaos continued, he would orchestrate a reunion. If anyone had a problem with this approach, they could mail him a letter and voice their concerns.

Hodge sighed in acknowledgment. He backed away, returning to his chair. "His father's terrorist connects." All the vigor had been sucked out of his words.

"It didn't go as planned."

"What happened?" Mazuski coughed. There was phlegm. There was blood. Six months seemed generous. "What the hell happened?"

Mazuski reached for a lozenge. Threw it into his mouth. Folded the paper into eighths. Recited a familiar line. "On difficult ground, I would keep pushing on along the road."

Mazuski had revealed a clue. Blackbeard's father was a former asset. His own father died in Lebanon. Mazuski had a photograph with his father in Vietnam. They presumably maintained their friendship after leaving the land of "me love you long time." Did Mazuski allow his father to be killed by Blackbeard's father? Hodge wondered if Mazuski hoped that he would meet a similar end. The thought seemed insane. Mazuski was operating in the interests of the United States. But nothing was black and white. It was a game of chess. Pawns get sacrificed to place an opposing king in check.

The next step was to find a way to discover the truth about his father. Maybe Mazuski would never reveal the full story. If Mazuski aimed to do so over a period of time, he might die before the story was complete. Perhaps Hodge himself would meet a similar fate as his father in some Middle Eastern wasteland. Hodge understood that he had to take the initiative and not simply wait for Mazuski to bestow the information. Three days before he deployed to Iraq, Hodge filed a Freedom of Information Act request for the release of his father's personnel files from the United States Marine Corps. Hodge hoped that by the time he returned from Iraq—if he returned—the records would be among the pile of junk mail slipped under his door, but he did not count on it. The only guarantee was that a response would be given within twenty business days. The delivery could be quite a bit longer. Even if it did arrive, there was no guarantee that Mazuski or one of his operatives wouldn't pick his lock and seize his mail. Mazuski might have even put the kibosh on it beforehand, knowing that Hodge would make this move. It was a desperate effort, and anything sensitive was likely to be redacted in the name of national security. This was the best move that Hodge could make at the moment.

20

FALLUJAH, IRAQ

JANUARY 2004

There was only one new face on Hodge's team at Camp Fallujah. Boogie was a wannabe rapper and former USMC Devil Dog, MARSOC. He had grown up middle-class in Carson, but visited his grandmother in Compton every weekend, where he saw the carnage that the gangs had unleashed in her neighborhood. N.W.A. released *Straight Outta Compton* when he was twelve. That album was an epiphany. Boogie had a gift for wordplay and rhythm. He longed to emulate the grim outlook of life on the streets that his favorite rappers had made millions from after they shared their talents with the world. Murdering your enemies and making money was the name of the game. The street way of doing that had been done to death. Boogie considered himself an innovator. His rhymes were all about putting bullets in the head of terrorists rather than rival street gangs and dope slingers. Boogie would have to find a creative way to spit rhymes about his last two years as a contractor. If he shared anything about what he had seen or done, or about his current line of employment, Boogie would get a cap busted in his ass faster than Fu-Schnickens dropped bars.

Hodge had resolved to take a more active role in November Team's dynamics. For his first three missions as team leader, he had sought to maintain a professional distance between himself and the team members that he had selected. Bozo had been with him since Somalia. Uggo had joined him on several missions within Yemen. There was only one new man on November Team. All his men loved poker. Hodge decided to join in the fun on their first full day at Camp Fallujah. They would be here for a while. The deck of playing cards that Hodge and his team had received was decorated with all 52 targets that they would have to hunt down in Iraq.

Boogie shuffled the deck. "Ain't no one in my family understands shit." His mother was a bookkeeper. She had no idea why her son would join the military. She had no idea why he would try to pursue a career as a rapper. His father had been a jazz musician who left his family after meeting a woman in Gothenburg while on tour. When his father eventually returned to the States after a decade in Sweden, he couldn't wrap his head around the fact that Boogie had chosen to fight for a country that he believed disenfranchised Black people. His father hated hip-hop. To him, it was just spoken poetry. There was no technique. The music was lazy. In his father's opinion, anyone could do it. It had been several years since that last visit. Boogie had yet to hear from his father again.

"You can't be too hard on civs. How could they understand?" Bozo asked.

Boogie started dealing out the cards. "Bitches the worst, though."

"You actually have relationships?" Uggo would not admit it to his teammates, but he had given up on love after he caught his wife in bed with another man after returning from a deployment. He had roses in his hand. Another man was inside her mouth. Uggo believed that was women's nature. Men could not fight it, so he decided to embrace the suck. Uggo was handsome and a former soldier. It was not difficult for him to find women to bed when back in Minneapolis. His only caveat in his dealings with the fairer sex was that he would shut off all contact if he sensed that they wanted to move from his bed to his heart. Uggo would not permit that to happen ever again.

Bozo found Uggo's whole "I'm miserable so let me make you miserable" deal tiresome. Whenever Uggo exposed himself for a gibe, Bozo seized the opportunity. This was no exception. "What? You're the love 'em and leave 'em type, pindick?"

"Fuck off."

"Y'all ever see *Clueless*?" Boogie posted the big blind in the team's preflop round.

Bozo was surprised at Boogie's reference. The guy seemed pretty hood. He may have been from California, but Boogie did not strike him as a Valley girl. "You're the homo of the bunch?" Bozo said with a smile.

Boogie gave Bozo a twin middle finger salute. "My bitch looked like Stacey Dash. I still dropped her like a bad habit when I enlisted. No time for that love shit."

Love. What a trite conversation. Hodge had wanted to join his men for some Texas Hold 'Em, not for an episode of Dr. Phil that masqueraded as a locker room conversation. He called and then switched the topic. "I don't trust our haji's information. He's a snake. They're all snakes."

Bozo raised. "You can tell by their eyes. I know when I'm looking at a liar. That's what I see in that guy."

"We can complete a million ops, but change their beliefs? No way." Uggo folded. It was a bad hand. There was no way he would play.

The guy with the briefcase refused to look Hodge in the eye. He was a straight arrow, a Lieutenant Colonel in the Army. Contractors were messy. This Lite Colonel did not do messy. He passed his briefcase to the CIA operative on base. The Lite Colonel could deal with those types because orders were orders and protocol had to be followed. After the O-5 left, the spook passed Hodge the briefcase. This guy looked him in the eye. Smirked too. Hodge nodded in assent. In twenty mikes, Omar would have this briefcase. First, Hodge planned to have some fun with his haji. November Team had been in Iraq for over three months and poker had become impossible with their deck. There were only six targets left to eliminate. Hodge knew that this might be his last chance to mess with this massively overpaid snake.

"I swear." Omar was from a professional-class family. During his teenage years, he had begged his parents to import role-playing video games from Europe for his Super Nintendo. He had convinced them that playing these games helped him learn English better, which would be useful when he pursued an engineering degree abroad later in life. There was little chance that Omar would ever satisfy his dream of becoming a computer engineer in the U.S. The Americans paid him too well for his most natural skill – being so convincing at acting like a stupid slimeball that occasionally he was able to score some useful information. Hodge would concede that Omar had the talent to be a social engineer if he actually displayed skillful deception rather than just operating from his natural state.

Omar clutched the briefcase against his chest. He could endure the threats. He could endure roughhousing. He could endure anything as long as he kept getting paid. Most of his friends and their families who had stayed in Iraq struggled with the collapse of Saddam Hussein's regime. Omar would pass around twenties and fifties to his buddies, reveling in being the big man. "My information – it's the best."

"We trust you, Omar," Bozo said, playing the good cop. "We know that you have no reason to lie; however, I'm sure you understand why my friend here may view it as suspicious that you require an initial payment."

Hodge slammed Omar into a fence. The briefcase flew out of his hand. He had claimed to have information on who was behind the recent murders, mutilations, and hangings of several PMCs. Omar's information had almost always been accurate. Whatever he would reveal was probably true. He never disclosed how he received this information. Hodge was convinced that Omar was playing both sides. Ten targets had been eliminated because of Omar's information. Once they smoked the last one, Hodge wished that he could unload a clip into this punk's skull. "If your info is bad, I will personally kill you. I'll track you down, kill you, and kill your family too."

Omar wet his pants. Bozo feigned sympathy for the asset. "Put him down." Bozo shook his head at Hodge in mock disappointment. "Put him down, Smith," Bozo said, calling Hodge by the alias he had used during his time in the sandbox. Hodge flashed Bozo a nasty look. It was all part of the game they had planned beforehand.

"My information is the best information! May Allah strike me dead if my information is not the best information!" Hodge released Omar, who fell on his ass right on top of the briefcase. If his information was not the best information, Allah could take this one off. Hodge would save him the trouble.

Ali Muhssan Al-Araji was an Iraqi-born, London-raised, proponent of eternal jihad against all whom he perceived as enemies of Islam. After graduating from the Islamic University of Medina, Al-Araji had risen to power as a prominent cleric on a multinational Islamic television channel, which he had used over the course of a decade as a vehicle to spread thinly veiled calls to arms against apostates. Al-Araji's list of enemies was extensive, but he targeted his actions primarily against the Shi'a community of Iraq, the state of Israel, the United States of America, and the moderate and pro-Western elements in his country. In the aftermath of the Iraq War, Al-Araji's thin veil of terrorist dog whistling had morphed into a full-fledged wail.

The city of Fallujah was entirely controlled by insurgents sympathetic to Al-Araji's call to strike against Western aggressors in the name of Islam. Despite this fact, Al-Araji had judged that his safety inside the city was no longer assured. His cohorts were equipped for war and would continue to fight battles on his command against the Americans and their allies, while he engaged in the call to jihad from a considerably safer location. Al-Araji's plan was to live in isolated luxury in Saudi Arabia, guarded from the spotlight until able to reengage in a more active role. In three days, a convoy would attempt to usher him to safety. If it failed, he would die a martyr. If it succeeded, many more would die.

Omar had revealed to Al-Araji that the Americans aimed to strike, promising the terrorist that his information was the best information. The boy's revelation served as a tipping point for Al-Araji's determination to remove himself from Iraq. Al-Araji had offered Omar a proposal after suspicions about his character and dealings had been raised. If Omar shared information about future attacks directed against him, he would compensate him twice as well as the Americans. If Omar refused, he would be beheaded. Al-Araji had found that when an offer was fair, both parties walked away satisfied.

In coordination with several other teams of PMCs, including a group from South Africa, one from the United Kingdom, and another from Nepal, November Team had secured two buildings. One was a klick away from Al-Araji's complex in the Jolan District near the Old Bridge. Hodge and Boogie were on the roof of this building, ready to eliminate the target when the opportunity struck. Uggo and Bozo were half a klick away on top of another secured building, ready to take the shot if the target exited from the backside of the complex.

Fallujah sizzled under a heat wave. The temperature exceeded one hundred degrees, twenty more than the standard high for early April. Boogie wiped the sweat off his forehead and drank from his CamelBak. "Hotter than a motherfucker." He had grown up in Southern California, where seventy-five and sunny was the forecast for most of the year. As the months rolled by, Boogie knew that wherever he deployed to next, the temperature would continue to rise.

"Welcome to paradise." Hodge had embraced the heat. It was just one other inhuman aspect of an inhuman land. His hometown was a place of stagnation; Fallujah was a place of radicalization. The desert climate bred a people comfortable with extremes. The four seasons bred a people who moved through the years in a tepid cycle. Maybe his mother had the solution. Instead of offering these people McDonalds, give them air conditioners. The results could not be any worse than the current situation.

Mustafa, armed with an AK-47, blocked off the front of the open hole of an entrance to Al-Araji's base. Mustafa had been mesmerized by Al-Araji's message of the infallibility of Islam's path towards the domination of the world. His father had served in Saddam Hussein's Air Force and died in the Gulf War. Mustafa viewed the Ba'ath regime of Hussein as weak and foreign in orientation. The suppression of Islam was its downfall. The Muslims had conquered much of the world when they were united and strong in their faith. Mustafa believed that they could do so again, and he aimed to be a part of Islam's return to its former glory. The sense of adventure, even in the mundane task of screening cars for Al-Araji, was irresistible. Mustafa's life had purpose. He was playing his small part in Islam's restoration and the defeat of all who would oppose Allah's plan for humanity.

Mustafa stopped a 2003 Kia Sorento. The man inside was wearing a black turban and robe. He was a Shiite. Al-Araji had shared the dangers of deviation with all his men. One of the telltale signs of apostasy was that a belief was outside of majority interpretation. Most Muslims were Sunni. Shiite Muslims were among the deviators and apostates. Mustafa understood that this man in the vehicle was an enemy of true Islam.

The last thing that Mustafa heard before the driver reached under his robe and detonated a suicide belt were the words "For Allah." Flames rose to the sky. Smoke bathed the complex. Mustafa himself was not privy to the spectacle, but many of Al-Araji's insurgents survived the blast. The Shiite cleric's attack was only a harbinger. Minutes later, swarms of young Shi'a men were engaged in battle with Al-Araji's forces. One by one, they began to pick each other off in close combat.

Chris Hodge observed the scene from the comfort of his sniper scope. Fallujah was plagued with ridiculous numbers of terrorists, but the irony of the situation was that the bad guys operated like ghosts. The city had been one big firefight since the start of the war, but it was rare to see the faces of the enemy. Casualties abounded, mostly for the insurgents, but PMCs and traditional forces also took heavy losses, often from roadside IEDs. Hodge radioed in. "Got a Charlie Foxtrot." Hodge had no problem with Al-Araji's men losing their lives to another terrorist faction rather than at his own or his men's hands, but the situation appeared to have spiraled out of control. Fallujah was a hellhole, and Hodge expected that every situation would have an attached air of unpredictability, but the completion of this mission was essential regardless of the circumstances. If the situation went haywire, Hodge and his men would have to exfil, but that was only a last resort. They were not paid to have rooftop parties in exotic locations. That was fine for Mirele and the other young elites he left behind when Mazuski decided to unveil his hidden hand and inform him that he was relevant. Mirele and her ilk could party in Rio or Bangkok or Ibiza. There were no parties in Iraq. No ladies ready to engage. No rivers of alcohol. No DJ's thumping beats to enhance the ambience. There was only an endless cycle of death, dirt, and monotony.

"Still deliver that present?" Boogie was unsure if their job had been completed for them courtesy of internecine strife within the radicalized Muslim community. How could they even know if Al-Araji had survived the blast? After the attack, their target might have holed himself up in the complex, but there was also the possibility that he may have been charred to bits. Boogie wondered if he and Wild Man's lives were at risk when their target was already KIA. *That would be a messed-up way to die. Mission complete, waiting for a target to appear that had already had his ass smoked, and then some Muj notices a very white and very black guy on top of a building and all hell breaks loose. We could take that dude out. Ten, twenty, thirty other tangos too. But not a whole army. Not by our damn selves.*

"Take out our target. Birds'll do the rest." The complex had caught fire from the blast, but the bomb itself was less than impressive. The chance that Al-Araji had died from the attack was slim. Hodge would wait. Boogie would wait. Hodge's men on the other building would wait. Completing all missions was a basic requirement of the job and Hodge expected his team to be stellar employees.

Hodge watched the scene on the ground from above. It was the stuff of nightmares, but Al-Araji was a boogeyman who was nowhere to be found. Two vehicles had blown up outside of the complex. One had driven straight through the walls before it ignited. The bodies of Al-Araji's men and the outside fighters continued to amass, repurposing the complex into a makeshift burial site.

Al-Araji's reverie of a new life in Riyadh had shattered. If he remained inside, he would be enveloped in flames. There was no choice but to move. Al-Araji and his men would fire at the infidels as they escaped the area. If Allah willed it, he would survive. If not, he would rejoice in the Sovereign's decision and await the pleasures of Jannah.

Bozo had eyes on Al-Araji as he exited the back of the complex with three of his men. The target's men shielded him as they attempted to both shepherd Al-Araji to safety and fire off wild rounds at the other side. One of the target's men was immediately picked off by enemy fire. The others had stopped in their tracks and engaged in a shootout. Unbeknownst to them, an American on a building half a kilometer away had locked in on the upper chest of their leader. Seconds later, November Team's target lay dead on the ground.

Al-Araji's vision had been to unite the world in submission to Allah. Europeans, Asians, Africans, Americans – regardless of nationality, in his utopia all would be subservient to Allah. Through his understanding of Islam, a person's race held no barrier to being a proper Muslim; however, the Arabs were the people to whom Allah delivered his glorious revelation. The Arabs were one of the few people who overwhelmingly had devoted themselves to Islam. The language of the Arabs was the language of the Qu'ran. Al-Araji believed that there was a unique purpose that Allah had bequeathed to the Arab people. Though all would one day become Muslim or die, the Arabs must remain at the forefront of the leadership of the ummah. Blacks like the Somali were zanj. They were slaves. Many had become Muslim through the glory of Allah, but they were not the original peoples of the Prophet Muhammad. Still, despite his skepticism in having aligned militarily in jihad with a non-Arab, Al-Araji had been moved by the Somali's story. The infidels had murdered his wife and son after he had guided them in their attempts to destroy the ummah. At first, Al-Araji was wary of working with someone who had betrayed the deen, but the zeal to which Guuce Duale had devoted himself to jihad was unmatched by anyone, Arab or non-Arab, that he had ever encountered. When Al-Araji witnessed the Somali behead four American contractors, all his doubts disappeared. Guuce was a true warrior for Allah.

Guuce exited the back of the complex with ten other jihadists, many of whom had been badly injured by the fire, explosives, nails, and other shrapnel. Guuce ordered his men to keep moving and avoid remaining in a stationary position. He told them that their leader had been killed by a sniper and that they would be too if they stood still for more than a second. A glance at the angle of the bullet in Al-Araji's corpse and the sound of the shot allowed Guuce to trace the bullet back to its point of origin. It was basic physics, one of the many kinds of leadership training that Guuce had studied in the mountains of Afghanistan after the death of his wife and his son. Zigging, zagging, and remaining in motion like a squad of AK-47 toting running backs, Guuce and his men advanced towards Bozo's building. It was one of only five large apartment buildings in that direction. Guuce ordered his men to spread their fire. Half of the men targeted the building from which the shot that killed Al-Araji was fired. The other men focused on the rooftops of the other four buildings. Guuce had told them that there was virtually zero chance that all the infidels were camped on top of one lone building.

Hodge had seen the shadow. First he was in Yemen. Now he had followed him to Iraq. Did Blackbeard have a bug inside the IC that continuously alerted him to Hodge's present location? Hodge was uncertain of the specifics of how the shadow was able to pinpoint his location. He wished to end all further speculation with one bullet to Blackbeard's chest. Even the thought of that outcome did not put Hodge's mind at ease. He suspected that if there was any validity to the claim of life after death, then the shadow would be there with him in the next layer of sand-swamped hell.

Hodge and Boogie stayed low to the ground. Blackbeard's troops had sniffed out their position, and Bozo's building was taking the heaviest fire. It appeared that Blackbeard had only a handful of poorly trained soldiers at his command. Still, the terrorists were closing in on Bozo's location. If a few of them could be taken out before the showdown, the odds of November Team's safe evac after this skirmish would improve. Hodge and Boogie fired M4 rounds at the spread-out mass of jihadists and quickly ducked back down behind the safety of the lip of the rooftop. None of their rounds connected and Blackbeard was nowhere to be seen.

Hodge's walkie crackled, then he heard a message from his handler, "November Team, CAS five mikes away."

"Roger. Need to RTB immediately. Taking heavy fire. Over." It was only a matter of minutes before Blackbeard's men swarmed. Jihadists controlled the city. There weren't even a dozen enemies coming towards them, but that could easily change in this landscape. November Team's mission was completed. As much as Hodge wanted to put Blackbeard out of his misery, he did not wish to do so at the expense of his men's lives.

"We got you. Ten mikes, November Team."

A hail of bullets soared over Bozo's head as he dropped low. He had fired off a round that connected with one of the bad guys. There were still ten more and they had started to close in on their position.

"Watch your ammo," Uggo shouted. He had been far more conservative in his attacks than his teammate. The enemy combatants already knew their location. They would arrive soon and they weren't bringing roses. Uggo aimed to be prepared to greet them in the appropriate fashion.

"Muj look like they're five mikes away. Gotta keep 'em at bay." Bozo had a completely different opinion of the tactics that this situation required. The less terrorists they had to face in close quarters, the better. Wild Man relayed that they would have air support, but by the time that backup arrived there might not be any need for the assistance. By that time, if all went well, November Team would have dealt with every member of this seemingly unorganized mass of terrorists.

Al-Araji had stored multiple PG-7 anti-tank rocket launchers inside the complex. One of his men had the sense to shoulder one of the devices before he made his move towards the infidels' location. The Somali had pointed out the location from which the shot was fired that killed his leader, but he judged that a more severe threat came from a different location. Two of his allies had already met Allah at the hands of bullets from another rooftop. The terrorist aimed an RPG at that location and fired, a trail of smoke following behind. Fortunately for

November Team, he was inexperienced in using a PG-7. The terrorist had left the safety cap on in front of the fuse.

The tip of the RPG connected with Boogie's chest, failing to detonate. As the energy of the projectile knocked Boogie off his feet his head hit the ground. Hodge knew that his teammate was unconscious, but there was nothing he could or should do in response. Boogie would probably be alright as long as the forces charging November Team were dealt with before they had the opportunity to inflict further damage. Still, it was likely that Boogie had internal damage from the RPG and a probable concussion from the fall. Hodge fired at the unlucky son of a bitch who injured his teammate. Taking down that bastard was particularly satisfying.

Guuce and his men were only three mikes away from Bozo's location. He ordered the surviving members of his troops onward towards Bozo and Uggo's building. He moved in a different direction, firing his AK-47 at the roof towards Hodge. Guuce's shots were wide of his target, but not by more than a handful of inches.

Hodge could see the shadow. This was his second chance, an opportunity to correct for his inability to complete the objective in Yemen. *Friendship is forged over years, over strife, over reliability. Friendship is not forged over a brother forgetting his shoe in a masjid or sharing a samovar filled with tea. Friendship is not forged with an enemy. Were his reasons for fighting justified? No. His reasons were barbaric. Ethics may be in the eye of the beholder, but an enemy is an enemy. Blackbeard is my enemy.* Hodge rose up. Fired on the shadow. It was only a partial victory.

The bullet hit Guuce's shoulder. With blood coming out of his wound, he continued to fight. Guuce watched the slivers of blood. It was no comparison to the total annihilation of his wife and son. His pain was a trifle. Their pain would be with him for an eternity.

The Muj were closing in on the building, but Bozo and Uggo had whittled down their numbers. As far as Bozo could determine, only four enemy combatants were continuing to advance on their location. Bozo fired at the street and connected with another target. "See ya, bitch!" With every bullet, Bozo was doing his part towards pushing back against radical Islam. He was making Iraq safer for decent people of all faiths. He was making the U.S. and all peaceful nations safer by taking the fight to these rogue elements. The men he shot deserved to die. Bozo was playing a part in the remaking of the world into a more peaceful place. The irony of having to do so through combat was not lost on him. Everything in life seemed to be polarized. All good was born out of evil and the converse held true as well. Bozo had dwelled on this philosophy extensively, but in the moment, he did not think; he only felt the massive adrenaline rush.

"Where's the air strike?" Uggo asked. There were only three haggard terrorists left against two bonafide warriors. Uggo was intelligent enough to realize that anything could happen in urban warfare, but the odds were stacked in November Team's favor. Any bad guy who survived the rush to the building would still die; the only difference between the dead and the currently living was that the currently living would breathe their final breath in a different place from their comrades. The trouble might come from reinforcements. It looked like these last remnants were all they had to deal with, but the element of surprise was one of the foremost tactics in war. Uggo and his team used it. He had been in enough war zones to know that the terrorists used it as well.

Bozo spoke into his walkie, "Wild Man, ETA on that bird?"

Hodge had only wounded the shadow. The darkness still existed. An evac would be a failure. Their target was eliminated. The mission was over. One of his men was wounded – a fatal wound perhaps if left untreated. Yet Hodge wanted to continue the fight with every fiber of his being. *That feeling is my emotions overriding my logic. Emotions lead to dead assets. Emotions aren't relevant.* Logic dictated that he radio his commanding officer. "CAS coming?"

"One mike away, November Team."

Bozo had eyes on Blackbeard. He was covered in a mess of blood and firing wildly. Blackbeard fired at Hodge and Boogie, then at him and Uggo. Bozo knew how much it meant to Wild Man to put Blackbeard six feet underground, but not at the expense of his life or any other team member's life. Bozo rose up from his crouched position on the building to attempt to fire at Blackbeard. Before he could get off a shot, Blackbeard's bullet connected with his heart. Uggo raced over towards Bozo, but there was nothing that could be done. Bozo was an instant KIA. As Uggo stared into Bozo's lifeless face, the A-10 Warthogs arrived. Their Avenger Gatling-type cannons reduced all underneath to rubble. Whether or not the remaining horde was neutralized, all fighting ceased. Within minutes, the birds came to evac what remained of November Team.

Twenty minutes prior, Chris Hodge learned that Bozo had died at the shadow's hands. Now, he and Uggo had just arrived back at camp. Boogie was receiving medical attention. Bozo's corpse was in the fridge. All Hodge wanted to do was take a shower, eat a meal, and go to sleep. His stink could be washed away with water and soap. His hunger could be mollified by whatever was being served at the DFAC. His exhaustion could be rectified by eight solid hours of sleep. Bozo's death was beyond his control. The pain that emanated from that loss could not be eliminated. He had lost a team member.

November Team had dealt with the media throughout their time in Iraq. For Hodge, their ceaseless presence was a new and entirely unpleasant experience. Hodge had encountered a couple of reporters while in Somalia, but he had not seen a single one on mission in Sudan, Yemen, or during any of his earlier missions before he became a team leader. On a normal day, he considered the media yet another unpleasant aspect of being in Iraq, but today was not a normal day.

The reporter was hanging around the camp as Hodge and Uggo made their way inside. This upstanding member of the press carried himself with the same false sense of confidence that all the other cowards possessed. "Any drone strikes killing babies today, guys?" he asked as he swooped in on the intact half of November Team, desperate for the slightest bit of information that he could spin into a story.

Years of combat experience had drained whatever remained of Uggo's childlike hope for humanity. By the time he had joined up with November Team, Uggo had long since settled into full-on misanthropy. While Bozo was alive, Uggo held him in as low esteem as he did anyone else; however, as much as he disliked Bozo, he was his brother. *Bozo had died fighting subhuman jihadists. He had risked his life to try to make a hopeless world better. This asshole had the gall to insult a dead man and all the other dead men who chose to fight an unwinnable war. He was scum.* "You guys are pathetic," Uggo sneered.

"Guess that's a yes on the baby killing, huh?" the reporter asked, a leer on his pockmarked, asymmetrical, and barely out of college face.

"Why don't you go inside?" Uggo said to Hodge, motioning towards the entrance to his teammate. "You ever been in a fucking rumble?" Uggo shoved the reporter. Hodge held his teammate back.

"What the fuck? That's assault."

Hodge turned to Uggo. "That's not the way to handle his kind." Hodge switched his gaze to the reporter. His anger was at a steady boil. It simmered under the surface. "Never forget that our friend here's job is solely to sell ad space. He's not here to report the facts. All he wants is the sympathy card so that he can gain political influence and moral acceptance from the establishment." Uggo shouted insults at the reporter. "Am I correct?" Hodge asked.

The reporter had no answer, just a sheepish look on his face as he sulked away from the camp. Uggo and Hodge could have eviscerated this man with their fists in a split second, but Hodge had judged that the far better action in this scenario was to devitalize this reporter with the truth. If, however, he was left to his own devices—and even in this lawless part of the world there were some checks on his actions—Hodge would have chosen a far less diplomatic approach.

Michael Standish, nicknamed Standin, had joined November Team after Bozo's passing. The team had only five remaining targets to eliminate before their mission was completed. Boogie had just been cleared for active duty after three days on the mend. While Boogie was in recovery, Hodge and Uggo played hand after hand of poker with the new arrival. No one said much during those games. Even after Boogie returned, awkward silence permeated the base. No one spoke of Bozo, but his absence haunted November Team like a wraith.

November Team played another hand. About halfway through their mission, they had replaced their original deck of cards. The new deck featured scantily clad women, risqué only by pre-1960s standards. One and five-dollar bills and two of Standin's packs of Marlboro Reds covered the middle of the table.

Standin placed his cards face down on the table. "I fold." Boogie halfheartedly nodded. Hodge and Uggo remained stonefaced. "Bad luck tonight," Standin continued.

Boogie shook his head. "Heard it's nothing but bad luck with you every night, man." It was a shitty thing to say. Standin did not kill his buddy, but this guy was not supposed to be on the team. Boogie was supposed to hear Bozo's nasal Northeastern accent and ridiculous brags. But he'd never hear Bozo's voice again. His injury was bullshit. He was ready for more action. Bozo had been snuffed out by the enemy and a new guy was supposed to replace him. *Business is business. Missions are missions. Everything moved on and there wasn't a damn thing you could do about it.*

"You heard right." Boston was known for its curses. The curse of the Bambino. The curse of the Bozo. Hodge wondered if Bozo's replacement could ever win a hand of Texas Hold 'Em. Maybe Bozo was intervening from the grave. If that was possible, that would be the kind of stupid prank that he'd pull.

Standin shrugged. "That's how it goes sometimes." Standin had put a psychological whammy on himself ever since he joined up with November Team. The pay was great, but the price it required had worn on him. He was a small-town boy from Ohio. All he wanted to do was finish this mission and then join the Xenia Police Department like his father had done before him and his grandfather had done before his father. Standin hoped to settle back in with his wife, start a family, keep his town safe, and leave everything he had seen behind. The money had served him well, but the reality that he had come face to face with had forced his hand. This was not for him. As soon as he could, he would get out.

"Five more dead hajis and I'm out for good," Uggo remarked.

Hodge threw five dollars down in the middle of the table. "I call your five and raise five more." *Five more dollars. Five more dead hajis. The cycle never would end. Death would continue to amass. That was the way the world operated.* Hodge had left his reformer days behind on the campus of the Massachusetts Institute of Technology. *No reform was possible. The threat would continue as it had for over a thousand years.*

"I'm out." Uggo placed his cards face down on the table. Boogie called, but Hodge collected the pot.

Hodge stood outside of Mazuski's office. All he could hear inside were the sounds of incessant coughing. Never before had Mazuski's coughs continued without pause.

Hodge entered the office. Mazuski's mouth didn't move as he gestured for Hodge to sit opposite him at his desk. Mazuski's mouth didn't move, but still the sound of his coughs kept ringing in Hodge's ears.

Mazuski folded a lozenge wrapper into eighths. "I warned you to be careful."

"Careful of what?" Hodge asked.

"Your questions put those close to you at risk."

"Who?"

"I'm your superior. You need to learn to follow orders, Chris." As Mazuski spoke, the coughs continued in endless repetition.

Hodge stood up. "Are you even listening to me?" He waved his hands in front of Mazuski. His handler gazed off into the distance, ignoring Hodge's gesture. "What are you looking at?" Hodge turned around and looked through the door. His father was behind him.

Behind Christopher Hodge, the area began to transform into a military barracks. Fifty Marines stood staring through the door. Christopher Hodge walked into the barracks. The men saluted him.

Mazuski's arms grew like tentacles. He reached out towards Christopher Hodge, but it was too late. Christopher Hodge had already returned to his destination. "Your blood is on my hands!" Mazuski stared into his hands. "Your blood is on my hands."

All Chris Hodge could hear was "Blood on my hands." The phrase kept repeating, slowing, mixing in with Mazuski's coughs. Chris

Hodge could not stop the words. He could not stop the coughs. He could not rescue his father. "Don't go in there, Dad!" Christopher Hodge's son called out, to no avail. He was already lost forever.

Chris Hodge rushed through the door into the barracks. He gripped his father in a bear hug, but Christopher Hodge ignored the intrusion and continued to march forward in precise, measured steps, almost like a machine. He was walking into the bombing with dead eyes. Chris' power gave way as his father brushed him off. Chris Hodge fell flat on his face in the barracks as the men followed Christopher Hodge into the abyss. His father and the men disappeared into an explosion, but Chris Hodge felt no heat.

Mazuski's coughs continued to ring out. Chris Hodge heard his handler's words continue to echo. "Blood on my hands." In a split second, the barracks had transformed into Blackbeard's home in Mogadishu. A boy held a wooden giraffe as he walked out of the explosion and sat next to Chris Hodge. The boy played with the giraffe, oblivious to Chris Hodge, oblivious to everything. The boy never revealed his face, keeping it tilted low to the ground. Even before he spoke, Chris Hodge knew the boy. "Giraffes. They're so tall. Do they have them where you're from?" Sharmaarke raised what would have been his eyes. There were no eyeballs inside, just sockets with rivers of blood streaming down.

Hodge shared his living quarters at Camp Fallujah with the three other members of November Team. Unless necessitated by a mission, the men were usually asleep by 0100 and awake at 0700. While Hodge typically kept to the routine, tonight he woke with a start, panting in fear from his nightmare. The small clock to the side of his sleeping quarters showed it to be only 0345. Hodge took several deep breaths, wiped the sweat from his forehead, and put his head back on the pillow. If it was possible, he would return to sleep tonight. If not, he would make this time useful and reread *The Art of War* by the night light near Standin's cot. Hodge had read that book so many times that, like Mazuski, he could now recite its passages from memory.

November Team had completed all their objectives. The thought of leaving Iraq after four months in this primitive shithole should have thrilled everybody. It didn't. Hodge could ascertain that Bozo's death had sucked the spirit out of everyone on the team. For him, Bozo's death was a tragedy, but so was the inability to put down Blackbeard, so was the fact that while terrorists kept getting crossed off his list, there was no shortage of other radicals to take their place. It was unwinnable. All Hodge had known as a young man was victory. Even in triumph, there was no victory in performing his duties.

Standin broke the ice. "Boogie, where will you be in five?"

"Same as where I'm gonna be tomorrow, man. In the hood."

Bozo's death had hit Boogie hard. He wouldn't rule out working as a PMC again, but it was time for a break. Boogie planned to make another go of it as a rapper and record producer. Unlike before, he was now open to other options in case his dream never materialized. Boogie understood that the likelihood of his success in any facet of the rap game was slim, but not impossible. He had started to put serious thought into deciding whether he should earn a degree. With an education in business, if he was unable to make it as a rapper or producer, then he could just

purchase a slick suit and go the corporate route or learn from his
mistakes and try another venture.

"Uggo?" Standin asked.

Uggo shook his head. "I don't know. You?"

"Police back in Xenia. Need a new way to test my luck. Wild
Man?"

"Wherever is appropriate." Hodge was relevant. The others
could return to mediocrity. Boogie could try to become a rapper and fail
miserably. Uggo could become a Chippendale dancer and entertain
bored housewives in Minneapolis. Standin could patrol the mean streets
of Xenia in his father's squad car. Hodge would go wherever Mazuski
assigned him. He was in this to the end. The thrill had gone, but that
wasn't what this was about. That was never what this job had been about
for him.

21

CAMBRIDGE, MASSACHUSETTS, U.S.A.

MAY 2004

Boredom had evolved into soul-crushing depression. Hodge had been back for two weeks and had barely left his bed. The amount of effort he needed to push himself to get up and perform his morning workout increased exponentially day by day. He didn't return Spencer's phone calls. He didn't return his mother's phone calls. He didn't visit Landmark. He didn't take a trip to South Amboy. He didn't check in with Mirele and see how her relationship was faring. It was all meaningless. Hodge was relevant. The mundane nature of love and friendship and current affairs and everything else people numbed themselves with was irrelevant to his life. Instead, Hodge would wait out the days until Mazuski contacted him, expending a bare minimum of energy. He ate, showered, exercised, and read, checking off the days like a prisoner until he was back behind a rifle with sand whipping against his face and the shrieking nonsense of a muezzin providing the score. That was reality. This was not. This was counting off the days of his sentence.

His father's personnel file glared at him on the night table. Hodge fixated on the document every night before sleep. It had become his perverse bedtime story. Even having obtained the file, his father remained an enigma. The Marines had embedded a photograph of his father on the heavily redacted document. The only useful bit of information was his credentials. Hodge had known that his father was a Marine, but he was puzzled by his father's affiliations with the State Department, DoD, and CIA. Everything that he had gone through in the last few years seemed even stranger with that revelation. Hodge knew that the IC was not big on legacies, but here he was, presumably walking in his father's footsteps.

Hodge was performing his nightly ritual of staring at his father's file, observing his face, scanning the lines, trying to read through the black, when his BlackBerry started to ring. It was a restricted number. He answered the call. "Hodge."

"Set to hat up?" Mazuski asked.

"Set for the next Charlie Foxtrot." Hodge could deal with a million clusterfucks. Being relevant was easy. Another week of monotony in Boston would be equivalent to life in a coma.

Mazuski arrived the next morning in his Lancia Beta. When Hodge entered Mazuski's vehicle, he had no idea where he would be deployed. It didn't matter. All that mattered was returning to the action. Maybe he'd find out about his father, or maybe Mazuski would keel over. Maybe he'd kill Blackbeard, or maybe he was already dead. Maybe his new teammates would nix the bullshit, or maybe they would amp it up and only be frosty when it mattered. There was no certainty one way or the other. There was no certainty that Hodge himself would not face a bullet in the head, maybe from Blackbeard. There was no certainty, but Hodge didn't need certainty. Combat was his respite.

Combat was his solace. That was why he was relevant. That was why Mazuski told him that he was heading to Afghanistan.

"1500?" Hodge asked. The number of targets sounded preposterous. November Team had 52 targets and it took them four months to complete just their portion of the quota. One of his men died in the process. 1500 was unfathomable. His father didn't have any gray when he passed, but his mother started coloring her hair at 33. If he had any of her genetics, by the time he was done in Afghanistan the top of his head might blend in with the snow-capped peaks of the Hindu Kush.

"Over 1500. In eight months. Up for the challenge, Chris?" Mazuski handled the wheel with one arm, coughing into his other. For a dying man, he still retained an amazing amount of dexterity. *Once a Marine, always a Marine*, Hodge supposed.

"Are you serious?"

"POTUS wants progress. So do I."

Hodge performed the calculations in his head. "That's approximately 6.25 kills per day."

"Are you still relevant, Chris?" Mazuski wiped the blood that was pouring out of his mouth onto his starched white shirt.

Hodge took a deep breath. The task was staggering. How many teams were going? How many were already there? 1500. It was crazy. If Hodge were like some of the other men he had worked with, he would ride off into the sunset after this tour, if he survived. With some wise investments and a move to some tropical paradise, he would never have to work again. But it wasn't about the money for Hodge. It wasn't about providing a safety net for his family. It wasn't even about combating terrorism anymore. It wasn't about the adrenaline-packed nature of the

action, although that was a nice side benefit. Hodge was relevant.
Mazuski had developed him because of some unique abilities that he
saw in him. His handler was elusive and had yet to even share the full
story of his father, but Hodge appreciated the fact that Mazuski believed
in him. Regardless of what situation he was thrown in, Hodge would
perform his duties. "Yeah...I'm relevant. Have I let you down yet?" In
Hodge's mind, his words were a lie. He understood that his erratic
behavior regarding Blackbeard had raised questions in Mazuski's mind.
1500 targets in less than a year must have been Mazuski's way of
throwing down the gauntlet and testing his asset's mettle. Hodge
resolved to do his best in this unwinnable situation and avoid letting his
handler down.

Mazuski let a smile cross his face as he took advantage of the
red light and popped a lozenge into his mouth.

"I need to know if you were involved in the Mogadishu drone
strike." It was rare for him to have an opportunity to interface with his
handler; Hodge knew that he needed to seize this moment to try to get to
the bottom of some of the questions that remained in his mind.

"Failures happen."

"But you were concerned about my friendship with
Blackbeard?"

There was another red light. Mazuski folded his lozenge
wrapper into eighths and placed it carefully into the stack of lozenge
wrappers in the Lancia Beta's cup holder. "Let go of your hubris. This
wasn't because of you. Life is random and meaningless."

"Air support in Fallujah corrected for my error?" Regardless of
how Mazuski answered, Hodge suspected that he would have to deal

with the shadow again. Unless he saw Blackbeard's dead body with his own eyes, he had to assume that his shadow escaped.

Mazuski chuckled. Like every other of his actions, it brought on a coughing fit. Mazuski choked out his words. "You better hope so."

"And his brother?"

"Taken care of."

"Was he actually involved, or was he taken out for a goddamn video?"

In a sense, Mazuski viewed Hodge almost as a son. Like in dealing with any child, boundaries had to be established. Certain types of conduct were acceptable and other types unacceptable. His faux son had to fall in line. "It's not your place to judge what's mission critical. That decision was way above your pay grade, Chris."

Hodge was aware enough to avoid pressing Mazuski any further. In less than twenty-four hours, he would be in a base outside of Jalalabad. One day, he might receive the answers to his questions, but that day would not be during his next eight months in Afghanistan. When Hodge returned, there was no guarantee that he would receive any further information. Mazuski's cancer was progressing, albeit slower than expected. Only two more months remained on his original prognosis. Hodge hoped that Mazuski would somehow find a way to avoid taking his answers to the grave.

22

AFGHANISTAN

MAY 2004

Afghanistan offered Chris Hodge a new start. Every member of Bravo Team, though highly vetted for their skill and experience, was new to Hodge. There was a stability that permeated the entire team, a cohesive killing unit. Bond seemed to be as stoic as his namesake. Squint was not only a talented medic, but one of the few contractors who spoke Pashto. He was a great shot too, but with his gold-rimmed glasses, slight frame, and youthful appearance, he looked more like a teenager used to getting stuffed in lockers than a PMC used to smoking Taliban. Hector "Gonzo" Gonzalez had a bit of snark to him, but mostly he enjoyed zoning out and nodding his head to the gangster rap that he constantly listened to on his iPod. Biggie was six foot two, the maximum height allowed for an operator. His personality was a bit rough around the edges; however, he was a warrior through and through who had not yet failed to meet an objective in three years of work as a PMC. Arjuna and his parents had moved to Edison, New Jersey from Ayodhya, India a few months after the destruction of the Babri Masjid in 1992. His parents were ardent Hindu nationalists who had instilled in their son a deep skepticism of Islam's claim to be a religion of peace. After six years in the US Army, including three years in Delta Force as a special operator, Arjuna decided to become a PMC. Above all, what Hodge liked most about his new men was that they were stable. Everyone who Hodge had worked with had been dynamite in the field, but more than a few were headaches away from the action. It appeared to Hodge that less management would be necessary with the men that he had assembled this time around. The only problem that Hodge could foresee would be meeting their objectives in a prompt fashion without having their heads served on a skewer by the Mujahideen.

It was Bravo Team's first day on base. On the second day, they would prep their kits. They would not actually track down targets until their second week. Every member of the team was relaxing in the FOB's welfare and rec center this afternoon. Squint was teaching Arjuna how to play the fantasy card game *Magic: The Gathering*. Bond was engrossed in Tom Clancy's novel *Clear and Present Danger*. Gonzo bopped his head to the gangster rap that blasted from his iPod. Biggie had just finished working out with free weights, slamming them down on the ground.

Hodge entered the welfare and rec center with a deck of cards in his hands. "Why don't we get a game going?" He passed Squint the deck.

Squint inspected the deck. It was a standard set. "No targets?"

"Nope."

"I'm not used to this kind of deck." It was routine for team leaders to be given a deck of cards emblazoned with their targets' faces on all but the shortest missions. In his two years of work as a PMC in Iraq, Squint had never been on a lengthy mission without seeing those familiar cards.

Biggie shook his head. "You two brains know a way to fit 1500 targets on 52 cards?"

Bond turned his eyes away from his book for a split second. "No one that's bright, Biggie." Bond returned to his novel.

"You in, Bond?" Squint asked.

Bond placed the book on his chair. "I'm always in, bros. Always in."

"Arjuna? I'll teach you *Magic* some other time. You up for a game?"

"Definitely."

"Yo, Gonzalez!" Squint shouted.

"Heard you, bro. I'm down." With Gonzalez's assent, Squint shuffled the standard deck of cards, then dealt out six hands.

Biggie examined his cards. A 3 and an 8. It may not have been the absolute worst way to start, but it was pretty awful. "Look, I'm the first to admit that I'm no math genius, but I do understand that you can't put 1500 targets on a damn deck of cards. What I don't get is how they won't even give us some ladies."

"I get it," Hodge deadpanned.

"Come on. You gotta admit it's crazy, Wild Man."

"We have 1500 targets. The Commander-in-Chief needs everyone's energy and full attention for this mission. There's no time for you to pull your pud, Biggie." His men laughed, none aware that Hodge's intent was not to kid around with their teammate, but to impart a deathly serious message. They all had excellent track records, but excellence would not be enough for this mission. Their sights had to be set far higher.

That night, in his dreams, Hodge met the shadow behind the pashminas at the souk in Mogadishu. It had felt like ages since their last interaction. Lately, all they seemed to do was try to kill each other. The recent past had dissipated into a new present.

"Your name is Hajj?" Blackbeard asked in Somali-inflected Arabic.

"It is." Hodge responded in American English-inflected Arabic. He had never revealed his real name to his friend. Chris Riley. The name sounded false to his ears. Hodge was certain that the shadow could see through his lies.

"And this is your pilgrimage?"

"This is where I was sent."

Blackbeard chuckled. "Why didn't you kill me, Baseball?"

"Because it isn't true." All the facts were deceptions. The drone strike never occurred. Jamilah and Sharmaarke were alive. They had never fired on each other. He stayed in Somalia. He never trained with Al-Qaeda. He was never in Fallujah. He was never in Yemen. None of that happened. None of that was real. It was all a big lie.

"It isn't true," Blackbeard confirmed.

"We need you on comms." The deceptions were getting in the way of the missions. These miscommunications were putting innocent people's lives at risk. Everything needed to be cleared up. The lies needed to be revoked by the power of truth.

"You need me on comms."

"I'm making a zebra for your son." Sharmaarke was a playful boy. He would appreciate the token.

"He likes zebras, but he loves giraffes."

"What can I get your wife?" Jamilah was a graceful, patient woman. She deserved something special.

The shadow smiled. "Your presence is enough."

"Your brother needs another pair of shoes." Erasto was responsible, but he had an absentminded streak. With enough pairs of shoes, Erasto would never have to borrow another pair from his brother ever again. Shoes lose cushioning and support. Wrinkles develop in the shoe sole. Holes form on the inside. Soles wear.

The shadow chuckled. "I am sure they will be very much appreciated."

"How about you?" Friends looked out for each other. Blackbeard had helped him and his team secure safe access and learn about a totally foreign land. The money provided to him went to his rent and his son's education. Selfless. He was selfless. But even the most selfless individuals deserved a little generosity from time to time.

"A cleared name. Bring me in from the cold, Baseball."

It was not an unreasonable request. The cover story couldn't be true. His friend, his shadow, this was not a terrorist. This man was a warm-hearted family man who owned one pair of shoes and lived with his brother and his wife and his son and he couldn't be an extremist. That just wasn't reality. The terrorists were the others. The ones only known on dossiers and seen through sniper scopes. They didn't call you Baseball. That's not what terrorists did. "I'll bring you back into the fold."

The shadow offered a hug. Hodge offered a slap on the back. A second later, it was over. Hodge was awake. The conflicted fantasy world his mind produced had disappeared. Now, Hodge had to return to his new reality and prepare for his first of countless missions in Afghanistan.

The bird dropped Bravo Team in a valley 110 klicks from the mountain village of Anjoman, which intel reported had been coopted into a center of terrorist indoctrination. Bravo Team's orders were to consider all who entered or exited that base a target and eliminate them, but the primary objective was Atta Mohaqiq, a minister in the Taliban's government. An attack from above by U.S. or allied forces would attract unnecessary attention, necessitating that PMCs be utilized to eliminate Mohaqiq. Hodge's plan upon reaching the location was to have his team perform recon on Mohaqiq's base and track all who entered and exited the location. To avoid detection, whenever a lone individual or small group entered or exited the base and left the village, Bravo Team would pick them off to reduce the numbers, targeting the leaders at the first available opportunity. If the team's presence was detected, Squint and Gonzalez would act as decoys and create a fake trail to leave the impression that their unit had moved in a different direction. Once Squint and Gonzalez circled around and linked back up with Hodge and the rest of his men, Bravo Team would ambush the Muj.

Bravo Team moved only in the cover of darkness, which suited Hodge and his men perfectly. It had been more than two weeks since anyone on the team had been on a mission. Their bodies had readjusted back to American time. To sleep through the day and move by night was in line with their current circadian rhythms.

The hump to the village in ideal conditions took between six to ten days; however, that timetable was contingent on the avoidance of any major hitches. The Soviets, a people renowned for their willingness to fight until the last bullet, were defeated in Afghanistan by ragtag groups of Afghan peasants on mules who fought until the last drop of blood. Even Alexander the Great, leader of the Macedonian Phalanx that had not known a single defeat during thirty years of battle, faced brutal difficulties while engaged in guerilla warfare within Afghanistan. Hodge expected that somewhere along the way Bravo Team would face at least one major hurdle. The main trails into Anjoman, including the Khawak Pass through the Hindu Kush that Alexander had utilized more than two thousand years ago, were filled with Taliban. Bravo Team, like most other special operators in Afghanistan, had to advance outside of the already substandard main trails that cut through this mountainous terrain. If the elements or the Taliban bested a member or the entirety of the team, there would be no recourse. Since the mission would stretch over several weeks, it was unlikely for Bravo Team to have access to reasonable comms and any subsequent support. Food, water, and ammo all had to be rationed. Bravo Team would only have four supply drops. One was on the route to Anjoman, three klicks northeast of Pesenta. The other was on the way back to their exfil point, ten klicks southeast of Mersmel. The remaining two were yet to be determined. Hodge expected that none of his men would entertain the thought of gorging on the scant supply of tasteless MRE battle rations.

The burnt orange jagged formations of the sand-dusted mountains were bathed in moonlight. Hodge thought that Afghanistan might as well be a different planet. Years ago, it was a different planet.

The women wore miniskirts and the nation was part of the hippie trail to "enlightenment." Now, a liberated Hazara woman in a miniskirt or a Western peacenik with flowing hair and a groovy smile would both be immediate targets for decapitation. Bravo Team were only three days into their journey, yet Bond had already become afflicted with fatigue from altitude sickness. Hodge halted the team to allow Bond time to recover, even though they had moved less than ten klicks that night. Bravo Team had advanced at a breakneck pace of between fifteen to twenty klicks on the first two nights; however, Hodge led with an understanding that the team's ability to function effectively should take precedence over speed. Hodge found it amusing that this was the easy season in Afghanistan. He and his men would remain in the land that sparked the beginning of the end for Alexander for another eight months. The snows had cleared for now and though the temperature dropped to near freezing at night on a regular basis, in winter it reached negative twenty-five degrees Celsius. The wind, elevation, frequent landslides, and difficult ground would remain when the snow returned. The Muj would not be going anywhere either. The killing season was over for a while.

The six hundred milligrams of ibuprofen that Bond had taken the previous night had served its purpose, despite the off-label use. Bond had recovered to the point where he was able to continue the journey. In order to safeguard against a backslide into illness, Hodge had ordered that Bond reduce the load he carried in his MOLLE, or Modular Lightweight Load Carrying Equipment backpack. Hodge divided the power bars and energy drinks that Bond had stored in his MOLLE between himself and the other members of Bravo Team. He had done so to reduce Bond's load and guard against a recurrence of altitude sickness brought on from the strain of carrying twenty pounds of gear while advancing through ground that was over ten thousand feet high.

Hodge's plan had worked. Bond was able to maintain his stamina and Bravo Team moved eight klicks without any difficulties. Hodge halted their advance when Bravo Team neared a collection of stone huts in a valley, commanding his men to wait it out until the next night. Throughout the rest of the night and into the day, two team members would remain on watch, switching-off every four hours. Some of the villages in Afghanistan had been able to resist Taliban control and were perfectly safe in the hands of their local elders. Others had become overrun with Mujahideen. There were obvious ways to tell one type of village from the other. If children were around, that was a good sign. If women were around and did not appear to be cowering in fear, that was a good sign. If Kalashnikov fire was not heard in the background, that was a good sign.

Hodge's men slept behind a large rock formation that provided adequate cover and obscured the villagers' view of their presence. Hodge remained on guard throughout the rest of the night, unwilling to rotate off duty and sleep. He observed the ground through his binoculars. An hour after sunrise, a girl with dirty cheeks in a pink dress rode her bicycle. Bravo Team would still move at night, but this village appeared to be clear of any visible threat from the cave-dwelling clowns who had overrun Afghanistan. Once he had established that the villagers were unlikely to present a threat, Hodge allowed himself to get some rest.

Two nights later, approximately eight klicks southeast of Mersmel, Bravo Team experienced their first encounter with Taliban fighters. A landslide had barred the road two klicks east of their position. A large platoon from the Afghan National Army were engaged in a firefight with the surviving members of a small group of Taliban fighters. The terrorists had veered higher into the mountains to shoot mortars at the troops, unaware that Bravo Team was less than a klick away. The Talis were badly outnumbered, but they had an advantage by nature of their position and their ability to utilize the mountains as a shield. They were only two mikes away from Bravo Team's position when Hodge's protective mentality prevailed and he gave the order to fire. Within minutes, the last seven Tali's blood had stained the sandy orange mountains.

After nine nights of humping through the extreme winds, frequent lightning storms, and scorching sun that was par for the course when traveling through Afghanistan's mountainous terrain, Bravo Team had neared their destination. The village was located at a high altitude, about six klicks away and three thousand feet below Bravo Team's path. The only way for Bravo Team to eliminate their targets in Anjoman was to follow the path further up the mountain. The journey had taken a toll on the members of Bravo Team. Hodge could see that some of his men were struggling to keep up with his pace. Bond paused to catch his breath and wipe off the dust from the evaporated sweat on his forehead. "Un-ass yourself. Our vantage point to scope out the village is six klicks away."

"Roger." After Bond's bout of altitude sickness, he had adjusted to the elevation with no more of a struggle than anyone else on the team. Still, Bond felt like he had let his team down by their having to shoulder an extra load. Leadership was central to Bond's mindset and he believed that the most critical aspect of leadership was earning the respect of others through demonstrating your integrity. Before he became a contractor, Bond had earned his MBA from the University of Virginia. After graduation, he had planned to take his father's furniture manufacturing business into the 21st century. Houston Bond was a genteel member of the Southern elite whose world revolved around handshake deals at the Rotary Club and arranging company picnics for his employees. Automation, outsourcing, and attorney-reviewed contracts were as foreign concepts to him as drinking unsweetened tea or not putting sugar or butter in grits. Bond was loyal to his father and respected the blood, sweat, and tears that he had poured into his business for over three decades, but was concerned about the potential damage to their relationship through irreconcilable views on the business. On a lark, Bond decided to visit UVA's career fair during his second to last semester. Most of the recruiters and representatives sought to staff positions that were of little interest. The only pitch that caught his eye was from a recruiter for the CIA. Bond's father had made a show of disapproval when his son called home and told him that he had decided to take a different path, but it was only a show. Houston Bond enjoyed the fact that he would have another decade or more to run his business his way. He doubted that any of the esteemed professors at his son's business school had ever been involved in the furniture industry or understood the way that business was done in High Point, North Carolina. Regardless of what his bright but stubborn son thought, he knew what was best for his own business. While Bond's father continued to relish his position as one of High Point's business leaders, Bond worked in intelligence for four years throughout the Middle East. After the events of September 11th, he transitioned into a role as a PMC in order to take a more active approach to the elimination of Islamist threats. Bond was the only other PMC Hodge had worked with who did not have direct U.S. military experience. While Hodge respected all his men for their bravery and skill, Bond was the only man who he could envision as relevant to larger purposes beyond their missions.

Bravo Team had made it one-third of the way by daybreak. Altitude sickness had struck Bond again, but this time he refused to admit his pain. He paused to catch his breath as he struggled to gain a foothold to continue his climb up a narrow part of the path. Bond was thirty-one. By his age, many PMCs had already retired or been forced out as too old for the intense physical rigors of the job. Bond was a realist who understood that he didn't have much more than a year or two before he would no longer be able to get hired, even with his exemplary record. His father had stage two bladder cancer and was undergoing chemotherapy, yet he powered through and worked most days. Bond was torn between the choice of returning to the IC or taking over the family business once his father passed. He hoped it would be a moot point.

When the foothold crumbled underneath him, Bond had to rely on his upper-body strength to hang on and gain another foothold. Even with the altitude sickness and being an "old man" compared to his twentysomething teammates, Bond's adrenaline had kicked in and he had found a way to survive. The thrill was exhilarating. Discussions with senior executives about the implementation of agile manufacturing strategies could never compare. If it were possible, Bond would remain a contractor until he was forty, and probably longer than that. But that was not likely. Every body ages. Eventually, they weaken and falter.

The blinding sun had begun to beat down on the mountain. Gonzo could see that some of his teammates were struggling with the terrain. "How y'all crackers feeling?" Gonzalez was born in Santo Domingo, but he had moved to the Bronx with his mother when he was five. She was light, a Dominican mostly of Catalan and French ancestry, but Gonzo's father was dark. As more of his mother's family immigrated to New York, Gonzo had heard them belittle his father, inaccurately labeling him a Haitian. After seeing how badly Wild Man, Squint, Biggie, and Bond were doing in the elements, he was prouder than ever of his complexion. Biggie had vomited behind a rock a little further down from their current position. Wild Man's face was chapped and red. Squint had to pour a few drops of water on his cracked lips. Bond also had cracked lips and couldn't deal well with the altitude. Gonzo had been in the military and worked as a contractor long enough to receive more than a handful of friendly jabs about his race; he felt that now was an appropriate time to throw one back at the white guys on his team. The only problem was that his teammates would not take the bait. To Gonzo, they seemed like some of the straightest guys with whom he had ever served. "Air up here's thinner than a bitch on meth."

Hodge ignored Gonzalez's remarks. Normally, Gonzo was in line with the team's laser-focused attitude. Occasionally, he slipped into the gallows humor and playful joshing typical of soldiers on their downtime. Hodge accepted that if you put your life at risk on a daily basis, you were entitled to some degree of bullshit, but he never found much value in the practice. When the path widened, Hodge handed Bond an inhaler from his rucksack. "You and Squint can share. Helps your lungs take in more oxygen."

"Can't flake out on this party." When Squint first enlisted in the Marines, his Drill Sergeant laughed in his face. Squint was short, four-eyed, skinny, and a technology buff. His profile did not fit that of the typical Marine and the Drill Sergeant made him aware of that fact for the first four weeks of boot camp. By the end of the seventy days, Squint had more than earned his respect. The Drill Sergeant even called him a tough son of a bitch. Squint had enlisted because it was an honorable thing to do. The strength of the United States military served in the interests of protecting the weak from tyranny. Squint had gained quite a bit of musculature since he first joined the Marines six years ago as a fresh-faced high school graduate, but the Drill Sergeant's words continued to resonate. He was a tough son of a bitch and he proved it whenever necessary by pushing himself to an incredible standard. Squint's innate grit had served him well as a contractor and pushed him on through the worst of situations. In Afghanistan, Squint knew that there would be plenty of those and welcomed the opportunity to rise above every hurdle.

Bravo Team pushed on for another hour, until Hodge ordered his team to rack out inside a cave. Even though his body felt like that of a rainbow after his first day of basic training, Biggie wanted to keep going. "Wild Man, why didn't you tell us it was our spa day?" His teammates laughed, but Hodge remained stonefaced. "What's the big deal? We're only a few hours away."

"Not today." Hodge was exhausted from the hump, but everyone on Bravo Team other than Gonzo looked in even worse shape. A day's rest to recuperate would keep his men sharp for the upcoming engagement.

"Must be summit fever," Squint added.

"Just wanted to get the job done, bros." Biggie was the last into the cave.

After he addressed his team inside the cave, Hodge ordered Gonzalez and Arjuna to stay on watch outside. It was typical for Hodge to push himself and be on watch while his men rested. Leaders always eat–and sleep–last was a principle by which Hodge lived; however, Gonzo appeared to be operating with close to a full tank even after a lengthy hump and Arjuna also seemed to be hanging in there. Today, those two men would start on watch. At 1300, Gonzalez and Arjuna would turn in and Hodge and Bond would take over outside, but for now, after a night and morning that had pushed his body to the limit, Hodge felt that he had no choice but to turn in for a few hours.

The mountain's peak reached an elevation of over fifteen thousand feet. Although it was the middle of May and Bravo Team's current location was several thousand feet below the peak, a light layer of recent snowfall blanketed the terrain. Labeling the settlement further down the mountain a village was a linguistic stretch. The settlement of Anjoman was comprised of a handful of stone and mud houses centered around two dirt roads that crossed each other. Its population appeared to consist entirely of sheep and cattle. Anjoman had no electricity and no

shops, but intel had informed Hodge that it was rich in one supply –
Taliban fighters.

Hodge had advanced Bravo Team to a fortified point behind a
large group of boulders. From this location, the plan was to observe the
village and track the Taliban's movement, taking out their target when
appropriate. After more than a week of traveling across brutal terrain,
Hodge and his men enjoyed the relative boredom of remaining in a fixed
location to gather intel on their target. Hodge ensured that Bravo Team
was vigilant in their watch, with the members switching off in teams of
two to observe the village and gather intel on the Tali's operations.
During their first twenty-four hours of reconnaissance, no one exited the
compound or any of the other homes. The village appeared to be
deserted.

The threat to Bravo Team's position did not arrive from the
village. Squint spotted it coming from further back on the path. Mohaqiq
had ordered his second-in-command and most of his forces to attack a
nearby village. Although the Taliban governed a majority of the rural
settlements in the province, the targeted village's militia force had
consistently managed to thwart the Taliban's assaults. After years of
successful resistance, Mohaqiq's platoon had finally been able to
overpower the militia. Once Mohaqiq's men had broken through the
villagers' defenses, they murdered the adult men and women of the
village. Their process was systematic, a methodical AK-47 round to the
head in each case. One young man barely out of his teenage years was
the lone adult survivor. He had been kept alive in order to spread the
Taliban's propaganda and encourage submission to sharia law. Like
most of the other boys, he would be brainwashed and repurposed into a

role as a bomb builder or militant. The girls would all become Taliban brides. Two of the preteen boys faced an even more nefarious fate. These boys were seized as "honey traps," child sex slaves who would be used as trojan horses to mount insider attacks on Afghanistan's military and police forces, who were known for their penchant for the traditional pedophilic practice of bacha bazi. The terrorists justified their murder, seizure, and sexual slavery of the villagers through Islam. The villagers had resisted the Taliban's implementation of sharia law; therefore, they were not perceived as practicing Muslims. They were apostates, and Allah demanded that they not be offered peace and restraint, but that they be seized and killed. The Taliban forces reveled in their carnage, an action they viewed as permissible given that not a single verse in the Qu'ran or in any hadith stipulated that to do so was haram or makruh.

The Taliban were natives of this harsh land, and as such they understood how to exploit irregularities to determine enemy position. Even the movement of a goat in these mountains generated dust in the air. Despite Bravo Team's best efforts to restrict movement and eliminate all non-essential communication, the Taliban had discovered the team's general location. Although the Muj could not yet pinpoint Bravo Team's exact encampment, they had begun to fire wildly in the team's direction. Attacking from a lower elevation was one of the gravest sins of tactical combat; however, the Taliban were guided by more than martial principles. For them, to be slain at the hands of the infidel was a blessing from Allah. If a member of the Taliban was slain by the enemy while engaged in jihad, it was believed that he would enter paradise and be rewarded for his actions. Death was meaningless to the Tali, be it their own lives, the lives of their countrymen, or the lives of the ANDSF or any force of Western infidels determined to oppose their jihad.

Even with his poor eyesight, Squint's binoculars allowed him to see every follicle on every beard of every jihadi that was approaching from further down the path. "About fifteen goat-suckers twenty mikes away."

"Engage." Looking back, this command was Hodge's first error in Afghanistan. The platoon of Tali were traveling up the winding path in three separate squads. Squint had only noticed one of the squads. The others had been obscured by the features of their homeland.

Bravo Team laid down suppressive fire to try to halt or slow the Taliban's advance, but their efforts were ineffective. Within minutes, Hodge realized that an entire platoon of Taliban was heading up the path at a brisk pace, and they had chosen to extend no consideration to their fallen or injured brethren.

Hodge had realized from an early age that he could avoid panicking in tough situations if he slowed his mind down. This practice had ensured clarity of thought whenever decisive action was needed and no obvious solution was apparent. Although it seemed counterintuitive in time-sensitive situations, this approach to solving problems had always worked. Now, with Bravo Team facing a Catch 22, Hodge processed the options. The typical strategy to utilize in this situation would be for his team to engage with the Taliban given their slight advantage in elevation and significant advantage in skill; however, to do so almost certainly ensured that Bravo Team would fail to meet their objective. That outcome would be an inauspicious start to an already difficult placement. Hodge suspected that Mazuski would view that failure as an indication that he was no longer relevant. Then, he would never know the truth about his father. Then, he would never gain revenge against his shadow. Then, he would be barred from his life's purpose. Hodge surmised that he'd lose whatever survived of Mazuski's respect if his team failed for any reason. He would rather be facing unwinnable odds in Afghanistan than alive in a corner office at a think tank or in some research university's political science department with the weight of Mazuski's disapproval forever looming on his conscience. Hodge believed that he had stumbled into a crossroads. Circumstances demanded that he break with conventional martial logic. The group of Taliban that were approaching was a far larger force than the amount described in his intelligence briefing. Perhaps there were additional forces nearby or more Taliban camped out with Mohaqiq in the village. The risk was immense, but Hodge had processed the options and realized that there was no better move in this circumstance than an unorthodox one. "I'm your rabbit luring the Muj down the draw. Bond, Squint, Gonzo, complete our objective. Hold your fire and find a fortified position further down the side path to take out our target. Arjuna, Biggie, drive those bastards towards me. Hopscotch uphill and put down fire every fifty meters, then link up with the team and complete the goddamn mission."

"You'll get toasted, homie." Although he knew that Wild Man could more than handle himself in a rumble, being outnumbered by what appeared to be forty to one struck Gonzo as nothing but an easy way for his team leader to meet Allah.

"Fuckin' move," Hodge commanded as he shoved Gonzo in the direction of the side path. His men had no time to argue. They had no time to even think. Biggie and Arjuna raced uphill as the terrorists continued to advance and fire wild shots at the encampment. The remainder of Bravo Team headed towards the narrow side path. After his men had followed his plan, Hodge darted towards a clearing that offered a better ability to scope the Muj's position as they advanced. They were lower, he was higher. It figured that the bad guys could not gauge how many members were on his team. Hodge operated on instinct as he rotated fire from his M4, 9mm, and .40 caliber automatic pistol, shooting two of the firearms at a time. It was impossible for him and only two of his men to present the impression that they were part of a massive force, but Hodge figured that at the very least this tactic would change the direction of the Tali's movement and lead them to believe their enemies were far more numerous than a team of six. Despite sacrificing pinpoint accuracy, Hodge had sent a few Taliban to meet their god before the platoon was no longer in his line of vision. The whole objective of the mission he had been assigned was to ensure that no quarter was given to anyone affiliated with the Taliban or the complex. Hodge intended, if possible, to wipe out the entire group.

On Hodge's command, Biggie and Arjuna had sprinted eight hundred feet up the hillside to provide overwatch for their team leader. Biggie scored the first scratch from around two hundred yards, an impressive feat given the fact that he had taken out a Tali without yet having caught his breath. Arjuna scored the next three scratches. An inherent competitive streak appeared to be a prerequisite for employment as a PMC, and Biggie and Arjuna nailed that qualification. For both men, thinning out the Taliban from above was not only linked to loyalty to their teammates and their personal honor and values, but to a bet which they had made. Whoever had the fewest scratches would have to foot the bill to purchase a new Xbox and two games at the PX. At present, the FOB was woefully unequipped for multiplayer video gaming sessions. The only video game system in the FOB's welfare and recreation center was an old Sony PlayStation that had to be balanced on its side to get the discs to read. Oftentimes, the games still wouldn't load. Clean and deadlift competitions were always fun, but even the members of Bravo Team needed recovery time. There were only so many cigarettes to bet for poker, and no one on Bravo Team even smoked. Arjuna had tried playing *Magic: The Gathering* with Squint, but found it too AV Club for his tastes, and none of the other team members had the slightest interest in Squint's game of choice. Rare as it would be on this mission for the team to stay overnight on base, Bravo Team could benefit from another outlet for their downtime. Biggie and Arjuna agreed that their "gaming tax" was a fair punishment for whoever proved to be the poorer shot.

"Comeback time," Biggie called out as he leapfrogged Arjuna further up the hill. He was now down three to one. Biggie took a few deep breaths, aimed his M4 at the charging mass of Tali, and fired.

Arjuna raced up the hill after Biggie laid down his fire. "Still three to two." Arjuna fired, but his shots were off by the slightest of margins.

Biggie laughed as he speeded up past Arjuna's position, crouched down, and fired. "One more scratch."

"Tiebreaker." Arjuna scaled the hill. The Tali would be out of range once they followed Hodge down the draw. Arjuna knew this might be his final chance to win the competition.

Bond's back was directly against the rocks as he crossed the side path. If he had lost his footing, Bond could have tumbled down four thousand feet, but adrenaline overrode his fear. Bond's father had served in Vietnam. He had taught his son from an early age that soldiers felt fear and that the common perception that soldiers were machines without emotions was hogwash. But he also explained to his son that to act in the face of fear was what separated a good soldier from a dead soldier. If Bond had the freedom to tell his father about his experiences, he knew that the old man would be proud. Bond did not have that freedom. Instead, the old codger thought that his son had lost his mind in deciding to leave the CIA to open a beer bar in Thailand. Bond understood that there were no heroics in this job, at least none that could be shared with anyone in the civilian world, even with an old sham shield like his father. Survival was a small victory.

A lucky bullet whizzed by Hodge. The shot missed him by inches. A significant distance remained between Hodge and the Taliban, but any further closing of the gap could signal his premature death. When Hodge first met Bling in Somalia, he was puzzled by his approach to life. Hodge understood Bling's unwillingness to socialize. The grave stakes of the job seemed an odd juxtaposition for slapstick and bullshitting, although Hodge understood that type of behavior was a defense mechanism that shielded his men from their bitter reality;

however, Bling's fatalism haunted him. In one of their few private conversations, Bling had expressed that he was "awake" to the reality of his situation. No one gave a damn. No one would ever give a damn. He was expendable. Money didn't salve any wounds. All it did was allow you to escape afterwards into some false hedonistic third world fantasy that would be colored by disillusionment in the end. Bling had perceived that nothing he did or could do would ever matter. If he died, it wouldn't matter. After a betrayal from a terrorist he had mistaken for a friend, constantly being strung along by his handler, burying a partner, and realizing how mundane the civilian world back home was and would forever be after these experiences, Hodge had begun to understand Bling's perspective. Even death would be meaningless, but the action itself was fulfilling and putting rounds in the bad guys remained powerful and purposeful. Until he stopped feeling those sensations, Hodge would choose to stay alive over being buried in a box six feet under.

Gonzo crossed the path without a second thought. Gonzalez was aware of the potential for a devastating end if he messed up, but he had been a soldier or PMC his entire adult life; the threat of death was old hat. Squint was right behind Gonzo. He advanced over the rocks, careful to maintain his balance, as a heavy gust of wind blew in his face.

Gonzo laughed as his teammate crossed over to safety. "Bet you didn't think you'd get blown out here, bro."

"Thought I'd have to wait to be deployed to the Philippines," Squint whispered.

Gonzo cracked up. "Hear that shit, Bond? My boy's got jokes."

Hodge had started to lay down more fire with his M4 and .40 cal pistol as he broke for the draw. His efforts introduced a few more terrorists to their betrothed seventy-two virgins. Hodge could see that some of the other Muj had been injured from non-lethal shots and the physical challenge of rushing up the path while taking fire. Even with Arjuna and Biggie helping to carry the load, a majority of the Muj's platoon remained ready for battle; however, his tactic had protected the encampment. The Muj had begun to split their fire between Hodge's position and towards his men providing cover. If the Tali followed Hodge down the draw, the rest of his team could remain on task and complete the objective. Whether he survived or not, Mazuski would respect his commitment to the job. It would cast all his doubts aside. Hodge's actions would prove to Mazuski that he was relevant; at least that's what he thought. In truth, Hodge had always set the bar for himself far higher than what was expected, even when measured against the demanding standards of the job. His constant need to overachieve had served him well throughout his entire life, including in his recent engagements as a PMC. Hodge had guaranteed his success in every endeavor by always choosing to go above and beyond, a tendency motivated partly out of his own idealism and partly out of his eagerness to earn the approval of his superiors.

Hodge tucked his chin, lowered his body down, and rotated forward into a shoulder roll off the cliff and into the draw for the thirty-foot drop. Upon reaching the bottom, Hodge heard an unmistakable sound come from inside his body. The bone made a hollow cracking snap like a tree branch hit by lightning under low barometric pressure.

Hodge's brain had registered the injury and knew it was bad, yet the rush of adrenaline and endorphins facilitated a painless experience.

Hodge's original plan had been to continue to attack the Tali. Now, with an injury having left his mobility suspect, Hodge would have to evade them. If the terrorists discovered his new position and had the stones to follow him down the draw, he would be a dead man. Hodge understood that a dead asset is not relevant. Mazuski had believed in him all those years, developed him, and now he was in this position. He was failing. Worse, he had let his handler down. Soon, he might be dead. The Taliban were aware of his location. They had to be. And if by some miracle they lost his trail, then his men were screwed. That outcome would be a million times worse than his own death. It had been over a decade since Hodge's Confirmation. He had not visited the Church afterwards except for a handful of funerals and one Midnight Mass on Christmas Eve with his mother and Uncle Joe when he was sixteen. Hodge was desperate for a miracle and hoped that works were valued above faith in the bestowal of grace.

As Bravo Team's second-in-command, Bond signaled for his teammates to be silent by moving his open hand over his mouth. The Tali kept their mouths shut. This was their land. They knew that it took a special pleasure in revealing secrets. Bond understood the rules of the game and the necessity of enforcing them. His teammates picked up on the message. Jokes were fine in their place, but Bond's goals were to complete the objective and ensure that none of his teammates' throats were slit. The three members of Bravo Team moved like silhouettes until they found a fortified location several hundred feet down. No one said a word as Squint passed Bond the binoculars.

Hodge's method of treating his gruesome ankle injury was problematic under normal circumstances. Serving as your own doctor rarely qualified as a normal circumstance. The likelihood of a swarm of Taliban heading in your direction was hardly a normal circumstance either. Hodge unfastened his medkit from the straps of his rucksack. He wrapped the outside of his boot over his ankle with tape and then applied a combat tourniquet as an extra precaution. Afterwards, Hodge found a nearby branch from a tree and affixed it to his leg. This makeshift apparatus made it much easier for Hodge to move with what he thought was a severe fracture. Now, instead of stepping on his injured foot, most of the pressure went to Hodge's knee. Hodge hoped that his men would be able to take out their target and make it to their exfiltration point. He hoped that he could survive long enough to meet them there. There was no other option because Hodge realized that he had made yet another mistake—he had not thought to devise a backup plan.

Direct combat with the Taliban fighters in his position was a fool's errand. Hodge was dealing with an escape and evasion. He had prepped for these types of situations since his earliest months on the Farm. In Syria and Iraq, his teams had faced these dynamics together. Now, this was the first time that he had to confront a non-simulated situation where he must evade the enemy alone. With a broken ankle and Taliban fighters expected to head his way, Hodge was aware that he needed to maintain absolute discipline regarding noise, light, and litter to eliminate, or at least greatly reduce, his signature in this barren environment. Hodge covered both boots with his wool socks to muffle the noise that they produced. Fortunately, his CamelBak was full. Bravo Team had shared their water rations through their journey to avoid excess noise from the faint rattle of partially filled water containers. Next, Hodge secured the straps on his rucksack, and then he jumped up with his pack strapped to his back to check if his supplies made any noise that could tip off the bad guys. After he secured for sound, Hodge switched his attention to light. His flashlight had a red filter, which was far superior to a typical white light in these circumstances, but Hodge was skilled enough to avoid the use of a flashlight altogether; he could travel by the light of the Moon. Hodge flipped his watch around to prevent glare from the glass. He had prevented an ambush from miles out in Yemen because the sun had reflected off a terrorist's watch. Hodge would not make the same mistake as the jihadist who his team had slain. He took care of the basics last, rolling his sleeves down and using camo on all his exposed skin. Although Hodge had been able to find a branch for the apparatus attached to his leg, there was not enough vegetation in the mountains to make a ghillie suit. If any of the Taliban had night-vision goggles and Hodge was not in a secure hideout, then all his precautions might be for naught because the outline of his body would be visible. Hodge could hear the Mujahideen closing in up on the path. They sounded like they were around ten mikes away. Pain or not, Hodge had two options. He could find a series of hideouts to evade the Taliban fighters if they followed him down the draw or he could die.

Bond, Gonzo, and Squint had settled into a new location approximately six hundred feet down the side path. This spot afforded them cover while they observed the village. There was an element of risk in remaining stationary anywhere other than near the peak. Additional Taliban fighters could arrive at any time, but Bond judged that they needed to take that risk in order to complete their objective. Once more, the three team members readied themselves to perform the slow and arduous process of performing recon on the village. If everything went according to Hodge's plan, Arjuna and Biggie would soon find the team of three's location. The whole situation struck Bond as odd. He did not need a third wheel. It made no sense to have a third man on the village when two could snipe and scout the target if he appeared. A second man should have gone with Wild Man down the draw. Bond understood that leadership in this environment meant one needed to often embrace creative moves, but this seemed like an obvious miscue.

Arjuna inspected the village through his binoculars. No action. He and Biggie had found the team's encampment easily enough once they headed down the side path. The leapfroggers had joined the rest of their team less than an hour after the others had arrived. The situation in the village had not changed. There had been no movement from the complex during all of Bravo Team's time observing the village. Once nightfall arrived, Arjuna would have to switch up the recon duties. He passed Bond the binoculars.

"Nothing to do except wait," Bond whispered, more to himself than to Arjuna or the rest of the team. Everyone understood the situation. This wasn't the fun part of the job, but it was necessary. Maybe their intel was faulty, but Mohaqiq undoubtedly had enough supplies inside to hole up for a long time. Without backup, any other move on his part would be foolish. The complex appeared to be a structure that was insulated from sound. Unless one of his men had been able to alert him, it was not likely that Mohaqiq had even heard the engagement. Bond's orders were to ensure that Bravo Team remained focused on the village until Mohaqiq made a move; however, the severe risk of Wild Man becoming KIA and the lack of movement in the village made Bond question if a different course of action was appropriate.

      The first leg of Hodge's plan had been executed to perfection. The remnants of the Taliban fighters who had survived the initial engagement and the subsequent firefight with Hodge, Arjuna, and Biggie had followed him down the draw. Some of the Tali had been injured. One had died from a fall; however, enough of the bad guys made it unscathed, including their commander.

      Ghakhtalay Khak ordered his men uphill to the peak. He had judged that a majority of his enemy's forces were stationed at a higher elevation. After Khak realized that his enemies were no longer uphill, he led his men to the draw. Khak thought that it was possible, but improbable, that their attacks had killed the infidels. It appeared that one squad had retreated down the draw, although the uphill squad's whereabouts were an open question. Khak granted his men rest for the night after hours of fruitless searching for the infidels. There was nothing else to do, other than try to alert Mohaqiq as to their predicament. Khak reached for his Nokia. If Allah willed it, he would have reception.

Squint was on watch. He assessed the entirety of the environment, alert for any threat to Bravo Team's position. Gonzo had his sniper rifle locked on the back of the complex, ready to score whenever the objective emerged. Arjuna and Biggie were halfway into their scheduled forty winks. Bond would rouse them in seventy-five mikes to relieve Squint and Gonzalez.

Unlike his other four teammates, Bond had been too restless to sleep. Instead, he had kept his M4 aimed at the front of Mohaqiq's complex for the last five hours, ready to support Gonzo with suppressive fire when the endless silence of inactivity reached its inevitable conclusion. The more that Bond pondered the situation, the greater the pull he had towards breaking with Wild Man's plan. It was a near certainty that Mohaqiq was inside. There was almost no way that Mohaqiq would have been a part of the force that they had engaged earlier. He was an old man – a cleric not a warrior. Mohaqiq was the type of man who sent other men to die for his ambitions. If Bravo Team destroyed the complex with a few .50 rounds, Mohaqiq would not be privy to a clear signal that there was trouble and escape; he would receive what he had wanted all along, a one-way ticket to Allah to cash in his overdue rain check for seventy-two virgins. It was obvious that Wild Man wanted the same thing that he wanted, to complete the objective; however, his approach belied his character. Wild Man wanted to take all the risk and save his men even the slightest chance of blame. Bond had set a timeline. If his body was ready to pass out and Mohaqiq had not emerged, he would give the order to blow the complex to hell, deal with any mess, and then head to the rendezvous point to make sure that Wild Man had taken care of business.

His teammates found reconnaissance too dull for their tastes, but Squint appreciated the pastoral quality inherent in the watch. He compared recon to golf and baseball, his favorite sports. The wait for the slightest movement. The thrill of silence punctuated by the pounce when the situation broke open. His teammates didn't need to understand its appeal. It was only fifteen mikes until Arjuna would take his place, but Squint watched and waited with the same dogged focus on the village that he had summoned for the last four hours.

Khak's Nokia managed to eventually have enough reception to alert his boss as to what had happened. He informed Mohaqiq that there had been a skirmish with multiple forces higher up on the mountain. Khak told Mohaqiq that the infidels, at present, had escaped Allah's judgment, but promised that would change.

After hearing from Khak, Mohaqiq informed the few fighters who he had ordered to remain in the complex with him that there had been a change of plans. Now, they were to carry out their jihad against the infidels. Mohaqiq did not know whether the infidels were internal agents of Afghanistan's apostate regime or external agents from the Great Satan or one of her allies, but either way they were to be slaughtered for the benefit of the ummah. Mohaqiq did not join his four subordinates when they scrambled out of the complex, two from the front and two from the back.

"Movement! Front and back!" Squint threw down the binoculars, grabbed his M4, and laid down fire on the targets of opportunity. The two Taliban fighters who had exited the front of the complex tried to maneuver away. In an instant, Squint gunned them down. Gonzo scored an easy two-hundred-yard hit on the other side of the complex. The other Tali who had emerged from the back tried to retreat inside. Bond eliminated him with a hail of M4 fire. Arjuna and Biggie were late to the party, but Biggie was already setting up his long gun, ready to support.

"Our target's in there. No use waiting. We're blowing the whole structure to hell," Bond commanded.

Biggie laughed. "Fuckin' A. I got this." After Bond nodded his assent, Biggie fired several .50 BMG rounds at the complex. The structure was less of a shield and the target was eliminated. No one exited. Bravo Team had completed their objective.

Bond addressed his men after additional reconnaissance. "Time to hump." He hoped that Wild Man would be waiting for them at the rendezvous point with a big shit-eating grin on his face. Bond could deal with a rescue mission. He hoped that he would not have to deal with something he could never unsee, like discovering the decapitated corpse of his team leader.

Bravo Team had reached their rendezvous point two thousand feet below Anjoman after five hours of humping down the mountain. Under a less pressing situation, the team would have been preparing to find a fortified and clandestine area to turn in for the night, while two men remained awake for several hours until their teammates relieved them on watch. The hump uphill to the draw would take another five hours at best. Neither Bond nor anyone else on the team had thoughts of sleep enter their minds. If they had to perform for three days without rest, then that's what would be done. The members of Bravo Team had been trained for this level of exertion. Their commitment to each other reinforced that training. Death was a constant companion which turned teammates into brothers. Brothers razzed. Brothers fought. Brothers had each other's backs.

Two hours from the rendezvous point, Gonzo shattered the eerie silence that hung over the team, pointing out the elephant in the room. "Hope Wild Man ain't dead."

Bond was team lead in Wild Man's absence. It was his duty to project leadership. This was not a book club or a group therapy meeting. His men had to do their job and emotions could not cloud their decisions. In Afghanistan, emotions led to death. "Keep humping."

"Need to save our bro," Biggie replied.

"He's a brave bastard," Squint added.

Arjuna nodded. "Really is."

"No tipoffs." Their sentiments were appropriate, but Bond nixed the eulogies. Nobody would be left to eulogize himself and the other members of Bravo Team if they were ambushed.

The dawn was rising when Squint spotted the remnants of the Mujahideen huddled around a campfire. Only one member of their unit was standing watch. Bond considered it a fortuitous sight that the Taliban were by the draw. If they were not around, it would have indicated that they had completed their objective and that Wild Man had possibly been killed or taken hostage.

Bond signaled for everyone to take cover behind a large formation of boulders. The Tali were only five mikes away and outnumbered Bravo Team by more than three to one, but Bond and his men had two distinct advantages: All five members of Bravo Team were awake as compared to only one of the bad guys; and they had elevation.

The watchman was Bravo Team's first scratch. Biggie had fired a suppressed shot. He remained on overwatch in a strong position to cover the other four team members, who were on M4s in close range. The watchman had been eliminated with barely a peep from the rest of Mohaqiq's jihadis. Bravo Team scored a few more easy scratches before the rest of the slumbering Talis were roused, although even these fighters were quickly put down by the M4s. The battle was over. It had been almost too easy. Bravo Team had decimated the entirety of the Taliban's unit, while facing only the weakest of retaliations.

"Should we keep—" Bond cut Arjuna off before he could ask the question, pointing at his eyes to signal that the team would continue to search for Wild Man. The idea that anyone would want to camp out at this point was offensive. The immediate threat of Taliban had been neutralized, but one of their own was nowhere to be found. Bravo Team's foremost priority was to complete their objectives, but their second-greatest priority was that every teammate walked away from each mission in one piece. Sleep should be low on the totem pole of his team members' priorities. Bond figured that anyone who wanted to could sleep when they were back at the FOB.

The sun was bright and hot when Bravo Team found their team leader. To evade the Taliban on his own, Hodge had stealthily moved between a series of crags, small caves, outcroppings, and other natural cover. Hodge ceased his movements only after he heard Gonzo's careless victory whoop and realized that the worst must be over. That's when the hurt started. Hodge soon passed out from a cocktail of immense pain and exhaustion that had previously been subdued by his adrenaline and endorphins.

Squint shook Hodge awake. "Good initiative, bad judgment, Wild Man."

At first, Hodge was startled to see his teammates. He then laughed at Squint's remark, but didn't say a word in response. His plan had worked, but once Bravo Team reached their exfil point and returned to base, that would be it for him. *It was a good run, but now I'm nothing more than a lame duck. Mazuski set me up to fail, to prove that I was not relevant, and everything went as he expected. Life will have to return to research on JSTOR and drafting white papers. Life will have to return to battling on ideological grounds with the useful idiots that academia keeps propping up. Life will have to return to trips to New Jersey for my mother's red sauce. Life will have to return to trying to sleep through Dennis' maximum volume midnight Gamecube and screwing sessions with his good-for-nothing girlfriend. Life will have to return to nights out shooting the shit with Spencer at Landmark.* At one time, Hodge believed that his actions might change the world. That ideology was long gone. A new identity had been forged in its place. Hodge had become a meat eater. His purpose was intertwined with combat. He would not be returning home in a box, but Hodge felt like he was already dead.

Biggie noticed the splint that Hodge had made for his leg. "What the fuck happened to you, Wild Man?"

"Part of the job."

"Get on your back, Wild Man. I need your packs, bros." Biggie gathered everyone's medical supplies from their rucksacks. The injury was gruesome. Biggie determined that the best that he and the team could do right now was patch Wild Man up. His team leader could get better treatment once back on base, but that would be a week at best.

Arjuna grinned as he knifed off Hodge's tape job. "I don't buy them dinner first either, bro."

Biggie attempted to push Hodge's ankle bone into place, doing his best to realign it and reduce the protrusion. "You're gonna be alright, bro." Biggie packed the injury with gauze, then rewrapped and bandaged Hodge up before giving him four shots of lidocaine to alleviate his pain. If they had enough supplies, Biggie would have given Wild Man triple the dose.

"Bury that tape, bro." Gonzo called out to Arjuna.

"On it," Arjuna replied.

Hodge laughed. "It should have been an air strike." Mazuski must have wanted him and his team to enjoy the scenic route through the Hindu Kush even though a simple air strike would have destroyed the entire complex and every Tali inside.

"The hell you talking about?" Gonzo asked.

"The Blackwater boys were hung over a bridge only, what, two months ago? You know we'd make great headlines for the media and you know they'd find some way to sniff this out if it went down. They'd run with us for a day. What kind of plan was it to send us out here? If we died, the optics would be terrible."

"Where's your head?" Bond asked.

Hodge cracked up with laughter. "Don't worry about me, Bond. I'm wide awake. No one gives a damn. No one will ever give a damn. We're expendable."

"Biggie, stay on watch with me. The rest of you turn in." It was not Bond's order to give, but his teammates followed his command.

"Have fun, Bond," Hodge deadpanned.

Bond nodded as Wild Man followed the rest of Bravo Team into the cave to catch a few hours of sleep. Hodge knew that his conduct was inappropriate, but he had already lost everything. His team's respect was no more than the final thing he needed to discard.

Hodge figured that the quick and unremarkable trek to the team's exfil point served as a fitting end to his brief sojourn as a contractor. The closest Bravo Team came to action was when they performed recon on a village that had a few bearded jihadi types with AK-47s on patrol. These jihadis were not on Bravo Team's mile-long list of targets, so they ignored and evaded. When the team reached the exfil point, they were four days ahead of schedule. The date and time of extraction had been arranged in advance as a matter of protocol. If Bravo Team had missed their exfil, it would have been another three days before they could be extracted. The times and locations of extractions shifted almost randomly; predictability gives advantage to the enemy. Hodge had survived, but the pain continued to test every last bit of endurance and pride that he still possessed.

Bravo Team was camped out near a cave only a couple of klicks from the exfil point. Gonzo and Arjuna were on watch. Biggie was giving Hodge another treatment while Squint assisted him as secondary medic. "We're out of lidocaine," Biggie informed his de jure team leader.

"This injury is bad. We gotta fight this infection," Squint added.

Bond shook his head. "You need to make a fire."

"Where's your head, Bond?" Hodge could admit to himself that he had made many plenty of bad decisions since the drone strike, but the thought of building a fire and giving the Taliban a beacon to their location struck him as beyond the pale.

"Really no other choice," Squint replied. It was either build the fire or Wild Man might become an amputee. Bravo Team could deal with the Tali if need be.

Bond continued, "We'll dig a hole. We should be fine, Wild Man." Biggie nodded in agreement.

Gonzo strolled over to join the rest of the team. "Bet you want me to dig the hole, right? It's 'cause I'm Black, isn't it?"

"Yep," Hodge responded in a pitch-perfect rendition of Steam's West Virginia twang. Maybe he could go down to Wheeling and hit the bars with Steam. That would be a fitting end.

The fire blazed in a deep hole that Biggie and Squint had dug in the ground. Biggie heated up a knife in the fire. "It ain't gonna be pretty, Wild Man."

"God loves ugly."

Biggie began to use his knife to scrape out Hodge's wound and cut away the infected and necrotic tissue. Hodge winced. Three days later, Bond managed to radio into Jalalabad Main. Just as promised, the bird was there to exfil Bravo Team in thirty mikes. Hodge shipped out to Frankfurt the next morning.

23

EAST COAST, U.S.A.

SEPTEMBER 2004

An opening had somehow appeared on Dr. Martin Tsien's otherwise booked schedule the day after Hodge left Jalalabad for Germany. Tsien was generally regarded as one of the top ten orthopedic surgeons in the world. Eleven weeks after the Shenzhen-born surgeon with the thick German accent performed his ankle surgery, Hodge had been cleared to walk without his knee scooter by Dr. Raymond Ruland, who had overseen the remainder of his recovery stateside at BWH. The x-rays had shown that Hodge's ankle was healing properly. Ruland was confident that his patient would regain full mobility without even the slightest bit of discomfort during any routine tasks within no more than a year. Hodge did not pose the question, but he assumed that climbing up mountains in Afghanistan to eliminate targets did not qualify as a routine task. Hodge's treatment had been the final parting gift that accompanied his walking papers. Mazuski, unbeknownst to Hodge, had arranged for the full cost of payment for surgery and his subsequent treatment and physical therapy visits at government expense. Hodge had earned a substantial amount of money through his former job, but a health insurance plan had never been part of the offer.

After the prescription drug-induced daze of his first two weeks back in the States had worn off, Hodge did his best to adjust his mind to a new reality. It was impossible that a cripple would ever be offered a second chance in the field. Despite being aware of the nature of his situation, Hodge slept with his BlackBerry on a side table. He hoped that Mazuski would give him a call. The call never came. Hodge wondered if the call would ever come; it was two months past Mazuski's expiration date.

Hodge was aware that it would be difficult for him to settle back into the expected career track of what seemed now like his former life. Graduating summa cum laude from the Massachusetts Institute of Technology did present a strong impression, but whatever challenges he planned to address in life would from now on have to be accomplished entirely through his own merits. There would be no hidden hand to unveil opportunities; however, Hodge remained confident in his talents. The overwhelming depression of his first month back had faded to a faint malaise by September. Every day, Hodge busied himself by keeping abreast on the latest research on all matters related to Islam, terrorism, and foreign relations. Spencer had helped Hodge not only work his therapy hard, but he had also found an ambitious freshman to serve as his research assistant on a new project. Hodge paid his assistant fifteen dollars an hour to run errands and find and sort through material for his unfinished manuscript on the history of Islamic imperialism. If the narrative dictated by the doves and the left was that imperialism was a subjugation of oppressed people by dominant empires that must be decried, then Hodge would beat his opponents at their own game through a comprehensive exploration of Islam's martial and expansionist mindset over fourteen centuries. Despite his credentials and the soundness of his argument, Hodge was not surprised that all twenty-four literary agencies that he had queried had passed on his proposal. While publishing houses were businesses that focused on the bottom line, certain groups were not to be offended, regardless of truth or sales potential. Hodge did not choose to write the book for the promise of a gratuitous paycheck. If Hodge could not find a publisher, he would release his work for free online. The mission was what guided him in this endeavor. Since battle with M4s was no longer an option, he would have to change his strategy. Now, as he had planned to do before he met Mazuski, he would try to win the war against the bad guys with words.

Hodge expected that the line would be dead. It wasn't like Mazuski's number was in the phone book. To the best of his knowledge, Mazuski maintained communication with his assets through multiple black phones. Hodge had dialed Mazuski's number countless times during his first two weeks back in Cambridge, but the calls never connected. It was a Hail Mary to expect a different result more than three months after he returned, but there was nothing to lose in trying. Later that night, Hodge received in his email a one-way ticket for a flight to Washington. The next evening, he was back at Langley.

It had been four months since Hodge had last seen his former handler. Mazuski had looked in poor condition before, but now the cancer had overtaken his body, accelerating his natural degree of gauntness to the point where he bore a closer resemblance to a skeleton than a person. The outline of quarter-inch hairs on his shaved head showed large bald spots on a hairline that had been solid for a man in his sixties. His coughs were relentless. Hodge had grown used to their previous frequency. Their change was akin to a move into quick time from double time. Hodge had placed his copy of *The Art of War* on Mazuski's desk. He reread the book on the flight and planned to read it again in his hotel room after their meeting. Hodge wondered if Mazuski could read in his condition or if he was plagued by blurry chemo vision. It was a borderline miracle that Mazuski seemed to be able to maintain his responsibilities at Langley in his condition. Hodge believed that if the roles were reversed, he would do everything in his power to match his former handler's dedication.

Mazuski managed a chuckle through his stream of coughs. "As I'm sure you can deduce, Chris, my time seems to actually have reached its conclusion."

"No use hoping for a different outcome." Judging by his current appearance, Hodge estimated that Mazuski would be dead within a month. The hope that events would play out in a different fashion for his former handler was not realistic. An expectation that this dying man would recover was an even greater flight of fancy than if Hodge were to expect Mazuski to inform him that they had intel on Bin Laden's location and needed him to lead the team set to eliminate the Saudi mastermind. That sort of hope was nothing but a foolish delusion.

Mazuski reached across the table with a trembling hand. He picked up Hodge's copy of *The Art of War* and paged through the book. A smile formed on his sunken cheeks. "You managed to hold onto this."

"It's my last connection to my father." Hodge had brought the book with him on his recent trip to New Jersey. During his last visit to South Amboy, his mother had decided, on her therapist's recommendation, to come clean to her sons about one problematic aspect of her husband's character. While Christopher Hodge was still alive, Donna had discovered that her husband was a chronic womanizer who had sired another child with one of his girlfriends. Donna Hodge never learned the names of her husband's mistresses or the illegitimate child, but she had received a call from one of the other women three months before Christopher Hodge's death. Donna's husband had told her that he needed to fly to San Diego for what he described to her as private and confidential business. There had been a nasty spat about child support while he was away and the mistress decided to go nuclear. When Christopher Hodge returned, he was only able to remain in New Jersey with his wife for two days before he had to ship out. After that, she never had a chance to see him again. Donna told her sons that she would have divorced their father when they were old enough to handle a separation, but his death overseas changed her plan and left her racked with guilt. Hodge had been shocked and disappointed to learn this fact about his father, but appreciated what had resulted from his mother sharing this information. Since that trip, Donna no longer needed her anti-anxiety medications. When she called to check up on him, Hodge heard life in her voice for the first time since he was a child.

"How many times have you read it, Chris?" Blood and phlegm stained Mazuski's handkerchief through an almost endless string of coughs.

"I lost count. It was the only book that I brought to Afghanistan. In Iraq, there were a few Tom Clancys at the FOB." Mazuski laughed through his coughs. "Do you need a lozenge? Can I do anything for you?" Mazuski had nixed his further use after the debacle in Afghanistan, but Hodge could not help but continue to view him with respect and fondness.

Mazuski's response was a simple declaration unblemished by pride, "I wouldn't want you to." His eyes lit up as he continued, "I promised you information."

Hodge had always held Mazuski in great esteem, but for over two years his perception of the man had been colored with resentment because of Mazuski's failure to keep his end of the bargain. Hodge's bitterness had dissolved into a quiet acceptance after he had been ordered out of Afghanistan. Now, months after being declared not relevant to the plan and with Mazuski on the verge of death, his former handler appeared to be ready to change course. "You did," Hodge replied in a stony tone.

"Your father and I served in Vietnam. I went into intelligence afterwards; he was a leatherneck through and through."

"What was he like?" Christopher Hodge had been an enigma to his namesake for two decades. His mother's revelations about his father's personal failings had disturbed Hodge, but these new facts did not diminish his curiosity.

"He was a friend, one of the few men to whom I would apply that term. He trusted me. I was his handler. In Lebanon. We thought Duale's father was working for us. The mission went south. He fed me deceptive intel. Chris went into the barracks because I told him it was safe based on that intel. He was not safe. And I have had to live with that, Chris. I shouldn't tell you this, but I'm about to be a dead man anyway." Mazuski had struggled to release the words. Hodge was unsure if the difficulty stemmed from emotion or the cancer. Mazuski reached for a lozenge, but it fell out of his hand and onto the ground. He kept coughing. Endlessly. Hodge just stared in amazement, waiting for Mazuski to continue. "You are his son. When the higher-ups made the decision to tap you, I did everything in my power to ensure that I took your case. I promised myself that I would handle you better than I handled your father. I wanted to do right by him."

"When am I shipping out next?" Hodge knew that the presumption behind his question was an incredible reach, but Mazuski had already stunned him with the unexpected once tonight.

"How's your ankle?"

"I made it here. It's healed enough."

"Are you relevant?"

"I'm relevant."

"There might be a new role in your future, Chris. Expect my Lancia Beta in front of your building at 0800 on Tuesday."

Hodge nodded. Working as an operator gave him the respect, honor, and even reverence that he craved. Hodge believed that without that purpose, nothing was worthwhile. No offer had been tendered and Mazuski had used the word "might," but even opening the possibility of reinsertion into the plan was the best news that Hodge had heard in his entire life.

It was 0400 on Tuesday morning and Chris Hodge remained wide awake. The anticipation about his new role had made it impossible for Hodge to fall asleep. His mind raced with possibilities about the nature of his next assignment. Hodge and Mazuski had not communicated since their meeting at Langley. The next chapter in

Hodge's life was still a complete unknown. In four hours, he would learn what awaited him. Until then, he watched *Platoon*. Barnes fragged Elias in the Vietnamese jungle. Elias maintained his smile to the end. Hodge shut off his DVD player and television. He put his head to the pillows, but his mind would not shut off.

Hodge stood in front of his building at 0745, yet the Lancia Beta had not arrived. Hodge had dialed his number twice, but the calls would not connect. He waited until 0800, his anxiety heightening with every minute that passed. At 0800 on the dot, his BlackBerry began to ring. It was an unlisted number. "Where the hell are you?"

"This is Keyes. You are to report to my office at Langley at 1000 tomorrow morning."

"What about Mazuski?" The line went dead.

Hodge had secured a three o'clock flight. The early trip would allow him enough time to be fully rested for his meeting with Keyes. Since their initial meeting at Landmark, Hodge had always been in direct communication with Mazuski. Now it appeared that Keyes had taken him on for his future role in the plan. Mazuski would work until he passed. It seemed an impossibility to think that he was still alive. Hodge viewed the situation as an initiation into manhood. The initial excitement of the change in direction in his life had worn off, he had faced an array of internal and external pitfalls, and now his guide was gone. He would have to face whatever the next leg of his journey had in store for him alone.

The cabbie's identification card was affixed to the bulletproof glass that kept him separated from Hodge. Sharmaarke Absame.

Sharmaarke the Somali was bulletproof. He looked about forty-five. If the boy had survived, maybe in 2040 he would have been driving Hodge to Boston Logan. But the boy did not survive. "Your name means protect from evil."

Sharmaarke's voice was gleeful and soaring, almost boyish. "Yes, sir. It does. How did you know?"

Hodge did not respond. *They're not your friends.*

"Have you been to my country?"

Let the enemy talk. Use his words to sink him.

"You don't speak Somali, do you?" Sharmaarke changed to his native tongue. "Speak Somali, brother?"

"I used to know someone who spoke Somali," Hodge scoffed. "I don't know him anymore." Sharmaarke attempted to continue the conversation for the next fifteen minutes. Hodge refused to engage. When they arrived at the gate, Hodge stiffed him on the tip. *Fuck him. Fuck all of them.*

24

AFGHANISTAN

OCTOBER 2004

The FOB in Eshkashem was at the far side of the Wakhan Corridor, a narrow strip of land that connected Afghanistan to the western edge of the People's Republic of China. Omega Team had assembled in the FOB's welfare and recreation center. Standin was glued to his laptop screen, immersed in a live newsfeed centered on the war on terrorism. *Maybe I'll take out the big names they keep mentioning in some future mission.* In Ohio, his wife was pregnant again with their third son. When she dropped the big news three months after he returned from Iraq, Standin gave his two weeks notice to the Xenia Police Department. The strain of providing for three young boys and a wife on a little over twenty-five thousand a year was an unreasonable proposition, even in the rural Midwest. Standin planned to take a few more jobs as a PMC until he had saved enough money to ride through the years in dignity, if not in comfort, with his family back in Xenia.

Boogie's rap moniker was Thirty Rounds, a reference to the standard magazine for the M4 carbine which held thirty 5.56 x 45mm rounds. In his years as a PMC, Boogie had only twenty-seven scratches attributed solely to his hand. He told himself that the reason why he was back on the job was to get those last three kills so that his name carried weight on the streets. The truth of the matter was that he missed the camaraderie and excitement. Boogie had only known Squint for a few hours, but he could tell that he was a solid little dude. He could also tell that Squint was very white. Boogie had been trying to teach him a handshake, but the process had been an abject failure. He hoped that Squint had quicker reflexes in battle than he was showing right now.

Steam snorted derisively. He had already made his mind up about his three new teammates. "Motherfucker. The hell was Wild Man thinking? Y'all are a sorry bunch of bastards." When Hodge had called to ask if his old bones could manage the freezing winds of Afghanistan, Steam jumped at the chance. Wild Man could not promise him anything more than the one mission, but if this was his swan song, then it would be one hell of an exit. The endlessly flowing beer and constant supply of cheap pussy in Wheeling could wait for a month or two now that Steam had the chance to take out a few battalions of Taliban for the fourth and final time.

"Motherfuck yourself, man." Steam rubbed Boogie the wrong way. Boogie thought that Steam was nothing more than a loud, obnoxious motard. In his opinion, this West Virginia redneck was a laughingstock. The guy was a couple years past thirty and he still acted boot as hell.

"Still don't know why they let y'all off the plantations."

"Forget you, man." Boogie had heard it all before. The first time he took his PT test, his drill instructor had gotten in his face for only scoring a 290. Afterwards, that racist old smokey bear would find a reason to get him alone and then it would be monkey this, boy that, coon something else. Back where he was from, brothers would put a slug in a white dude's chest if one of them came into the hood and talked that mess, but Boogie had to take it at Parris Island. They were just words. Steam was not worth his energy. As long as that piece of white trash had his back against the Tali, he could run his ignorant mouth all he wanted.

Arjuna carried an Xbox and three games as he entered the welfare and recreation center. He had just visited the FOB's PX to pick up *Madden NFL 2004*. Biggie had purchased the console itself and *Mortal Kombat: Deadly Alliance* and *Counter-Strike* after Bravo Team eliminated Mohaqiq and returned to base. It had been a close competition, but Arjuna scored the victory with four Tali scratches of his own to only three for Biggie. "Who's up for some *Madden*?"

"Where the hell's my goddamn M4? Who let this Tali onto our base?"

Arjuna placed the Xbox and games down in front of the television. "I'm not a Tali, bud. I smoke Talis. Hey Squint, this clown on our team?"

"He's cool, Arjuna. Don't sweat it."

"He ain't cool," Boogie snapped.

The tension between Boogie and Steam had made it impossible for Standin to concentrate on the news. He slammed his laptop shut and stepped between his teammates. "You two keep this up, we'll all be dead. We're brothers here. Remember that."

Squint turned to Standin. "They're professionals. Don't worry. They'll be frosty it counts."

Steam puffed his chest out as he looked Squint up and down. He lowered his Oakleys and glared at the peacemaker. "You my manager?"

"No." Squint had seen this before, all the way back to middle school. Guys who wanted to play the big man who tried to trap you by posing a question with no reasonable answer. If he said yes, he would be called out for the obvious bullshit. If he said no, he would be called out for stepping over the line. There was no way to win against them except to not play their games, but in Afghanistan the stakes were too high to refuse. Squint aimed to ensure that Omega Team was cohesive from the beginning, even if it meant that he had to play the martyr.

Steam's response was exactly as Squint expected. Defensive posturing with a dig on his glasses. He was surprised that Steam didn't throw in a Bill Gates reference. "I can speak for myself, you four-eyed jackass. Why don't you go on and watch some Bill Nye, Mr. Wizard?"

Steam behaved like a greenhorn, but Standin was confident that Wild Man would not put anyone on the team who wasn't one of the finest warriors on the planet. "How many missions you been on?"

"Hell of a lot," Steam replied in a self-righteous tone.

"And you're still this hotheaded after all you've seen?" Standin asked.

"Yep." Steam figured that every man dealt with life in the way he chose to see fit, but he would be damned if anyone else tried to tell him how to live, including any member of Omega Team. His experiences in combat were what had turned him hotheaded. Almost half a lifetime ago, he was a snot-nosed punk who had no idea that there was a world outside of Wheeling. In the fourteen years since he first enlisted, Steam had discovered the reality of the world and it wasn't pretty. There was no use for nice words and polite gestures. The world was a fucked-up place filled with fucked-up people. It was at war and would always be at war. The best that he could hope for was to smoke as many of the enemy as possible and have some fun in the process. If his teammates didn't like him, big whoop. He'd save their lives in a heartbeat and take out a target faster than that. If they wanted more than that, screw 'em.

Bond entered the room. When Hodge had offered him a new role as team leader, he added a suggestion that it was paramount that he strive to find a balance between developing a rapport with his team members and maintaining discipline. Just as he had seen Wild Man do as a member of Bravo Team, Bond allowed his men some time to acclimate to each other before he stepped into the dynamic.

"You our team lead?" Steam asked.

"That's right." Wild Man had warned Bond during their intake meeting that Steam was a character, but he had also told him that there was no better man to have on your side when it mattered.

Steam pulled up his Oakleys. "Goddamn, man. Be happier with the spade, the nerd, the haji, or the downer."

"Dumbass redneck." Boogie was trying to remain above the fray, but Steam's attitude had pushed all the wrong buttons.

"Enough. Get on task." *Balance. There was a time for discipline and a time for rapport. Now, the former was needed; later, the latter would emerge.* Wild Man had stressed how critical it was for a team leader to avoid unnecessary emotion in his decision-making process, explaining that those types of emotions were what had caused problems for him. Bond had no intention of letting his new handler down.

When Bond first entered his trailer, Hodge felt as if no time at all had passed since they had worked together to eliminate Mohaqiq in Anjoman. Hodge gave Bond a brotherly hug, then patted him on the back. "Really good to see you, Bond. Sit down."

"How's the ankle holding up, Wild Man?" After the ignominious end outside Anjoman, Bond never expected to see his former team leader again.

"It's fine."

"When are you making your return to the glorious battlefield?" Bond posed the question despite already knowing the answer. You do not get second chances in this line of work. The fact that Wild Man was given a new strategic role was a surprise in and of itself. Bond figured that Wild Man had some powerful connections to advocate on his behalf.

Bond's question rankled him, but Hodge tried his best to put on a brave face. Hodge had been removed from active combat by the higher-ups. Keyes had informed him that since the debacle in Afghanistan, Mazuski had worked tirelessly to get him back into the fold via a new opportunity commanding teams. The brass had initially judged Hodge unworthy of even a more traditional role in the intelligence community, yet Mazuski continued advocating on his behalf behind the scenes. After he had called in enough favors to his allies and made some noise about the exposure of skeletons in the closet to the rivals he had made over the years, Mazuski had been able to secure a return for Hodge, albeit not the full return that Hodge desired. "Let's stay frosty, Bond. Your men are to take care of Jalaluddin El-Hashem in coordination with Foxtrot Team. Ready to move tomorrow?"

"You bet."

Hodge could tell that there was a trace of invective in Bond's words. He did not mind the edge in Bond's voice either. Hodge believed that he deserved to be treated with a degree of skepticism after his actions. Bond would give no quarter in any situation; he was going to make one hell of a team leader. Hodge passed Bond his father's copy of *The Art of War*. He had stored the book in the same rucksack that he had worn when Bravo Team humped along the Hindu Kush. Hodge had repurposed the rucksack to store some of his most valuable items as he traveled to the worst parts of the world not as a warrior, but in his new role.

"What's this?" Bond had read *The Prince*, but *The Art of War* had never crossed his radar.

"It's a good read, but it gets old after about sixty times through." Hodge's words were lies. Sun Tzu's military treatise had been as engaging a read the sixtieth time through as the first; however, Bond could benefit from reading the book quite a bit more than he could, given the limitations placed on him.

"You read this book sixty times?" Bond was a voracious reader, but he had read his favorite book, Cormac McCarthy's *Blood Meridian: Or the Evening Redness in the West*, only three times. The thought of reading any book sixty times seemed further proof that Wild Man's moniker was accurate - and not in the way intended.

"It's a page turner," Hodge quipped.

"Guess so."

"Open it to page fifteen." Bond started to page through the book. Before he reached the page, Hodge began to quote word for word from the text, "It is the rule in war, if our forces are ten to the enemies one, to surround him; if five to one, to attack him; if twice as numerous, to divide our army into two. If equally matched, we can offer battle; if slightly inferior in numbers, we can avoid the enemy; if quite unequal in every way, we can flee from him." Hodge paused for a second. "I don't like that last part."

"We'll follow your plan and have twelve men scattered in six different positions. Your intel said to expect a force of ten Tali. I don't imagine he'll have numbers on us, Wild Man."

"I already gathered that you're not the imaginative type." Hodge admired Bond's determination and strength of character; however, it was important to knock him down a peg. They were not equals. Hodge was his handler in Afghanistan and there remained a clear disparity in their power dynamics.

"What do you mean, chief?"

Hodge allowed Sun Tzu's words to speak on his behalf, "He wins his battles by making no mistakes." Bond reached page fifteen and scanned through the page. He could not find the quote. Bond started to flit through the book. "Making no mistakes is what establishes the certainty of victory, for it means conquering an enemy that is already defeated." Hodge laughed. There was a degree of satisfaction in watching Bond struggle to keep pace. "That's page twenty-three." Bond turned to the page. "Read this. Memorize it. And pass it on when you're done." Hodge's protégé nodded. "Bond, whatever will happen, follow this advice." Hodge recited further wisdom from his favorite book, "On difficult ground, I would keep pushing on along the road."

"That Sun Tzu, too?"

"Yes. But I'm cosigning the statement."

Bond closed the book. "Thank you, Wild Man."

"Stay relevant." Bond nodded in response as he walked out of the trailer with Hodge's father's book in hand.

Most of the conventional U.S. and allied military forces in Afghanistan had a more defined objective. They primarily fought the Taliban in the southern plains of Afghanistan's Kandahar and Helmand provinces; however, members of the dark community such as Hodge's men in Omega Team and the members of Foxtrot Team had a far more difficult task. They were entrusted to run the Tali out of the mountains.

Omega Team and Foxtrot Team had been in their spread-out position five hundred yards above Jalaluddin El-Hashem's hideout for the last sixty-five hours. El-Hashem was holed up in a series of caves that intel concluded had been his home for the last month. Tajikistan was practically next door and Pakistan was only around twenty-five klicks away. El-Hashem had bounced between the sovereign states, finding refuge among the radicalized Pashtun communities in all three nations. He was an expert in blending in with the locals and had eluded conventional U.S. and allied armed forces, as well as PMCs, for over two years. Hodge had him trapped. His men had their sights on his caves. If El-Hashem left his mountain home, he would be dead.

The completion of the base at the foot of the mountain two months prior had led to a near-constant bloodbath for both sides, but it served as a visceral warning to El-Hashem that his days were numbered. While Hodge preferred that his team's target die by his own hands, necessity mandated that he settle for Omega Team and Foxtrot Team to do the wet work. It was not an easy transition for Hodge; however, with a string of horrors attached to his name, not the least of which being the public beheadings of two female schoolteachers for the crime of clandestinely educating young girls, Hodge was content to arrange for El-Hashem's death.

When El-Hashem finally stepped out of the cave, he was flanked on all four sides by his men. Squint did not have a clear shot on the target, but was able to eliminate one of the objective's flunkies. El-Hashem and the other three Taliban fighters immediately sped back into the caves to regroup. In the hours while their target was in hiding, Omega Team and Foxtrot Team had moved to fortified defensive positions only around 150 yards above El-Hashem's caves. The units were ready to strike when the target showed his grizzled, bearded, middle-aged face.

The terrorists reemerged ten hours later in the blackness of night. Both teams sprayed El-Hashem and his fifteen men with suppressive fire. El-Hashem ordered a retreat down the mountain after three of his men were taken out by the storm of metal. Foxtrot Team remained in their positions on guard to deal with the possibility of additional fighters and to provide cover, while Omega Team stormed down the path to overwhelm El-Hashem with their massive superiority in firepower and skill. The jihadis moved with a swiftness over their native soil that Omega Team found difficult to match. Arjuna fired his M4 towards El-Hashem's direction. The target seemed to have the luck of the devil himself, with another one of his subordinates taking the fall. A new Tali immediately stepped in for his fallen comrade as El-Hashem hurried down the mountain encircled by four of his men.

The gap had widened. It was becoming increasingly difficult for Omega Team to have clear shots on the target and his men. El-Hashem addressed his men in Arabic as they continued to rush away from the fire, "Grenades. That cliff." Omega Team was about two mikes from the cliff which led further down the mountain. Before they could reach it, one of El-Hashem's men had removed the pin from a grenade and hurled it up at the cliff. The cliff shattered. Although the rest of Omega Team evaded injury, Boogie and Steam were both nailed by fragments of shrapnel. Blood poured down Boogie's face from the bridge between his eyebrows. Steam bled from the back of his head.

"Motherfuckers!" Steam shouted.

"Motherfuckers," Boogie concurred.

Bond and Standin remained alert to prevent the possibility of an ambush if new enemy combatants emerged, while Squint and Arjuna rushed to dress the wounds of their injured teammates. Boogie and Steam had ugly injuries, but neither was dealing with anything life-threatening.

"Muj know their land better than we do," Bond snarled.

"What's the move now, boss?" Standin asked.

The terrorists would soon be out of range. With the cliff destroyed, there was no way for Omega Team to charge ahead. "A good man once told me this," Bond replied, "On difficult ground, I would keep pushing on along the road."

"What road?" Standin shook his head in frustration. "Muj blew the hell out of our road."

"That's a metaphor." Bond spoke into his mic, "This is Omega 5. Requesting exfil. HVT evac'd. Grenade KO'd our cliff. No way down. Shrapnel injuries to two of our men. No KIA's. Over."

The mic crackled as Hodge responded, "Any way for the Muj up? Over."

"None apparent, but it's their turf, so maybe. Over."

"Move to rendezvous point. Radio when up. Birds forthcoming."

"Roger."

Steam scoffed, "Ain't that a shit sandwich?"

Boogie laughed, "Couldn't think of a better motherfucker to hump up this mountain with than you, brother."

"Yep. Now knock off that mushy POG bullshit and get your black ass up, brother."

After the cliff had blown out, Allah had chosen to bestow his favor. Cell phone reception was always sporadic in the mountains, but El-Hashem knew where to get service and contacted several of his associates. El-Hashem had lost more than eighty of his fighters over the last month to the clandestine forces that had intruded into his territory. It was now time for him and his associates to teach the Americans a lesson that the Soviets and British had already learned.

Hodge could hear the forces on the move. It sounded like a large number of Tali were approaching. Within minutes, a large Taliban force had breached the wire and was entering the base. Hodge exited the trailer with his trusty M4. He moved behind one of the jingle trucks that the base had contracted from Afghanistan's official government, making contact with the Tali, sighting them in one at a time. One of the Tali fell. Another marched off to his seventy-two virgins. A third fell. Four. Five. Six. Seven. Even with imperfect mobility, Hodge remained a deadly shot.

Four teams had stayed on base in-between deployments. Over twenty-five Afghan and foreign non-military contractors were also stationed at the FOB. Dozens of Taliban had poured into the base in a disorganized frenzy. In short measure, the Talis had taken heavy losses, but not before they inflicted several casualties and numerous injuries in the process.

A bullet nailed Hodge from behind in the back of his good leg. Hodge collapsed to the ground. "Piece of shit mother-" Hodge spun around and saw his shadow hovering above him. He furiously rammed his M4 against Blackbeard's shoulder. There was barely any impact. His skinny was not so skinny anymore. He was wiry now. Blackbeard no longer looked like a twerp.

This is a fitting way for it all to end, Hodge thought to himself. *Just me and my shadow*. Hodge turned to Blackbeard. *Speak now or forever hold my peace*. "Your asshole of a dad was a terrorist. Now you're a terrorist. My dad was a patriot. Your father killed mine and now you're going to kill me. And it just goes on. Is this how it goes? That's how this ends?" Hodge's command of Arabic had not deteriorated at all for lack of usage.

Guuce butted his AK-47 against Hodge's face. Blood began to stream from his wound. "That's how it goes, Baseball. And it's on you. And we're winning." Guuce's Somali-accented Arabic had improved. With a few more years in the terrorist cells, he might be mistaken for a member of the Saudi royal family – at least until he showed his true color.

"I was doing a Black handshake. It's popular in the States. They do it as a way to bond. Like brothers."

Guuce pressed his Kalashnikov against Hodge's skull. As Blackbeard's body rotated wildly and fell beside him, all Hodge could do was laugh. Sun Tzu understood the game all along. Even the finest sword plunged into salt water would eventually rust.

EPILOGUE

LANGLEY AIR FORCE BASE

HAMPTON, VIRGINIA, U.S.A.

NOVEMBER 2004

The first thing Chris Hodge did after wheeling himself into his office was adjust the thermostat to sixty-four degrees. It had only been three days since leaving the mountainous north of Afghanistan and he had not yet adjusted back to the mid-Atlantic's more temperate autumn weather. The second thing Chris Hodge did was check his email. The most recent one had a subject line that read "Undisclosed." Hodge clicked it open and began reading. He snickered. Hodge had accumulated significant TIC. He had become normalized to the chaos, and his ultra secret and THA levels were very high. He smirked after he finished reading this "invitation."

Seconds after Hodge finished reading the ambiguous email, a fist began to pound against his door. The knocks were perfectly spaced, the sound resembling a metronome.

"Come in."

Keyes entered Hodge's office. "Did you check your email?"

"I'm not much for small talk either," Hodge quipped.

Keyes frowned. "You've been requested to handle this."

"Glad I know a thing or two about quantum physics."

"Are you ready?"

"Roger," Hodge replied.

Keyes left the room without any further conversation. Hodge logged out of his account. *Well, this is different.*

GLOSSARY

.50 Caliber - The diameter of a round often used as a sniper rifle to get through and knock down walls or similar.

A-10 Warthog - An attack jet aircraft able to deliver significant ordinance.

Adhan - The Islamic call to prayer.

Alhamdulillah - Arabic for "Praise be to God."

Allahu Akbar - Arabic for "God is greatest."

ANDSF - Afghan National Defense and Security Forces.

Avenger Gatling - Multi-barreled weapon mounted on an A-10 delivering significant and impressive rounds into its target.

Ba'ath - Saddam Hussein's Iraqi nationalist political party.

Bacha Bazi - "Dancing boys." An Afghanistani practice involving underage boys in prostitution and the sex trade.

Bird - Aircraft.

Black Phones - Phones not registered to an individual.

Blackwater - A renowned private military company.

Boot - Short for "Boot Camp." Indicating behavior associated with that of a new recruit.

Burqa - A garment worn by Muslim women that covers their entire body from head to feet.

BWH - Brigham and Women's Hospital. One of Boston's top hospitals.

Carbine - A shorter rifle type by way of the barrel.

CAS - Close air support.

Centcom - Central command.

Charlie Foxtrot - A situation that has become chaotic.

Comms - Communication. Often used synonymously with radio.

CQB - Close quarter battle.

Dark Community - Persons involved in spycraft or intelligence in a very clandestine manner.

Deen - The required, traditional religious observances for Muslims.

Desaparecido - A Spanish term for a disappeared person. Most commonly used in reference to individuals kidnapped and murdered by Argentina's military junta in the 1970s and early 1980s.

DFAC - Dining facility.

Dope Your Scope - The art and skill of setting up a rifle's scope for a long range shot based on current wind, the direction of the shot, and the ballistics of the round used.

Exfil - Exfiltration, a plan for leaving the mission.

Fajr - One of Islam's five daily prayer times. At dawn.

Fatal Funnel - Term used primarily in reference to building-clearing operations. Narrow areas with little opportunity for concealment should combat arise.

Fatwa - A religious ruling by a Muslim scholar.

Five-Sided Puzzle Palace - The Pentagon.

Ghillie Suit - Camouflage clothing that allows one to blend in with natural environments.

Gitmo - U.S. military base in Guantanamo Bay, Cuba.

Glasgow Scale - Also known as the Glasgow Coma Scale. A scoring system used to assess a person's level of consciousness after a traumatic brain injury.

Hadith - A series of sayings ascribed to Islam's prophet Muhammad that are second only to the Qu'ran in scriptural importance for Muslims.

Haji - A pejorative term for Arabs, particularly Iraqis.

Halal - Something deemed permissible for Muslims.

Haram - Something deemed impermissble for Muslims.

Hat Up - To leave.

Hazara - Shia Muslim ethnic group living mostly in central Afghanistan, which is a predominantly Sunni region.

High-Value Target - A targeted enemy needing efficient elimination.

Ho-Chunk - A Native American people whose historical land encompasses part of the Midwest, including Wisconsin.

Hump - Moving from point A to point B with all of your gear loaded.

IC - Intelligence community.

IED - An improvised explosive device. Easily-constructed bomb.

Imam - Individual who leads Muslims in prayer at a mosque.

Inshallah - Arabic for "If God wills it."

IRA - The Irish Republican Army. A paramilitary group that seeks to end British rule of Northern Ireland.

IR Thermal - Using infrared technology with vision devices to see where others can't see (i.e. in the dark).

"Israeli" Bandage - A quickly applied in the field pressure bandage.

Jahannam - A place of torment. In Islam, where evildoers spend eternity after they die.

Jannah - Paradise. In Islam, a place righteous Muslims go to after they die.

Jihad - Battle against perceived or real enemies of Islam. Can also refer to the internal struggle against sin for Muslims.

Jingle Trucks - Elaborately decorated trucks common throughout Afghanistan and Central Asia.

JSTOR - A research database.

Kalashnikov (AK-47) - Created by the Russians. The most widely built assault rifle in the world.

Khamiis - An ankle-length garment resembling a robe worn throughout much of the Middle East and parts of Africa.

Khutbah - An Islamic sermon.

Klicks - Kilometers.

Layli Goobalay - Board game played in parts of Somalia. It is a variant of the classical count and capture game mancala.

Lidocaine - Local painkiller.

Line-Animal - A Marine who finds combat exhilirating.

LRADs - Long range acoustic device. Projects sounds at great distances.

M4 - A carbine. Shortened, more compact version of the M16 rifle.

Madrasa - The Arabic word for any educational institution, either secular or religious.

Mashallah - Arabic for "God has willed it."

Masjid - Islamic place of worship. Also known as a mosque.

Mikes - Minutes.

Minbar - The pulpit in a mosque. This is where sermons are delivered.

Mossad - Israeli intelligence agency that oversees intelligence collection, covert operations, and counterterrorism.

Motard - A motivated Marine.

Muezzin - The man responsible for calling Muslims to prayer.

Muj - Derived from Mujahideen. Common term used to refer to Muslim insurgents, especially in Iraq and Afghanistan.

Mullah - A Muslim religious scholar.

O-5 - Officer rank in the U.S. military of the fifth level.

Pashmina - A large-sized scarf.

Pendejo - Spanish slang for an idiot.

PG-7 - Anti-tank rocket launcher.

POG - Person other than grunt. Non-combatant military.

Post Exchange/PX - A commissary on a U.S. military base.

QRF - Quick reaction force.

Rack Out - Go to sleep.

Rainbow - Fresh trainee.

RPG - Rocket-propelled grenade.

RTB - Return to base.

Rucksack - A backpack.

Saaxiib – Somali word for "friend."

Score A Grouping - Keeping the practice shots on a range within a certain predetermined space on a target. A measure of the shooter's accuracy.

Sharia - A legal system based on the Qu'ran and other Islamic religious texts.

Shaytan - Islamic term for the Devil or Satan.

Shi'a/Shiite - The largest minority denomination of Islam.

Sitrep - Situation report on an area's current military conditions.

Skinnies - Derogatory slang for Somalis.

Snatch Mission - Snatch and grab. Taking the target prisoner as opposed to elimination.

Souk - A bazaar common in Arab and Arab-influenced nations.

Spook - A spy or intelligence officer.

Stay Frosty - Slang term for be alert or maintain situational awareness.

Subhanallah - Arabic for "Glory be to God."

Sunni - The majority interpretation of Islam.

Suppressed Shot - A shot fired with a device that silences the rifle sound.

Surah - A chapter of the Qu'ran.

TACP - Tactical air control party. Close in air support on the tactical level. Deconflicts combat aircraft, especially during attacks.

Tangos - Targets or enemy forces.

THA - Threat hazard assessment.

The Suck - A term used to refer to the U.S. Marine Corps by Marines.

TIC - Troops in contact.

Tradecraft - The methods and procedures of an intelligence officer.

Ummah - The worldwide Muslim community.

Un-ass - To quickly leave a hostile area, often while under fire.

UNOSOM II - United Nations Operation in Somalia II. The second phase of UN intervention in Somalia during the mid 1990s.

UZI - A .9mm submachine gun accurate to 150 meters.

Viet Cong - Vietnamese soldiers opposed to the non-communist government of South Vietnam and the United States during the Vietnam War.

Walaalka - Somali word for "brother."

Walal - Somali word for "sibling."

Wet Work - An operation with an expected bloody end.

Zanj - Term used by Muslims to refer to individuals from southeastern Africa.

Zizou - A nickname for French soccer player Zinedine Zidane.

If you enjoyed *Relevant*, please leave a review on Amazon. Your support is appreciated.

Thank you,

Peter Zaccagnino